ALBUQUERQUE
Alibi

SIZZLING CITY SERIES
BOOK 2

ZIZI HART

*Stan,
Worry less,
laugh often,
+ love deeply.
ZiZi Hart*

Albuquerque Alibi
Copyright © 2024 by Zizi Hart.
Published by Secret Passage Press, LLC

This book is a work of fiction. Names, characters,
places, and incidents either are products of the author's
imagination or are used fictiously. Any resemblance to actual events
or locales or persons, living or dead, is entirely coincidental.
All rights reserved. No part of this book may be used or reproduced
in any manner whatsoever without written permission
except in the case of brief quotations embodied
in critical articles or reviews.

For information contact:
www.zizihart.com
www.secretpassage-press.com

Cover design by Miranda Lexa
Editing by Cyndi Rule

ISBN: 978-1-9644-6001-7 (paperback)
ISBN: 978-1-9644-6003-1 (eBook)

First Edition: October 2024

Secret Passage Press, LLC
Canon City, CO

Disclaimer

This book contains adult language, themes,
and sexually explicit scenes.
It is intended for readers 18+.

*To my Albuquerque crew and Santa Fe squad,
a shout-out and special thanks
for all your suggestions and hidden gems.
With the wealth of information
and hilarious anecdotes shared,
I had the absolute best time.
I'm amazed by your passion,
and hope that my brief descriptions
of hot spots inspire others
to explore your amazing cities.
I could not have done it without you.*

Prologue

Sofía

The streetlights swirled as I spun in a circle. I loved that off-balance, dizzy rush you felt when the world lost its axis. I collapsed on the lawn laughing. My date, and I use that term loosely since I didn't remember his name, grinned at me. When I climbed to my feet, I glanced at the small rip in my skirt. I shrugged it off, not caring. I was still a tomboy at heart, despite the figure I had developed over the last year. Boys were starting to notice me. All but the one I wanted to. I had no interest in them except Jac Dillon, a tall, dreamy senior, and my brother's best friend. My date stared at me with hungry eyes. Why couldn't Jac ever look at me that way? Oh, I remember. Varsity football players didn't date lowly freshmen. I glanced across the empty pool and spotted my girlfriend Vera making out with the guy she was dating. They were getting horizontal on some cheap lounge chair that looked like it might collapse at any moment. The house was under construction, so the party was mostly outdoors. Someone had jimmied the lock in case people wanted to use the bathroom, not that I had ventured inside yet. I overheard that one of the kid's family owned it, but the fact that he didn't have a key made me question if that was true. Not that I cared one way or another. I hadn't been paying that much attention when Vera's boyfriend had shared the details. After hearing that several seniors from our high school would be attending, I zoned out imagining Jac stopping by. That was all the incentive I needed to agree to his ridiculous terms. I was to be a 'date' for his friend. Vera owed me for this. I scrutinized the skinny twig of a guy in front of me. He wore a grey t-shirt and jeans with a red ball cap on backwards. I bet he thought it looked cool. I wanted to tell him all it did was make him look more like a dweeb. But I held my tongue, counting down the minutes until I could ditch the guy. When we entered the party an hour ago, he handed me a cup of spicy fruit punch. I had him fetch me three more throughout the evening. It was potent stuff and made me downright giddy. I had a good buzz, but I wasn't drunk. Not by a long shot. I had the Ramirez family's tolerance for hard liquor, not to mention that I had been sneaking booze from family parties for years.

"Why don't you take off your top, Sofía?" Red ball cap suggested.

I squinted at him and scowled.

"Kiss my ass, pendejo." I slapped my butt to accentuate my words.

It earned a grin from the perv and I rolled my eyes. My reputation as a chica with attitude had been with me since grade school. I was a fighter, and I left a string of boys with bloody noses and black eyes in my wake. It proved that my Ramirez blood ran hot. I wouldn't tolerate being disrespected. I'd kick him in the groin before doing anything I didn't want to. And if I really wanted him to suffer, I'd sic my brother on him. César would sweep the floor with this loser without breaking a sweat. And with César, always came Jac. They were a pair. No one messed with the two of them. Although tonight was an exception. César was on a date. It was the second reason I was here. I had double-checked before I left with Vera. Otherwise, I would have never risked coming to a party where my brother might show up. If

ALBUQUERQUE ALIBI

César saw me here, he would lose his mind. Dates were the only times when Jac and him weren't joined at the hip.

I ignored Red ball cap and made my way through the crowd to check out who else had arrived. Maybe Jac was inside the house. I took a stroll hoping to get a glimpse of him. Panting bodies in various stages of undress could be seen as I went from room to room. Power tools and loose nails were scattered across the kitchen counter. The furniture was covered in plastic. The air was thick with sawdust, and I coughed as I roamed the hallways. Exposed beams made me wonder just how safe it was to be inside the house. After my search was complete, I sighed, disappointed. My heart sank. Jac was a no-show. That was the only reason why I was here. It sucked. Big time. I kicked myself for being so stupid, assuming he'd show up to some stupid party. Jac was probably on a date just like my brother. He was never hurting for female attention, just like César. Although Jac wasn't nearly the player my brother was. At least Jac was discreet with his girlfriends. My shoulders slumped. Maybe it was for the best. If Jac had shown up, he would have figured out I had lied to mi mamá about sleeping over at Vera's. He would have insisted I tell my mother and brother. Then I'd have all three of them coming down on me. Tanning my hide would be the least of my worries.

I went over to check on Vera, but she was passed out. That didn't seem to stop the guy who had been making out with her. He was still groping her unconscious body. What a creep.

I thwacked him in the back of his head.

"Dude, she's out cold."

He turned bloodshot eyes at me. "No, she's not." He slurred.

I gave him a shove and he fell to the cement and grumbled.

"Whadya do that for?"

I took a seat on the lounge, guarding Vera from the big jerk. That's when I heard the siren.

"Fuck. It's the cops." Someone yelled.

ZIZI HART

Within seconds, everyone scattered.

"Help me with Vera." I said to the guy who had been having a grope fest with my best friend.

He released some expletives and shook his head, taking off between the houses.

"Coward." I yelled.

Great. I'd have to get her out of here myself, or we'd both be in trouble.

I lifted Vera's dead weight onto my shoulder and went out the back gate to the alley. It's crazy what you can do when necessary, especially when the adrenaline is high. I made it to the local park and had to take a breather. I let her body flop onto a bench and bent over wheezing. I needed help and fast. There was no way I'd make it to her place carrying her like this. I was stout and strong, but despite my workouts at the school gym, this was pushing the limits of my abilities.

I pulled out my cell phone and pondered who to call. Mi mamá would throw a fit. Gabby was too young, and César might end up being worse than my mother, especially if I interrupted his date. I scrolled through my numbers again, and it landed on Jac's name. He had been on my mind all night. Mamá had all our friend's and relative's numbers listed in a book in the kitchen. She made me enter them into my phone in case of an emergency. I had never called him directly. Taking a deep breath, I clicked the button. I could feel the pulse in my throat as I wracked my brain for something smooth to say. Maybe I should just hang up.

"Hello." He said with a gravelly voice. It was all sexy and deep, and the butterflies in my stomach spun and bounced in my belly. I had woken him. What was he wearing right now? That was the first question that popped in my brain. My imagination was doing somersaults. I glanced at the time on the phone. It was 1 in the morning.

"Jac?"

"Who is this?" He asked, clearing his throat.

"It's Sofía." My voice was soft and hesitant.

ALBUQUERQUE ALIBI

It sounded like he was shifting in bed. I heard the rustling of sheets. Maybe he slept in the nude. I inhaled a sharp breath. The image was going to make me hyperventilate.

"I. Uh." The image had me fumbling over my words. I let out a deep breath, and a girly giggle slipped from my lips.

"Is this a prank? Why are you calling me this late?"

I bolstered my nerve. "I-I need your help."

The sirens were getting closer. I hid behind a tree and hoped they didn't see Vera's shape on the park bench. I'm sure he overheard the sound in the background.

"Is someone hurt?"

I bit my lip. I didn't want to lie to him, but I also needed his help. Maybe if he assumed someone was in dire need, he wouldn't hesitate. The silence dragged on as I debated exactly what response would make him drive out to pick me up in the middle of the night.

"Why aren't you calling your brother or your mom?"

"Are you kidding? César would beat the shit out of me, and mi mamá would ground me for life. Please." I begged. "I need you. Can you pick me up?"

He grumbled and mumbled some incoherent words that I figured were swear words under his breath. "Where are you?"

I gave him the cross streets. "I will owe you forever." I said on a hopeful note.

"Yeah. Ok." He yawned. "Give me ten minutes."

I stayed in the dark shadows of the park while the police prowled further down the block, probably investigating the extent of the damage. The way everyone scrambled I had serious doubt that any of the kid's parents owned the house. The police were still investigating when Jac rolled up in his pickup truck. I grabbed Vera and zombie walked her over to the vehicle. She had woken up enough that I could steer her in the right direction. I none-too-gently shoved her into the back cab to collapse on the seat.

"Thank you." I said when I climbed into the passenger seat. "Can you take us to Vera's?" I rattled off the address.

Jac nodded and we drove in silence to her house.

He parked out by the curb and turned to face me. His blue eyes were piercing, and his dark hair was a mess. I noticed he hadn't put on jeans. He was still in his pajama pants and a t-shirt.

"You won't tell anyone about this will you?"

He frowned.

"I can't keep this a secret from your brother."

My shoulders slumped. "It was nice knowing you."

He chuckled. "Your brother is not going to kill you."

I shook my head. "You don't know him like I do."

"He's my best friend."

"When you find my dead body in a ditch, then you'll believe." I shrugged. "It'll be far too late of course."

"You're being dramatic."

I raised my brows.

He gave a long weary sigh. "Fine. I won't tell him as long as you promise to never do this again."

The dread that had been overwhelming every fiber of my being was suddenly lifted with his words. I screeched with happiness and jumped into Jac's lap. Without even realizing what I was doing I kissed him. It was automatic and pure reaction to the excitement of the moment. If I had spent more than half a second contemplating the action I never would have done something so bold. The kiss should only have lasted a second, but it didn't. Our tongues touched and I felt myself moaning into his mouth and squirming on his lap. Maybe it was the fact I had too much to drink, and he was barely awake, but whatever the reason, we were both into it. It left me feeling lightheaded when we finally parted. I could never have imagined a more perfect kiss in my wildest dreams.

My eyes fluttered open.

Jac looked like he was going to be sick. I frowned. I thought he had enjoyed the kiss as much as I had. Hadn't I heard him moaning as well? Why else would it have gone on as long as it had?

"That should never have happened."

The fluttering butterflies in my stomach took a nose-dive. How dare he make the beautiful moment we just shared ugly? It angered me. Maybe it was my Latina blood, but I wanted to say or do something to hurt him.

I punched him in the chest and got out of the car. "I guess we both have secrets to keep."

"Come on Vera," I said as I opened up the back door. She flopped out of the car, but I was there to make sure she didn't face plant.

I slammed the door, refusing to look back at him as we staggered our way to the front door.

Jac peeled from the curb with squealing tires. That was fine by me. His fury and frustration could match my own. I couldn't believe how bad this night had turned out. Something I had been dreaming of for years had finally happened. I had kissed Jac, and he had kissed me back. But somehow, it had all turned to mierda in seconds.

Vera started puking in the bushes. My sentiments exactly. That pretty much summed up the evening.

Chapter 1

14 Years Later

Sofia

The melody of birds singing traveled on the soft summer breeze. I took a deep breath smelling the fresh-cut grass and sighed. I was lounging in an oasis in the high desert. The lush green was a rarity. It was more common to see adobe brown, desert tan, and terracotta. Those were the colors that made up the palette of Albuquerque. However today, I was at Duck Pond at UNM, soaking up the beauty on campus. The sound of the fountain spraying in the background drowned out most of the squawking geese. To me, it was like being surrounded by a symphony of nature. It drowned out the city and all the worries that came with the outside world. I let it soothe me as I stretched my limbs, allowing the sun to do its work. My muscles relaxed. The warmth sizzled along my exposed skin, burning off the chill caused by the classroom's frigid air conditioning. I had mistakenly dressed for the weather this morning, wearing shorts and a sleeveless top. You think I would have learned by now. I had lived here my whole life, but I had been shivering through much of my finals. Not that it should affect my grade. As tempting as it had been to answer the questions quickly to remove myself from the uncomfortable situation, I forced myself to take my time, and believe it paid off. I was confident I had aced the exam. I curled my toes in the grass and sighed. To some it might have seemed like such a small accomplishment, finishing my first year at UNM at the age of 28, but I was still proud of myself. Even if I had to take a summer class to stay on schedule. Working and going to school full-time was challenging, but I had done it. Just three more years to go and I'd complete a bachelor's in business. Many of my friends from high school had graduated from college long ago. Sometimes, it made me feel like a failure. The average age of the students in my classes didn't help either. The majority were a decade younger. Not that I wanted to complain. I knew who to blame. Me. I should have started college years ago, but I had been too preoccupied with boys. Bad boys if I were being honest. Mi mamá, sister, and brother had no clue how involved I had been with the wrong crowd. Criminals and drug users as boyfriends, and plenty of my friends had been in gangs. Thank goodness I had separated myself from those toxic people. I had gotten out of that life and now had a chance to get on the right track. The pharmaceutical company I worked for was helping me pay for college. I owed my boss for recommending it.

"Sofía, is that you?"

I blinked my eyes up at the figure standing over me. I got up on my elbows and my stomach bottomed out. Dread crawled up my skin. It was the last person I wanted to see. Diego. My ex. Hadn't I just been thankful for getting out of that life? Why was he here now? I hadn't heard from him or seen him in three years. My torso shivered despite the heat of the day.

"What are you doing here, Diego?"

"Nice to see you too."

"Can the small talk."

He rubbed the back of his neck and glanced around campus. I followed his gaze. He stared at several college boys

ALBUQUERQUE ALIBI

running around in the grass, horsing around. They looked like jocks, just letting off steam after finals. No one was menacing except for the one hovering over me.

"I'm in a bind."

I rolled my eyes. "Nothing new there."

I didn't want to hear whatever sob story he was going to share with me lying down. I quickly threw on my socks and sneakers and placed my water bottle in my backpack. I started climbing to my feet wanting nothing but to get as far away from him as possible.

He helped me up by the elbow and I scowled at him.

"You're looking fi-ine." He said.

So did he if I were honest. Diego was still sexy on the outside. Why were all assholes so hot? Not that I would say that to Diego. His ego was already huge. I bit my lip, preventing myself from saying anything to encourage him. There was a reason I started dating him in the first place. Golden skin and dark curly hair that kept getting in his eyes. Unfortunately, the good looks came with a whole lot of drama and danger. I wasn't going to do anything stupid, I chanted to myself. There was a reason we had broken up.

I started walking to the parking lot, and he followed. Apparently, he wasn't taking the hint that I was trying to get away from him and this conversation. Subtlety had never been his strong suit. He needed more of a brick-to-the-brain kind of logic. I glanced around the walkway. Where was a loose brick when you needed one?

I arrived panting at my rusty Chevy Impala and put a hand on my hip. I had speed-walked across campus. He barely looked winded, and it pissed me off. Damn him and his long legs.

"Can you give me a lift?"

I huffed. "Where is your car?"

He shrugged. "Got repo'd."

I glanced at his worn sneakers and sighed. When had the sign 'sucker' been etched into my forehead? Or a better question might be, how the hell could I get it surgically removed?

I gestured for him to get in. The sooner I could get this over with, the better.

"Where to?"

"Thanks." He said and jumped in the passenger seat.

I closed my eyes and took a deep breath. The fact that he didn't immediately share a destination had me worried. Either he was still trying to decide, or I wouldn't like where I was dropping him off. I started the car in silence. Time dragged as I fiddled with the radio and the AC. He was clearly stalling.

"Address?" I asked.

He frowned.

"Do you need a ride or not?"

"I need your help."

His eyes turned watery. And despite my best effort, I felt sorry for him. I couldn't fall for this again, being dragged back into his world. I mentally kicked myself, commanding myself to grow a backbone.

I gritted my teeth. "What kind of bind are you in this time?"

"I owe money to some bad people." He rolled in his lips looking out the front window.

I shook my head. "Don't have it."

"I haven't even given you an amount."

"It doesn't matter. My savings are nil. I moved out of mi mamá's house. I have an apartment and expenses."

"But you got that sweet job at Biogen labs."

We had broken up before I got the job, and he hadn't reached out since then. That meant he was checking up on me. Spying. I didn't like that one bit. It was one more reason for concern.

"All my extra money is going toward college."

"Isn't your company paying for it?"

ALBUQUERQUE ALIBI

Again, information he shouldn't have.

"They pay a portion, not all of it." I frowned.

I wasn't about to tell him Biogen covered a large chunk of the tuition, as long as I made good grades. There was no way I was loaning or giving this asshole money. I had done that for years, and it had gotten me nothing but heartache.

"Why don't you ask Candy?"

"Aww. Don't be like that. She meant nothing."

I snorted. That made it so much better. He cheated on me for nothing. My pride had been hurt that day, but it had been for the best. My heart healed and I had grown stronger in the past three years. Now I realized it had been a blessing. If I hadn't caught him giving it to Candy, I might still be stuck in that toxic relationship today. I might have married the cheating bastard. Plus, his friends were nothing but trouble. I thought of the other reason I had left. The real reason. Mr. Torres. I swallowed hard. I didn't like who I was around Diego. I had done things I would regret for the rest of my life.

"How much is it this time?"

"Ten grand."

"What the hell?" I shook my head. "I told you to join gamblers anonymous."

"I tried. The meetings kept getting canceled."

"You are so full of it." I shook my fist at him. "Why are you bothering me? You know I don't have that kind of money."

He slid his hand on my knee, and I was tempted to break his fingers. My brother had shown me how to do it. Family on the police force had its perks.

"If I can't borrow some cash, info is the next best thing. That's all I need, baby."

My eyebrows rose. He was still touching me. Whatever he saw in my expression made him snatch his hand back.

ZIZI HART

"They're going to kill me." He slammed his fist on the dashboard. "Can you live with that? After all we've been through?"

"Why don't you ask your buddies to help you out?"

"I stopped hanging out with those guys. I got away from the gangs. Just like you."

While I was glad he made changes in his life, I didn't appreciate being reminded of my past.

"Your friends were troublemakers."

"It wasn't all bad. You used to have fun pulling pranks with us."

I snorted. "That's what you think? Really? You thought I was having fun?"

He shrugged.

I remembered back to that last prank. He and his friends had robbed a convenience store. Of course, at the time, I hadn't realized that's what they were doing. They told me they were playing a joke on their friend. I should have known better when they handed me a ski mask, but I was drunk and I believed the lie. Diego and his friends were going to freak out one of their friends, punking the guy. But when we got inside the store, I noticed that things didn't add up. The guy working behind the register was an older gentleman who went to my church. Mr. Torres. They beat him up and stole money from the register. I was horrified. I couldn't move. They managed to shove me back into the car. I remember their boisterous laughter and feeling sick to my stomach. We stopped at a fast-food restaurant, and I holed myself up in the bathroom, puking my guts out. They had left me there. Diego had gone out to some bar, partying with his friends. When I arrived at his apartment the next day, after a sleepless night trying to figure out what to do, I caught him and Candy together. She was his buddy's girlfriend, a skanky chick who worked at a strip club. That had been the final straw.

"After you left me, my life turned to shit. I knew I needed to change."

ALBUQUERQUE ALIBI

"Glad you found some sense, but I'm not taking you back."

"I know and I'm not asking for that." His shoulders slumped. "I made a mistake. Haven't you ever done something you regret?"

Yes. I had. Too many to count. Sad to say, but Diego wasn't even at the top of the list.

"We had some good times, too. Don't you remember?"

Yes. But I wanted to forget. Despite his gambling and ridiculous pranks, he had been a decent boyfriend for two years. He had gotten me through a tough period of my life. I had been deeply depressed after a previous breakup. I had a knack for dating losers. Diego had been the one to nurse my broken heart. He had been sweet, bringing me flowers and little gifts whenever I was down. He always managed to do or say something to make me smile. Diego was charming and funny. In the beginning, he seemed to be different from all my previous boyfriends. Before the robbery and his cheating, I thought he was a good guy. I was famous for wearing steel blinders when it came to my relationships. None of my boyfriends had flaws in the beginning. I couldn't be trusted to see the truth until it was too late. I wasn't about to make that mistake again. I might be sympathetic with Diego's plight, but he had done it to himself. He wasn't going to pluck at my heartstrings. If he had changed, then good for him. I'd encourage his progress from afar. I wouldn't kick him while he was down, like I wanted to. Even if he did deserve it. It's not like I wished him dead after the ordeal he put me through. Beat up, sure. But not dead.

"What do you want?" My question came out snarky as hell, but I needed to play it tough, or he'd walk all over me like he had in the past.

"Just schedules."

My mind whirled. What did that mean?

"Schedules of what exactly?"

"Deliveries."

I closed my eyes and inhaled. Did he mean Biogen? That's why he knew where I worked. He had been casing my company for one of his schemes. He hadn't changed at all.

"Hell no. Not gonna happen." I wasn't about to let him jeopardize my job.

"All right. If you aren't comfortable, that's fine. Relax." He held up his hands like I was going to attack. "How about a lift to Old Town? Can you do that for old times?"

My eyes narrowed as I stared at him. Why hadn't he fought me harder? It wasn't like him to give up this easily. Was he truly trying to turn his life around? I could feel the ache in my temples pounding. It tended to happen around my ex-boyfriends. I grabbed the crucifix dangling from the chain around my neck. The one I always wore. It was a gift from my long-departed abuelita. I searched for wisdom. I was trying to make smart decisions despite my past. I recalled the words my pastor had given me during last week's confession. He said I needed to let go of my anger and forgive. If he had known the extent of Diego's sins, he might not have been so keen on me offering forgiveness. I let out a breath and put the car in gear. I had been planning to visit my sister in Old Town this afternoon anyhow. She was working at Que Pasa's restaurant. Gabriella would slip me free soda and appetizers when the owner wasn't looking. My sister and I both had the attitude if we weren't caught, it wasn't a sin. My pastor sure had his work cut out for him with the Ramirez sisters. At the behest of my mother, he was trying to save me. He didn't need to bother. I had already saved myself. But mi mamá had her ways of persuasion. She should have been a lawyer. I dropped off Diego and waited for the other shoe to drop, but it never did. He thanked me and went on his way. I was almost disappointed. It was like waiting for the climactic ending to a movie, and having it just fade to black. Maybe he really had changed. I know I had. Was it such a stretch to think he could do the same? I drove around the downtown area hunting for one of the free two-hour parking spaces. I wasn't about to pay the parking lot fees. I finally found one a block away ten minutes later.

I entered Que Pasa's with a spring in my step anxious to tell Gabriella all about my final. My jaw dropped when I saw my ex sitting at the bar chatting with my sister. She let out a boisterous laugh at something he said, and the fury boiled to the surface before I could stop it. I shoved Diego off the stool and glared at him. He lost his hold on the glass he was holding. Alcohol sloshed over his shirt and the tumbler smashed to the floor. Everyone in the bar turned in our direction. My sister, ever the professional, quickly went into clean up mode. She propped Diego onto another stool and swept up the glass.

"Don't make a scene." My sister whispered in my ear and pulled me to the side. She knew my temper. Diego brushed ice off his pants and signaled for the other bartender to replace his drink. He gave me a cocky grin that I wanted to wipe off his face. Gabriella corralled me to a booth and told me to stay while she finished cleaning up the mess. I didn't want her to lose her job over something I did, so I forced myself not to move. I stared at the back of his head wanting it to explode, forgetting all the words of forgiveness my pastor had preached about. Diego must have felt the daggers coming out of my eyes, because he glanced back. Whatever he saw in my gaze gave him pause. He quickly paid and left without another word.

I breathed a sigh of relief when the door shut behind him. Gabriella brought over two sodas and some nachos and slid into the seat across from me.

"What the hell, Sofía?"

"Sorry." I mumbled. "That was an ex."

"Criminal?"

My eyes widened. I didn't like that she automatically assumed, but she was right.

"Yeah, and a cheating bastard."

ZIZI HART

She knew a little of my past, but not specifics. I tried to keep that part of my life separate from my family. I didn't bring boyfriends around to the house. There were good reasons for that. My sister knew I was drawn to bad boys. There was a time in my life when danger was exotic, and my choices in men had been horrible.

"I kind of had that feeling. Not by his looks, but by your reaction."

I never gave Gabriella enough credit. Her powers of perception were off the charts.

"I can put him on our board not to serve if you want."

"It's probably a good idea. He's a magnet for trouble."

"You got a picture of him?"

"Ha. I think I burned all my photos, but maybe I can find one on the internet. Thanks sis." I held up my glass.

"To terrible exes." We clinked our glasses together.

"May they stay in our pasts."

Chapter 2

Jac

I arrived early at Muldoon's and got a booth at the back. Each one had thick dark mahogany walls that created a privacy space that few restaurants these days provided. Even though it was early Thursday afternoon, the lighting was dim with a small sconce over the table. It barely allowed enough light to read the menu. A month ago, I had made the mistake of asking the owner, Sean Muldoon, if they had trouble keeping people from getting frisky in the booths, and he had told me this was a respectable business and stormed off in a huff. The busboy had been more forthcoming, flashing the heavy-duty cleaner he used with a grin. I knew I couldn't be the only one to think of lovers meeting for an illicit rendezvous. I wondered if my mother's fascination with Regency romance novels was rubbing off on me. I had filled her in on my complicated relationship with Sofía. My mother had offered some suggestions. That's in fact why I chose Muldoon's. The owner was discreet, and those from the force didn't come here until later in the evening and even then, they mostly stayed at the bar. It was the safest way to get together in public and yet not run into anyone. Not that we were doing anything wrong, or even compromising for that matter. We were just friends, even though I wanted more.

Sofía and I had been getting together once or twice a week since I moved back to Albuquerque. We would occasionally talk on the phone late into the night, just like we had in high school. It reminded me of that summer before I left for college when we had dated in secret. It felt like a million years ago. Of course, we weren't dating. Sofía had sworn off relationships and wanted to keep our lunches private. She thought others might assume and she didn't want to deal with any misunderstandings. I could get that. I knew those on the police force could gossip like nobody's business. They were sometimes worse than my mother's church group. Despite Sofía's bold attitude, she was emotionally fragile. Several ex-boyfriends had done a number on her, violating her trust. If Sofía needed us to meet like this to feel safe, that was fine by me. She was worth the wait.

Sofía strolled in and my breath hitched. She flipped her dark curly mane to one side. She wore a strapless peach and teal sundress that hugged her curves and complimented her honey skin tone. Everything she wore made me have dark thoughts, imagining things I had no right to of my best friend's sister. I must be a glutton for punishment to continue to be around her when I knew nothing could come of it. She hopped into the booth and her chest bounced. Momentarily distracted by her cleavage, I forced myself to meet Sophia's deep brown eyes. They sparkled with restrained laughter. The little minx knew exactly what she was doing. Sofía was torturing me, something she had enjoyed doing in high school as well. Some things never changed.

"Hello, Jac." She pointed to her necklace. "Do you like it?"

I focused on the turquoise stone that lay heavy on her chest. It was pretty, but that's not what held my attention.

"Yes." I cleared my throat. "Quite lovely." I took a deep drink of water.

ALBUQUERQUE ALIBI

"Mari made it for me." She turned the stone over in her hand and leaned forward so I had an even better view of her cleavage. "Feel the stone. It stays cool to the touch in the air conditioning."

"I'll have to take your word for it," I said desperately scanning the restaurant for our waitress. I needed something to focus on other than Sofía's beautiful breasts, or I might do something truly stupid like I had that one summer in high school. I dramatically gestured to the waitress and was grateful when she made her way over.

"Can we have some menus?"

She nodded and retrieved two large leather menus and asked if we needed anything to drink. Sofía ordered a soda, and I asked for another water and a Guinness. I needed something to cool my libido, although I doubted any amount of icy beverage would do the trick.

"Why do you need the menu? You always order the same thing." Sofía complained after the waitress left.

"I could be in the mood for something different today."

She scoffed. "Really Jac. You're so predictable, it's not even funny."

That riled me enough that I did order something different. I decided on a large Cobb salad and almost immediately regretted it. Sofía ordered my favorite, fish and chips.

While waiting for lunch, we chatted about work, the weather, and the places they wanted to visit over the weekend. Since Mari, her roommate, had only recently moved from Arizona to New Mexico, she wanted to see all the sights the state had to offer. She appointed Sofía her official tour guide. Not that Sofía minded. They got along great, otherwise they wouldn't have decided to become roommates after just meeting two months ago. Mari and César had been instantly attracted to one another, in those love-hate sort of relationships. César had been undercover when they met, a story I still cracked up over. Although their relationship hadn't been all fun and games. Mari had been forced to stay in César's apartment after a near abduction by a drug lord. It was clear the two of them were deeply in love, even after only a few weeks. But their relationship was still new, and César's mother, Irene, was ultra-conservative and very religious. She didn't approve of couples 'living in sin', as Irene called it. Mari had bonded with the Ramirez family over a weekend when César and I were taking down a drug lord. Apparently, the impact had been profound. Mari decided against moving in with César when he asked. Instead, she got an apartment with his sister Sofía. César had been floored by that. He wasn't used to not getting his way, especially when it came to women. It was funny watching the two of them. I knew that Mari still spent most evenings at César's, but in his mother's eyes, they were just courting. I knew Irene wanted grandkids, but she also wanted to see all her children married first. That was a hot topic these days at Sunday lunch. Now that I moved back to Albuquerque full-time, I had a standing invitation. I wouldn't pass up Irene's cooking for anything in the world.

 My promotion came with a hefty pay raise and had been contingent on me relocating from Santa Fe to Albuquerque. There were a lot more opportunities in a larger city, and after the success of my last bust, I had been excited about the move. The first month had been a pain, traveling between Santa Fe and Albuquerque while finishing up my cases, but now I worked full-time for the Albuquerque PD Narcotics Division. César worked in the same department, and we were spending more time together. It reminded me of how we were in high school.

 When our food arrived, I kicked myself for falling for Sofía's taunts. She always knew just how to rile me. Sofía slowly dipped the deep-fried fish into Muldoon's homemade tartar sauce and slid it between her lips. She made this ridiculous, almost orgasmic sound as she bit into the beer-battered goodness. Her eyes fluttered. I knew they were good, that's why I ordered them all the time, but she was laying it on thick. The little scamp was performing. Mocking me. She was waiting for me to react. Sofía smiled and took another bite. My mouth watered for more reasons than just hunger.

"You're missing out, Jac. Don't you want a taste?"

She waved the half-eaten piece of fish in front of my face.

I snagged a fresh one off her plate.

"Hey. That's mine." She complained.

I shoved the salad toward her. "Have some salad."

Sofía snorted. "You never could stand to be teased." She forked a bit of the salad and made a dramatic huff. "I guess we could share."

"So, I wanted to ask if I could swing by your parent's house when Mari and I visit Santa Fe this weekend?"

I choked on one of the chips. "Why would you be doing that?"

"Oh, I don't know. I figured Mrs. Dillon might have some recommendations and share some of her favorite places. Mari didn't get to explore much when she lived there with my brother." She sighed. "This week got away from me. I'm in a jam. Can you help me out?"

I wasn't quite sure what to think of this new development. Sofía had never asked to meet my parents before. She knew of them and had probably met them in passing years ago, at some sporting event that César and I had been at. We had done everything together in high school. Did this mean she wanted to push things to another level? Or was I overthinking it?

"My mom, huh? I didn't think you were close."

She shrugged. "We're not, but I figured if I knew someone who lived in Santa Fe, they would know all the best places to go."

That made sense, but why wasn't she asking me? I had lived there for years. Why involve my parents? We had an unspoken rule that we wouldn't involve family in whatever was going on between us. Not that I had exactly kept to that rule. My mom and I were close. At a brunch a month ago, she had weaseled the information out of me.

"I might have mentioned to my mom that we were seeing each other."

"What?" She screeched. "You told her we were dating?"

"Keep your voice down", I whispered. "I didn't use the word date. Just 'seeing', as in getting together."

"The woman must have assumed." Sofía's head collapsed into her hands. "You must know that."

"I didn't have a choice. She was ready to set me up on a blind date with her girlfriend's daughter."

"So, I was your excuse." Sofía glared at me. "I thought we weren't involving family."

"It's just my mom."

She sighed. "It's going to be awkward getting together with her. She might ask questions."

I grinned. I was counting on that. "You'll figure it out."

She rolled her eyes.

I didn't want to tell her that my mother was a romantic at heart. She was probably already planning our wedding. That's just how my mother was wired. I showed interest in something, and she was already 12 steps ahead. Maybe my mom's influence would help move things along, either that, or she'd scare Sofía off for good. I frowned.

"Maybe the two of you shouldn't get together."

Sofía's expression held disbelief, then defiance.

"Give me your mother's number." She demanded.

I handed her my phone. She transferred the number into her phone and in minutes had messaged my mother. A few minutes later, she received a response.

"There. It's all set. We are meeting her for breakfast on Saturday. She even offered us a place to stay Saturday night."

I blew out a breath. I was in it now. My mother was going to drill Sofía for details. And who knows what she would tell her. But since Sofía was pushing the boundaries, maybe that meant she was ready. This might be the push she needed. Sofía could have easily avoided the conflict, but instead willingly charged head-first into the fire.

"I wasn't going home this weekend. I have a stakeout."

She rolled her eyes. "I know. That's why I agreed to stay at your mom and dad's house."

I frowned. "Why would you have a problem if I was there?"

Sofía shook her head. "That would be worse. Trust me. It's going to be difficult enough as it is."

"Mari will probably tell César things she hears from my mother."

"No, she won't. We are best friends, and she knows the situation."

I'd sure like to know what that was. It would be nice to have it spelled out for me. Most of the time, I was clueless. But I never pretended to understand how a woman's mind worked. I knew whatever this was between us would come out sooner or later. Someone was going to see us and make assumptions. Maybe I had started the ball rolling. It had been a tactic to get my mother off my back, but it might work in my favor, as long as Sofía played along.

"Are you going to tell my mother the truth?"

Sofía smirked. "I haven't quite decided yet."

"She's going to set me up. Please." I begged.

"Don't worry." She rested her hand on mine, and I felt the touch like a bolt of electricity.

That's all she had to do to me these days. I was so wound up.

She licked her lips and pulled her hand back.

Maybe she needed a reminder of how good we were together.

"Do you remember hanging out at the park back in high school?"

Her eyes glittered. "I remembered doing a lot of things at the park. You have to be more specific."

I glanced around the restaurant. It was still slow. No one was looking our way.

My voice lowered. "You want me to remind you in graphic details."

Sofía inhaled sharply and reached across the table to hold a hand over my lips. Her brow furrowed and she shivered. She closed her eyes and licked her lips. As much as Sofía said she didn't want to escalate things further, her body betrayed her. I knew she had to feel the sexual tension between us. I refused to believe it was only one-sided. I could read a suspect better than anyone in my division. Body language didn't lie. Sofía was still fighting it, but she wanted more. My phone pinged twice. There were two messages; one from César asking me to meet at the gym, the second from my mom, wanting me to call her back, ASAP.

I picked up my fork and forced myself to eat the Cobb salad. I needed fuel for the workout César was sure to give me. At least with him, I didn't need to discuss anything. We could enjoy each other's company without uttering a single word. The call with my mom, on the other hand, would be nothing but talk. She was one of the best interrogators I knew, and she didn't even work for the police.

Chapter 3

Sofia

I can't believe Jac brought up the past. I spent every night dreaming about that summer. Fantasizing. I had been infatuated with him. In fact, I still was. He was tall at 6'4", with massive shoulders. Underneath his suits hid a powerful body with taut abs and virtually zero body fat. He always had a polished appearance, clean-shaven with his dark hair neatly trimmed. I wanted to muss up that perfect hair time and again over the years. But his absolute best feature was his icy blue eyes. One glance and you felt sucked in, drowning without a life raft. That had happened to me the first day we met, when we were both kids so many years ago.

Not that I needed a relationship right now, as tempting as Jac could be. Guys inevitably screwed up your life. I was the poster child for that fact. My ex showing up out of the blue yesterday was the perfect example. Jac needed to stay firmly in the friend box, no matter how much I wished things could be different. We left the restaurant separately in case someone got the wrong idea. Although, we had nothing to feel guilty about. We were both single and it was strictly platonic. Our relationship had always been complicated and by mutual agreement, we agreed to meet in secret. Well, it had mostly been my idea, but Jac hadn't argued. Sneaking around felt a little like it did in high school. Was I trying to recreate that old feeling without committing? Maybe.

I walked out of the restaurant feeling Jac's eyes on me. He always watched to make sure I got to my car safely. He had always been like that. Protective and kind. No other guy in my life ever worried like that. Well, except maybe my big brother. Although, César took protection to a whole other level. He went a little loco if you asked me. César would catch wind of a guy interested in me or my sister and threaten them, or just beat them up. He called it a warning. I struggled to find anyone willing to even hold my hand in high school. They were all scared of what César might do to them. His attitude and fists were the reasons I kept my love life private. If he had known Jac and I had dated in secret one summer in high school, he would have lost his mind. Being his best friend wouldn't have saved Jac from a beat-down. I still couldn't believe Jac had managed to keep that a secret all these years. But he had made me a promise. I had his word, and he had my trust.

I entered the apartment to Miles' meows of welcome. He was this sweet little kitten that Mari had rescued from a gas station in the middle of nowhere a few months back. He had nearly doubled in size in the last month and was more attention-hungry than an out-of-work thespian.

"You're home." Mari came out of the kitchen with a strand of beads dangling from a necklace in progress. She made them for her Etsy store and made pretty good money. Enough that she didn't need another job. I would love to have that kind of freedom, to be able to work from home, but I didn't have the same creativity gene she possessed. Miles jumped up to swat at the beads, and Mari yanked them up into the air, dancing around.

"Aaagh. He's jumping higher now."

I grinned at their antics. The two of them together was like watching a comedy show.

"Soon even putting them above your head isn't going to help."

ALBUQUERQUE ALIBI

"He's getting into everything lately. Miles knocked a whole box of beads on the floor today."

"He must have wanted your attention."

"Well, he got it all right. I had to lock him in the bathroom for an hour while I picked up all the pieces. I didn't want him accidentally swallowing anything."

I sighed knowing what that meant. Our toilet paper roll was most likely in shreds.

He did tend to drive us crazy, but he was also so darn cute, and such a little snuggle-bug. It was impossible to stay mad at him.

"How much time will you need to get ready for our road trip?"

"I have most of my stuff packed, although the majority is covered in cat hair. Miles decided he was going to come with, even if he had to sneak into the luggage."

"I'm sure he won't mind being stuck at mi mamá's house. Gabriella will be home during the days, and he'll be tucked in with Mamá at night."

"I didn't think your mom cared for Miles all that much."

"She complains, but that doesn't mean that she doesn't look forward to Miles' visits. She's been making toys for him out of old ribbons and bells. And I saw a bag of cat treats in her pantry."

"Really?" Mari giggled. "Well, then I'm glad. I didn't want to leave Miles with just anyone. He's had a tough life for such a little guy. I appreciate your family. They're the greatest."

Mari didn't have a family of her own. The last of her relatives, her brother, had died a few months ago. Investigating his death was how she met César. The Ramirez family was huge. Sometimes at extended family gatherings, it felt downright suffocating. Everyone knew each other's business. That's another reason why I was so secretive. Our big crazy family filled a missing piece for Mari, and she gave me an escape from mine. I had moved out of my family home when I was 18, but for the past three years had been living with mi mamá. Two months ago, I met Mari. We instantly clicked. Even though she was dating César and things seemed to be going great, she decided against moving in with him. Whatever the reason for her hesitation, I was grateful. She was the best roommate I ever had. But Mari was so much more, she had become my best friend. I wanted to thank her by making this weekend extra special and showing her all the wonderful things our state had to offer, just in case things fell apart with my brother. Not that I saw that happening. One day, I hoped to become her sister-in-law. As soon as my dumb big brother found the courage to pop the question.

I woke up Friday morning excited. I didn't take vacation days very often, but I sure needed it, especially after finals and dealing with my ex. I decided to recruit a few professionals this weekend, and by that, I meant tour guides and family.

First on the agenda today was the ABQ trolley tour departing from Old Town. After parking, we picked up our tickets at the Old Town Emporium on San Felipe. We had some time before the trolley arrived, so we decided to shop. It was a particularly hot day for the end of July, and we both noticed a shady alley filled with brightly colored storefronts. Wandering down the brick pathway between the adobe buildings, we came to the Patio Market filled with plants, flowers, and trees. Local artist shops and galleries lined the avenue. We grabbed iced lattes from Blackbird Coffeehouse; and browsed through Nikki Zabicki's Boutique. Across from the plaza were additional patios with more stores filled with local art, crafts, and clothing. We posed for some photos in front of the floral sign at Lillies Handmade Soaps. It was the cutest shop filled with soaps, lotions, and bath bombs among fairy lights and flowers.

"We better head back," I said as I noticed the time.

The trolley had pulled in on the other side of the plaza. We raced across laughing and hopped aboard. Our tour guide was hilarious, cracking jokes as he told stories about prominent

ALBUQUERQUE ALIBI

figures, historical buildings, and local landmarks. Being a native, and having lived in Albuquerque my whole life, I was surprised by how much I learned. Mari loved all the graffiti artwork and the unique architecture, especially the Spaceship UFO house. She was shocked to discover just how many TV shows and movies had been filmed here.

"I knew about Breaking Bad, but I had no idea that Transformers and The Terminator movies were filmed here too. That is so cool."

After our 90-minute trolley ride, we decided to have lunch at the High Noon Restaurant & Saloon, which was supposedly haunted. A little tidbit we learned from the tour.

"Do you think we'll see any ghosts today?" Mari asked.

"You never know." I grinned. "And if we miss them today, we could always come back in the evening. Old Town gives ghost tours almost every night."

Our waitress dropped off our prickly pear margaritas.

"Have you had any paranormal experiences while working here?" I asked.

"Well, I've seen the woman in white, back there in the Santos Room." She said, sticking her thumb over her shoulder, "And drinks have slid down the bar mysteriously. Both happen after hours when no one else is around." She gave a shiver. "The first time I closed, it completely freaked me out. Now it's just business as usual." She shrugged. "Sometimes I hear my name and know it's just the ghosts having fun."

We slipped into the Santos Room after our meal. Accent lights highlighted saint statues in small alcoves throughout the room. No ghosts visited, so we promised each other to come back in the evening closer to Halloween.

At the Indian Pueblo Cultural Center, we checked out the murals and explored the museum learning all about the 19 Pueblo Tribes in New Mexico. After that, we drove to the Hispanic Cultural Center for a paleta at Pop Fizz.

"These are popsicles?" Mari asked.

"It's made with fresh fruit and real sugar," I said. "These are way better. My favorite has chili powder. Sweet and spicy, just like I like it."

She laughed.

Her phone buzzed and she looked down at the screen. "Jac and César want us to meet up with them for dinner."

We headed to Two Fools Tavern, a good old-fashioned Irish Pub in Nob Hill.

"What an appropriate name," I said, gesturing to Jac and César. They stood under the sign outside the restaurant waving their hands dramatically, telling their tales to a group of guys.

"I bet you it's some football story," Mari said.

"My guess it's one of their big arrests. Ten bucks?"

"Twenty."

"You're on."

"And then César did this double Salsa twirl mid-sprint," Jac moved his hand in a circle.

"It's called a hook spin."

"Whatever," Jac shrugged. "The linebacker didn't know what was happening. He missed the tackle, and César ran in the winning touchdown. The crowd went wild. And that's how he got his nickname, the Salsa spinner."

I groaned and slapped a twenty in Mari's hand.

Jac and César turned around. My brother picked Mari up and whirled her around in a circle. Jac looked momentarily like he wanted to do the same with me. I raised my eyebrows, and he cleared his throat.

Once seated inside, we all ordered fish and chips and ale. It was always fun with the four of us. Now that Jac had moved down here permanently, we would be able to get together more often.

"Sorry to cut the night short, but we have to head out," I said. "We have an early start in the morning."

ALBUQUERQUE ALIBI

Jac and I awkwardly stood next to each other as Mari and César said their goodbyes, which was more like a grope-fest with a lot of tongue.

"Do you think they'll make it the whole weekend without each other?" I asked.

"There's a potential for withdrawals," He shrugged, "but I think they'll survive."

I snorted. Jac always had a dry sense of humor.

"Hope you have fun at Mom and Dad's this weekend."

"Are you nervous that I might find something in your old room?"

Jac swallowed hard. "Is that where Mom is setting you up?"

I shrugged. Let him worry about that. I couldn't wait to rifle through all his stuff. It's something I had dreamed of doing when I was a teenager. I wasn't going to pass up this opportunity.

"Sorry." Mari blushed, wiping her smeared lipstick. "Let's go."

Jac was ribbing César for being such a horny bastard when we left.

Early Saturday, we dropped Miles at mi mamá's house, then drove to the Petroglyph National Monument. My cousin Carlos worked at the information center. He met us there to take us on a private tour before his shift started. He droned on sharing dates and history of the carvings created by Pueblo tribes and their ancestors. I had heard the spiel before about the petroglyphs and theories on how the chiseled pictures were created on the rocks.

"Scientists have claimed certain images date back to 2000 B.C., but the majority were created between 1300 and 1680 A.D."

"Wow." Mari grinned.

I got caught up in her enthusiasm and found myself smiling.

"You can feel the history, the power in the stones."

"We think there may be over 25,000 petroglyphs within the monument." My cousin chuckled. "I hope to document them all. Maybe one day, I will have mapped out the whole 17-mile region."

"He wants to become an archaeologist."

Mari tilted her head. "That's an Interesting career."

"Your madre would use a different word." I grinned at Carlos.

"She doesn't understand my passion."

"Your Mamá wants you to get a better-paying job and move out of the house."

"She loves me too much to force me to move."

"Stop being such a nerd and get a girlfriend."

"You're one to talk Sofía," Carlos said.

I shrugged. "You have a point."

"Speaking of family, it's my sister's Quinceañera next month."

"Another one?"

"My youngest sister, Clara."

Another family event. And this one would be big. Maybe I would ask Mari to make one of her designer necklaces. I'd buy the supplies, and we could go in on the gift together.

"Mari's invited too, right?"

He grinned. "I'll make sure she gets an invitation."

Mari's face lit up with excitement.

"I've never been to a Quinceañera before."

We blasted our music on the drive to Santa Fe. With the singing and chatting, the drive took hardly any time. Mari's gasp as we drove into the downtown area was worth the trip.

ALBUQUERQUE ALIBI

"I just love the adobe architecture. Everything is so close and cozy here. It feels like we've entered another world. Stepping back in time."

"I guess that's the theme of this weekend. Some of the structures we will be seeing date back centuries. I'm amazed they are still standing. There is so much to see. I'm not sure we will get to everything on my list. That's why I wanted to recruit Jac's mother for help. She knows the hidden gems of Santa Fe. We are meeting Mrs. Dillon at Café Pasqual."

I pulled into a parking space, and we walked to the café. It was this adorable eatery downtown. Mrs. Dillon was already seated and waving us over.

She squealed with delight and gave each of us a hug in turn. I was a little nervous meeting with Jac's mother. I had known her for years and seen her at sporting events in high school, but we hadn't talked much, and when the Dillons moved to Santa Fe, I didn't have a reason to reach out to her. Mrs. Dillon had been to almost every football game. Since I cheered for my brother, and they played on the same team, our families often sat together. I had a crush on Jac back then, and if I were honest, I probably spent more time watching and rooting for Jac than my older brother. I wonder if his mother realized that I had a crush on her son.

"Thank you for suggesting this place, Mrs. Dillon." Mari turned her head, taking in all the colors that filled the bright, cheery café.

"Please call me Faye. I love this place. And there is an art gallery next door. I figured that would be a hit since you're an artist."

"Hardly. I just string beads and wrap stones with wire. It's just jewelry."

"She's modest." I grinned. "Mari is a genius. Her jewelry pieces are incredibly unique and super stylish. It's wearable artwork. I've had more compliments with her pieces than with any other jewelry I've ever worn. This piece I'm wearing right now is one of hers."

"Really?" Faye tilted her head, admiring the necklace I wore. It was a wire-wrapped design holding various crystals in a graduating teardrop pattern. It looked like dewy raindrops encircled my throat.

"I might just have to commission something special for one of my charity balls."

The Dillons were quite wealthy. Jac's father, Troy, retired as a financier after Jac joined the police force. I think he hoped that Jac would follow in his footsteps, but Jac had other plans. It was surprising that he hadn't chosen a more lucrative career path based on his upbringing, but that was Jac. He never followed the crowd. That's probably why we got along so well together. I liked to do my own thing, although my rebellious nature often got me into trouble.

"So Jac tells me you've been seeing each other quite a bit."

Faye's eyes were wide and hopeful. I pursed my lips, knowing this had been coming. I had prepared myself since Thursday's revelation.

"Yes, we have. It's great spending so much time together, now that he lives so much closer. César loves it, too."

"Well, of course César would. They have been like two peas in a pod since high school. The two of them were always getting into trouble together. I'm so glad they both turned to law enforcement instead of going the other way."

I grimaced. If Faye knew what I had done, she might not be so keen on me hanging out with her perfect son, corrupting him.

"I've heard stories." Mari giggled. "But I'm sure you have tons more."

Faye grinned. "Oh, the things I could share." Her eyes light up. "Let's get drinks first." She signaled for the waitress.

"So, do you have anything special planned for the weekend?" Faye asked.

ALBUQUERQUE ALIBI

"I was hoping you could offer some suggestions. There were a couple of places I had seen online, but other than shopping, I haven't explored a whole lot in Santa Fe."

"Oh, you are in for a treat. We are known as The City Different for a reason."

Faye revealed her favorite art galleries and museums, and Mari decided which ones she wanted to see. After breakfast, we rushed to say our goodbyes.

"I'm sorry, but we have to run. I set up a walking tour."

"No problem. Have fun. We'll have dinner at 6 tonight. Our chef is whipping up some Santa Fe specialties." She handed me a set of keys and the PIN for the gate. "You'll be staying in our casita. It's to the right of the garage. Once you are settled, follow the path from your patio to the main house."

"Thank you again for letting us stay with you." I hugged her.

"Of course. You're family."

Mari hugged her too. "It was so nice meeting you."

We had another comedian for a tour guide which made the time fly by. My brain felt like mush after the 3-hour walking tour.

"I have too much information," I said, grabbing my head, then making an explosion gesture with my hands. "My head feels like it's gonna explode."

Mari laughed. "Me too. It's hard to keep all the facts straight. Just as I expected, tons of history. I'm having so much fun. So where are we going for lunch?"

I pointed to the sign above her head. "How about The Shed?"

"Sounds good to me."

We entered a doorway that said Prince Plaza. It led to a courtyard and everywhere you looked was bursting with color. Peppers dangled from the rafters. Shelves and tables were filled with unique accessories. After putting our name in with the hostess, we strolled through the courtyard perusing all the items for sale. I loved the painted jack-o-lanterns in bright colors, while Mari was partial to the Day of the Dead dolls. When our table was ready, we were escorted through room after room to a window overlooking the plaza. Every wall in The Shed seemed to be painted a different color, from cheery yellow to hot pink and purple. Even the door trim had bright decorative stencils. Eclectic artwork covered the walls. Mari's head seemed to be on a swivel, catching every detail.

"So, what was your favorite part of the Santa Fe walking tour?" I asked.

"I'm torn. Maybe the Loretto Chapel and the miraculous staircase. That was an incredible story about the mysterious man who built the spiral staircase for the sisters."

I grinned. "I liked that one a lot. I also love the La Conquistadora that was in that side chapel at the Cathedral Basilica of St. Francis of Assisi."

"That's the super old statue of the Virgin Mary, right?"

"Yep. And did you get a chance to look through that book with her holiday costumes?"

She nodded. "I can't believe how intricate some of those gowns were. She has more clothes than I do."

We both laughed.

"What are we doing after lunch?"

"The New Mexico History Museum at the Palace of Governors?"

"That's the building that dates back to 1610, right? The one that is across from the plaza?"

"Yep, that's the one. Past all the Native American artisans."

"Are Jac's parents super rich?" Mari asked as we pulled into the circular driveway of the Dillon family home in Santa Fe.

"Yep. They are." I nodded. I was a little intimidated by how big their house was. It looked more like a grand hotel. It still had the adobe architecture, but it was spread out. I wondered how many rooms the home had. We brought our luggage to the casita and quickly got dressed for dinner. The winding path led to the back patio with a stunning view of the Sangre de Cristo mountains. We arrived a few minutes before 6.

Jac's father looked like an older version of him, just a slight graying at the temples and a few wrinkles around his eyes that were only visible when he laughed. He was nearly as tall as Jac, maybe just an inch shorter, which put him at 6'3. Faye had told us over breakfast that her husband liked to stay in shape. He played racquetball, tennis, and golf any chance he could at the country club. After hugs and introductions, we sat down.

"I can't believe how many dishes there are. How many people are joining us?" I asked.

Faye threw back her head laughing. "It's just the four of us. Our chef does tend to go a little overboard."

Everything looked like something you would see in a 5-star restaurant, and it all smelled divine.

"I think I gained ten pounds from the aroma alone."

"Dieting is not an option in this household. Not with our chef's cooking."

Both Faye and Troy told stories of Jac and César over dinner. It had us all laughing.

"So why did Jac decide to become a police officer?" Mari asked. "I know César had family on the force."

"Well," Faye looked over at her husband who had stiffened in his chair. He placed his hand over hers.

"When Jac was young, I got into a horrible car accident. I had been knocked unconscious, but Jac was still awake. He was only seven at the time. The car had crushed in on itself and the seatbelt had jammed. He was trapped and didn't know what to do. To this day, he still has a fear of tight spaces." She shook her head and sniffed. "Jac became hysterical. The first officer on the scene climbed inside the car and held Jac's hand. Whatever he said during those minutes until the fire department showed up made an impression," she smiled. "After that, Jac wanted to join the police. There was no dissuading him from doing anything else, much to my husband's dismay. Anyhow, that man became his mentor. I think he now works for the FBI."

She squeezed Troy's hand.

"I beat myself up every time I think about that moment when I could have lost you both. I should have been here for you, but instead, I was in New York, traveling for business."

"You couldn't have known dear."

Troy kissed Faye's knuckles tenderly, and I realized he was just like Jac, a romantic at heart.

After dinner, we were served dessert on the back patio while watching the sunset.

"Jac said the two of you are dating," Faye said.

"No. We aren't." I said automatically, so used to denying everything. My guard had dropped, getting too relaxed with the conversation and company.

"Well, in that case, I should set Jac up on a blind date. There are several very nice young ladies at the country club."

"Let the boy date who he wants." Troy said, "It's not like he's hurting for female attention."

I tilted my head. I didn't realize he had been dating other people. Jealousy clawed at my insides.

"But he's getting so old," Faye pouted. "If he hasn't found someone by now…"

"The country club girls are all gold diggers. Plus, it's not what he wants." Troy shook his head.

"Oh hush. All the girls come from money and are very respectable. Next weekend. Yes. He doesn't have a choice in the matter."

"You can't." I said before I could stop myself. I bit my lip. Everyone was staring at me. "I mean, he's taken."

ALBUQUERQUE ALIBI

"Care to elaborate, my dear?"

I cleared my throat. "It's a secret. I swore I wouldn't say a word. Just know that he's not available. At all."

Once I said the words, I couldn't take it back. Was I doing this for Jac, or myself? I just knew that the thought of Jac dating someone else filled me with such jealousy I could barely see straight.

Chapter 4

Jac

"Feel like a hike?" I asked while holding my cell. I was out on my townhome's patio watching the sunrise over the Sandia Mountains. The vivid streaks of orange and red were intense. It made me long to be out in nature.

I heard swearing in Spanish. "It's barely 6 a.m." César complained.

"Rise and shine."

"You asshole. It's my first day off in I can't remember how long."

"Come on. Mari is out of town with Sofía. And it's a beautiful day."

"I need my beauty sleep."

I snorted. "Your mom says you're too beautiful for your own good."

"The ladies do think I'm gorgeous."

"So glad you aren't vain." I chuckled.

"I'm going back to bed."

"Don't make me come over there with my super soaker."

It was a reminder of the time he had done that to me on a camp out. I had vowed revenge.

"That happened once."

"Payback's a bitch."

He knew I'd do it too. I had held that over his head for years.

"I hate you right now."

"Good. I'll see you in 20."

I hung up.

Slathering on sunscreen, I laid out my supplies. Three liters of water. Protein bars. Electrolyte packs. Sat phone. Emergency first aid kit. Bug spray. Jacket. And an extremely goofy-looking adventure hat my mom had bought me. The rim was huge, and it had a neck cape in the back. It had a rating of UPF 50. So as much as I complained about the thing, it was useful. Plus, I had promised my mom I would wear it whenever I went hiking. My Irish blood meant I tended to burn rather than tan. César always made fun of me when I wore it because of the design. It had tan and black spots all over it. He called it my bobcat hat.

César grumbled when he came out to my car.

"I still can't believe we are going this early. Where are we off to?"

"La Luz Trail in the Sandia's."

"Nothing easy, huh?"

"How about only halfway, since you're being such a pussy?"

César took a half-hearted swing at me, but I jumped out of the way. I knew he would go the whole trail. We had plenty of daylight. The view from the top would be worth it. And it was useful in our line of work to stay in shape. He would bitch and moan, but he loved hiking as much as I did, and La Luz trail was something special. The trail started in the high desert, then turned rocky, and before you knew it, you were surrounded by trees in the Cibola National Forest.

ALBUQUERQUE ALIBI

While appreciating the gorgeous views and rehydrating at the summit, I glanced over at César. He had this contemplative expression, and I wanted to wipe the worry from his face. That's why I had brought him along. I knew his current case was eating him alive. Not necessarily by his words, but by his demeanor. There were times that he had done the same for me. We needed that every now and again. To pull each other out of whatever hellhole we were stuck in.

"When are you going to pop the question?" I asked.

César spewed water and it sprayed me in the face. I think he did it on purpose because he was chuckling. He knew I was joking too. It was way too soon, but I wanted to get a rise out of him. César had been far too quiet lately.

"Why would you ask me something like that, man. Mari and I have only been together a few months. It's still new. She didn't even want to move in with me."

"You know that's because of your mother."

"But why is she listening to her? She hardly knows mi mamá."

"Irene has her ways of persuasion."

"Hmph. I love her, but she needs to mind her own business."

"Oh. I'm telling your mom you said that."

"You will not."

"I bet she could still whoop your ass."

"How 'bout I buy the first round of beers?"

"Deal."

We took the tram down and went to our favorite haunt in midtown, Louie's Bar and Grill.

"So how are things going with Carson?"

I made a face. "Don't ask."

He laughed.

Detective Carson was my new partner on the force. César and I had wanted to be partners when I moved down here, but the

Lieutenant had different plans. He wanted me to work with someone who played by the rules. Not that César wasn't a good detective. He just wasn't always so black and white when it came to certain crimes. I think that had a lot to do with how long he had worked undercover. The lieutenant probably thought César would corrupt me. What a laugh. I could have told him that was impossible. I had known César most of my life. If I hadn't been corrupted by now, I was immune.

The lieutenant also wanted to capitalize on my success in Santa Fe and give the Albuquerque PD some positive press. That's why I had been given this promotion and the reason I had moved down here in the first place. And of course, the other reason was that Carson was amazing in front of the cameras. He was always calm and composed. Said all the right things. Spun things on the fly. If I wanted to rise through the ranks, the Lieutenant made it clear I needed to learn the politics of the job, and how to work the press.

"I feel like I'm performing when we talk with journalists. Like we are actors in a play." I shrugged. "Carson loves that shit."

"He's a storyteller. Carson spins his yarns, and the press eat it up. Plus, he knows how to kiss ass."

"It just feels like a lie. And that doesn't sit well with me."

"That's because you aren't a hypocrite."

"So how are things with you and Mari?"

"Surprisingly great. Even though we aren't living together, which floored me when she told me no."

I think it shocked everyone when Mari decided to move in with Sofía instead.

"How about you man? It's been forever since you mentioned a woman or even a date."

There was a good reason for that. The only one I had any interest in lately was Sofía, and I wasn't about to talk with César about his sister. Maybe I could settle on a half-truth.

"My mom's trying to set me up on a blind date. Several country club pals have unmarried daughters."

ALBUQUERQUE ALIBI

"Not good. I'm guessing plenty of them have the whole butterface going on."

He swished a hand over his face in a circle and I laughed.

"She hasn't shown me any pictures."

"Bingo. I told you so. There's a good reason for that." He chuckled. "But seriously, you need to get out there and meet someone."

How could I tell him I already had?

"What is it with this interrogation? Now that you are in a committed relationship with Mari, you are some sort of expert?" I shook my head. "Why don't you turn your wisdom on someone else? How about Gabriella? Huh? Your youngest sister is single."

"Hush. Don't even talk like that. My sisters don't date. I'd kill anyone who even thinks about asking them out." He glanced up at the ceiling as if in heavy reflection. "I'm pretty sure they are both destined to become nuns."

"Now who's the hypocrite?"

"Hey. You should be on my side. Gabriella and Sofía are like your sisters too, since you are like a brother to me."

I agreed that Gabriella felt like a sister, especially with nearly a decade age difference, but not Sofía.

He looked me up and down and rubbed his chin.

"I guess you aren't too bad looking. I might be able to help you find a woman willing to overlook your flaws."

"Ha. Ha." I shoved César's shoulder. "Don't even think about it. I don't need charity or your sloppy seconds. I can imagine who you'd set me up with. Thanks, but no thanks."

After we got another round of beers, I noticed a young guy in his early twenties at the bar with a backpack. He looked around nervously.

"What do you think of that dude?"

"Like I said before. I can hook you up. You don't need to bat for the other team."

"You are such a shit."

He chuckled.

"Yeah. I noticed him when he walked in. He's probably selling."

César would know best. He could see the signs others missed.

"What kind of drugs?"

"Nothing high end. That's for sure. My guess is it's pharmaceuticals."

"There has been a lot of that going around lately. Pharma is big money. But I think you're right. He's small-time."

We watched the kid for a while, but the buyer either never showed or the kid finally got sick of waiting. He hadn't talked to anyone save the bartender, and he paid for the single beer in cash. The kid was lucky. At least this time. If we had witnessed something concrete, we would have taken him in, despite it being our day off.

"Word on the street is there are a lot of Fentanyl shipments being hijacked. Shipments all across the country." César stared at his glass, like it held the mysteries of the universe.

Now we were getting to why he had been in such a funk lately.

"Dangerous shit."

"I know."

"Who do you think would steal it?" I asked.

"Competition? Drug dealers aren't all that loyal. It's all about the money. If they can get something for free, that cuts their costs." He shrugged. "I've been trying to hunt down which gang, or ringleader is coordinating the hijackings, but I've come up with zilch."

"Who are they stealing it from?"

"Big Pharma companies."

He chugged his beer and sighed.

I signaled for the bartender to bring another round.
I patted César on the back.

"Don't worry. You'll catch them. You always do."

ALBUQUERQUE ALIBI

I held up my glass and toasted my brother in blue.
"Be careful man."
"I always am."

Chapter 5

Sofia

We arrived back at the apartment laughing. It was late, almost midnight, but we wanted to spend every moment of the weekend we could. I was so glad to be rooming with Mari. Despite the shared expenses, which granted, I wouldn't be able to afford the apartment without her help, but she was also a blast and a half. A kindred spirit. I threw my backpack to the sofa and slumped into it, sighing with laughter.

The doorbell rang.

Mari and I both groaned as we glanced at the door. Her butt was planted into the cushy recliner, with her feet already in the air.

I grumbled but pried myself off the couch and opened the door with a yank, thinking it was probably some neighbor complaining about the noise. Mari and I weren't exactly quiet when we got to talking or laughing. And it was late on a Sunday.

"Gabriella?"

She pushed past me, panting heavily. Under her arms was a cat carrier and a box.

"Didn't you see me waving?"

Mari and I both shook our heads. It was dark. The lighting in our apartment complex wasn't the best, and we weren't paying that close attention.

"Miles." Mari exclaimed running to unlatch the carrier and grab the little fluff ball. "I missed you so much." She said snuggling with him.

"Sorry, but we were cracking up about an incident that happened on our way here."

"Do tell." Gabriella took my seat on the couch and plopped the box she had been carrying on the coffee table. My sister loved gossip. That's probably why she loved working as a bartender. She would get the juiciest stories.

"Some kids driving into Albuquerque on I-25 were mooning all the other drivers."

"At night? How could you see anything?"

"They had the interior light on in the car."

"We got the full show." Mari snickered.

Gabriella grinned. "College boys?"

I shrugged. "Maybe high school. Who knows. We weren't exactly concentrating on their faces."

"But that wasn't the best part." Mari's eyes lit up. "They didn't pull their pants up quick enough and got pulled over by the sheriff."

"No way."

"Anyhow. It gave us a lot to talk about on the last part of our drive."

"Sounds like you had a great time."

"Yep. The whole weekend was a blast. We packed a lot in. Now we are exhausted."

"Well, I won't take up much time. I thought I would drop off Miles and this box, so you wouldn't have to stop by mom's house. I know she's angry that you missed Sunday lunch."

"Thanks sis."

"No problem. I just wasn't planning on running up the stairs behind you too." She shook her head. "I thought I would catch you in the parking lot, but you weren't paying any attention."

"Sorry about that. I know how much you hate exercise."

Gabriella rolled her eyes. She slid the package in front of me. I was seated on the other side of my backpack. "I'm dying to know what's inside."

"Who's it from?"

Gabriella sighed. "Didn't you get my text messages?"

I grabbed the phone from my purse. She had sent me a bunch of them. Diego had dropped off the box at Gabriella's work of items I left at his place years ago. Dread bubbled up in my belly. I had no desire to reopen that Pandora's box. My life with Diego was over. I didn't want to look back. I knew nothing good would come of it. I should toss it or burn it. Whatever I had left at his place, I didn't want back. At least I didn't think so. Certainly nothing of value. It would have been sold long ago if it had.

Gabriella's eyes were giant orbs. Expectant and curious. "Open it already."

"Curiosity killed the cat," I said.

Mari covered up Miles' ears. "Don't listen to her." She whispered.

I shook my head. Best to get this over with. "I'm surprised you didn't just open it yourself."

"I'm trying hard not to be nosy these days. It tends to get me into trouble." Gabriella shrugged her shoulders.

I wondered if someone was giving her a hard time at work. I called her a pest all my life. That was my job as her sister. She always was sticking her nose into other people's business, but that didn't mean I would tolerate anyone else saying that to her.

"You'd tell me if I needed to thwack someone, right?"

She giggled. "Stop delaying. Just open the damn thing."

My eyebrows lifted. Gabriella barely ever swore.

ZIZI HART

    I hesitated for a moment longer then tore off the brown paper. It wasn't wrapped particularly well, but it was sealed enough that I knew Gabriella hadn't peeked inside.
    It contained some photos and letters, a few DVD's, a ripped pair of jeans, a ratty sweater, two worn sandals, an old purse, and a few frames. The family photo in one of the frames was the only thing I cared about. Another frame I picked up had a picture of Diego's friends in them. I was with them, in the middle of a group of rough-looking hooligans. My outfit was slutty, and my pupils dilated. I didn't remember taking the picture, but there were a lot of blanks from that period of my life. A lot of drugs and alcohol, and poor decisions.
    "I have to use the bathroom." I said throwing the pictures back into the box and racing to the back of the apartment. I closed the door and breathed through the pain. The emotions and turmoil of our relationship came back full force as I had flipped through items from my past. I had been feeling so good about where I was in my life, and Diego had smashed through my defenses and did what he always did, stirred up trouble. He was a catalyst for destruction. No matter how much I wanted to forgive and forget, there were some people you just needed to cut from your life. I finished staring at my reflection in the mirror. I wouldn't stay back here and hide. I wiped away my tears and splashed water on my face. Once I was satisfied that I appeared half-way presentable, I marched back to the living room. It had been fifteen minutes at most. The girls had turned on a movie. I was relieved. I did not want to talk about my ex right now. They must have known. Vegging out in front of the tv and watching a movie sounded like a fabulous idea. Anything to zone out the memories filling my head. I slumped on the couch and Gabriella paused the movie.
    "I'm fine. Go ahead and play it."
    "Are you sure?"
    "Of course."
    She pushed play and my whole body felt like an electric current had sizzled my nerve endings. I recognized the setting. It

ALBUQUERQUE ALIBI

was a memory I had buried deep, pushed to the darkest corner of my mind. I was reliving a nightmare, stuck in a horror film, unable to run or scream. A team of thugs were roughing up some poor convenience store owner. I knew the man. He went to my church. My stomach seized. I was going to be sick. I ran to the kitchen waste bin. Gabriella dashed to my side, rubbing my back, as I heaved up dinner. When I was through, I rinsed my mouth in the sink and washed my hands. I glanced back in the living room. Mari was still sitting in the recliner, but the footrest was down. She sat with elbows on her thighs staring open-mouthed at the tv. The remote was in her hand. She had pressed pause. My face was on the screen. Frozen. I had an expression of sorrow and disgust. I was in a car with the rest of Diego's crew all in mid-laugh. It appeared I was the only one with a conscience. I had felt myself removed from the others even back then. I remembered this like it was yesterday, but I had no idea someone had taped it. Now my sister and roommate had witnessed my deepest secret. One that I could barely admit to myself.

"What is this?" Gabriella asked.

My sister was like me. She would give me the benefit of the doubt until the last possible moment. I knew she was hoping I'd give some sort of reasonable explanation, that this wasn't exactly what it appeared to be. Both my roommate and Gabriella were waiting.

I collapsed into the sofa, eyes averted, staring at the box. The source of my misery.

"That was my ex and his friends. They robbed a store, and they brought me along."

"I thought I knew you." Gabriella whispered. "Why would you do such a thing?"

I swallowed, realizing I needed to tell them the whole story.

"Diego gave me some pill to mellow me out earlier that evening. It's not an excuse for what I did, but that's how he convinced me they were playing a practical joke. One of their friends was working, and they wanted to scare him. He promised me no one would get hurt. I was barely with it when we all loaded into the car. Everyone was pulling on masks, and I just followed along."

I held up my hand when I saw Gabriella's expression of disbelief.

"I know. It was stupid. When they started kicking poor Mr. Torres, that's when I realized my mistake. I had trusted Diego, believed his lie. They had planned to rob the store. There was no friend working that night. No ridiculous prank. They shoved me back in the car when it was all over. Even with the drugs, I was smart enough to know that the crew had guns and tempers. If I told anyone, I would be dead."

"I had no idea you had been through all that." Gabriella said.

My head flopped forward. I was so ashamed.

"I broke up with Diego the next day."

"Good for you." Mari patted my hand.

My eyes lifted. I had forgotten she was there, my focus so intent on my sister.

There was no judgment in her tone. I knew Mari had a tough life. From what she shared, it had not been easy growing up with an addict for a brother and an alcoholic stepfather. I also knew her mother dying when she was young had taken its toll. She might be one of the few people who really understood mistakes and getting a second chance. I squeezed her hand, grateful for the solidarity. I knew I picked Mari as my roommate for a reason.

"Why didn't you ever tell me?" Gabriella asked.

My shoulders slumped. "You were nineteen at the time. The last thing you needed was more drama in your life. César was working with the police. I wasn't about to involve him."

"What about mom?"

ALBUQUERQUE ALIBI

"She had her own struggles raising us on her own. I didn't want to burden her." I blinked back tears. "I needed to clean up my own mess."

"Is that why you volunteered at the church?"

"You remember that?"

"Yeah. It was your voice that got so many people involved in bake sales and yard sales. Raising money to help pay for Mr. Torres' hospital bills and get him back on his feet after the robbery. I also remember you visiting him at the hospital quite a bit. You were such an inspiration."

Tears streamed down my cheeks. "I'm such a fraud." I sobbed. "I'm the one that caused his suffering."

"You did not," Mari said. Eyes fierce and voice strong. There was no doubt in her words. No judgment in her gaze.

Both Gabriella and Mari held me while I cried. They told me everything was going to be ok. I knew it was a lie, but I didn't care. I crumbled in front of them. At one in the morning, Gabriella took off demanding I stop over for dinner at the restaurant before her shift started.

I crawled into bed wondering if I would get any sleep. My phone pinged, and I turned to see the message. It was from an unknown number.

'Hope you enjoyed the video. I'm sure your brother will too.'

I bolted upright in bed. It was Diego, my dirtbag of an ex.

What did that mean? Was he sending a copy to my brother?

I lay under the covers for hours thinking about everything, unable to close my eyes. I debated messaging back the number, but I decided doing nothing would be better. If I didn't respond, maybe he would think I hadn't gotten it yet. I watched as the sun rose and the light filtered in through the blinds before I finally gave up. Sighing, I went to take a shower and get dressed for work. Waiting for the coffee to brew, I unpacked the rest of the box, sorting it into piles to keep and donate. I added a third pile of items to burn. That included certain pictures of my ex and that video that had reminded me of a time I wasn't proud of. Both my sister and roommate had seen me at my absolute worst. I was grateful neither had rejected me, but I didn't want anyone else to witness it. I couldn't bear it if my mother found out, or my brother or Jac. What if Mr. Torres saw this? I couldn't imagine what he would say. At the bottom of the box was an envelope with my name on it. It looked new, not old like most of the other papers. I poured myself coffee, added the creamer and sugar and sat down at the kitchen table. I stared at the envelope as I sipped my coffee and nibbled on some toast. My curiosity got the better of me and I opened it. It was an old notecard with my initials on the front. I flipped the card and the coffee turned to acid in my gut. I dropped the card to the table, re-reading the scribbled words from my ex.

'Give me what I want, or this goes public. -D'

Chapter 6

Jac

Waiting in our normal booth, I thought about Sofía. What would she be wearing? What snippy little comment would she be bold enough to say to me? How she teased me and kept me laughing. I needed that in my life right now. The negative things from my job tended to stick with me if I didn't re-focus on the positive. Too many times I saw people at their worst. Criminals making horrible decisions, endangering the innocent. Sofía was the light in the midst of darkness. I needed that balance to stay sane, but she had been avoiding me. Any messages she sent were brief and cold. It didn't feel like the normal playful banter we shared back and forth. After the trip to Santa Fe with Mari, things had changed. I wondered if it had something to do with my mother. My mom had been pestering me about this so-called commitment that Sofía had mentioned. She wanted more details. We both did. That's why I was looking forward to this lunch, to finally get some answers. I needed information before I talked with my mom.

Sofía marched in wearing ridiculously high heels. The tight pencil skirt and low-cut silk blouse had blood flowing south. I shifted uncomfortably in my seat. She fanned herself with a pamphlet. Her hair had come undone and was spilling from the neat bun she often wore while working. Curly tendrils framed her face. She slid into the booth and glared at me. I wondered if I was in trouble for some reason. Had I been focused completely on her body? Who could blame me in that outfit?

"My air conditioning died on the way here."

"In your car?"

"Yes. My car. I wouldn't have lasted at the office the whole day with no a/c."

"Sorry?" I said, not knowing quite what to say. From her words, it was like she was blaming me. I'd offer to look at her car. But I wasn't sure if it would get my head bitten off.

I stared at a bead of sweat as it made its way down her neck into her cleavage. I slid my glass of ice water over to her.

"Have some. It looks like you're going to pass out."

She scowled at me. It only made her more beautiful. I smiled. Sofía snatched the straw and flung it on the table. With a sigh she took a long drink of water, draining my glass. Some dribbled down her chin and dampened her shirt. I licked my lips. I signaled for the waitress to bring us menus.

She brought over another glass and a full pitcher of water. The waitress was definitely getting a big tip.

"Do you want anything else to drink besides water?" She asked.

Sofía opened her mouth, but then shut it after looking at me.

"Do you want a margarita?"

She didn't respond, just put her arms over her chest, and stared at me.

"It looks like you could use one," I said.

Her eyebrows rose.

"A margarita and a Guinness, please." I ordered.

The waitress walked away.

"I don't need you to order for me."

"I know you wanted one. Why were you hesitating?"

ALBUQUERQUE ALIBI

"Why do you always have to be such a know-it-all?"

I sighed. Sofía was being a pain. Some days I just didn't understand her. I decided she needed to cool off. I'd keep my mouth shut and let her stew.

After a few minutes she huffed.

"Why aren't you saying anything?"

I quirked a brow.

"Fine. I know I'm being a bitch. I've just had a really bad day. Or rather week."

"You want to talk about it?"

She opened her mouth and closed it.

"It's just fate catching up with me."

What did that mean?

"Go on," I said.

"Having conversations I'd rather not have. Stirring up the past."

"We never did discuss what you and my mom talked about on your trip."

The waitress dropped off our drinks. Sofía's eyes lit up when she saw the margarita.

"You want to start there?" She asked.

Sofía took a few sips and then large gulps of her margarita.

"You'll give yourself a brain freeze."

"Then something on my body will finally be cold."

I shook my head, chuckling. She nearly finished off her margarita before beginning.

"I kept our pact. Your mother is not going to rope you into any more blind dates, at least for the moment."

I breathed a sigh of relief. "What did you tell her?"

"That you were already taken."

I wondered if that meant she wanted to push things further. Did she imply as much to my mother?

"Woah. Back it up there. Your eyes got way too hopeful. I didn't say it was with me."

Of course, she would smash that sliver of hope to pieces. "I see."

We ordered another round of drinks and sat in silence. I know I was upset over what she said. I wondered if it was pointless, our relationship. She obviously only wanted to be friends, despite the attraction. If she wanted to lie to herself, maybe I should take my mom up on her offer to set me up.

Sofía fiddled with her straw. She clearly didn't like the silence between us.

"I'm sorry." She sighed. "I wish things were different. Maybe, then." She gazed into my eyes. I saw the hurt. Sofía was obviously in pain. And here I was ready to bail. I rested my hand over hers.

"Is something else bothering you?"

She turned her head away, whispering, "Just running into people I'd rather not see."

Anger flared. I snatched my hand back. "I can always leave."

She whipped her head back around. "I didn't mean you. How could you think that?"

"Then talk to me. Who is bothering you?"

Sofía shook her head. She shivered, rolling her shoulders in and putting her hands in her lap. Someone had frightened her. That someone was going to pay.

"Give me a name." I said through gritted teeth.

Her eyes were like saucers.

"No. You can't."

"Why not?"

"It's complicated."

"When is it not?"

"He can do things. Just let me figure it out." She pleaded with me. "You can't be involved."

Why was she so concerned about keeping our friendship a secret? I knew the kind of men from her past. I had beaten one of her ex-boyfriends to a pulp three years ago. Sofía never failed to call me when she was in trouble. Why was she reluctant now?

"You know you can trust me."

"It's not that." She sniffed. "I just don't want to take you down with me."

Sofía might be in real danger. I had done background checks on the thugs she used to hang around. Some of them had criminal records, petty theft and drug possession. Mostly low-level stuff. One had abuse charges. Was someone hurting her physically? I stared at her. Reaching across the table, I lifted her chin. I couldn't see any bruising, but the lighting was horrible. I needed to check her over in the daylight. Was she covering for some asshole ex?

"I'm going to check out your car when we leave."

Sofía shook her head. "No. I don't want to be seen with you."

I didn't let her words bother me. She was saying it to irritate me in an effort to get her way. I wasn't falling for it. Not this time. I glared at her.

"You don't have a choice."

She blew out a breath and she crossed her arms over her chest. "You always were an asshole."

I snorted. No one else who knew me would ever call me that. I was a nice guy, and she knew it. I just wanted to help, but she kept pushing me away.

She dangled her car keys in front of my face. "Why wait until we are done. It's right across the street. You can't miss it. I think I'll wait here in the cool air conditioning." She leaned back into the booth. "You don't mind, do you?"

Sofía and her damn secrets. I snatched the keys and left her sitting there thinking she had won this battle of wills. That was fine by me. I wanted to do some snooping, anyhow.

I walked across the street to her beat-up Chevy Impala. She needed a new car. I knew Sofía was struggling for cash even though she had been working for a big pharmaceutical company for a couple of years. Sofía was paying her debt while going to school and working full-time. I was so proud of her. Sofía had told me for years how badly she wanted to move out of her mother's house. I'm glad, with Mari's help, she finally did it.

I unlocked her car and popped the hood. While I was inside the vehicle, I searched the glove box and under the seats. I found some receipts that I pocketed to look at later. There was a slightly pungent odor of aftershave and tobacco. There was some man in her car recently, and it wasn't César. I knew his brand of aftershave, and it wasn't anything quite so harsh. I glanced in the middle console and found an envelope. It said simply, 'I'm waiting.' Inside was an AC cap and a Schrader valve. I wondered if this was why Sofía's air conditioning was on the fritz. What I couldn't understand was why someone would do this. After looking under the hood, I confirmed the contents of the envelope were the missing pieces from her HVAC. Walking back to our booth. I threw the envelope and her keys onto the table.

"We need to talk."

Her jaw fell.

"Where did you find this?"

"In the car's console."

"Why would you be looking in there?"

I crossed my arms over my chest.

She avoided my expression and focused on the envelope. After studying the words, she peeked inside.

"What are these things?"

"They go to your HVAC system. It's why your car's AC sucks right now."

Sofía pinched the bridge of her nose.

"I see. "Do you know how to put these parts back on?" She asked.

I shook my head. Not at the question, but this situation. I actually did know how to put the parts back in, I just didn't have the tools to do so. Not that she needed to know that.

ALBUQUERQUE ALIBI

"Who did this?" I asked.

I saw the recognition in her eyes when she stared at the writing on the envelope. She knew. But it was clear after a few minutes of silence she wasn't going to talk. I had seen that resolute expression before.

My head flopped back. She wasn't going to give me answers. Again, keeping me in the dark, even though I did everything to be there for her. Let her brother handle it. I knew she would have to call him next. Maybe he could get answers.

"There's this thing called trust. Right now, we don't have it."

I stormed out of the restaurant. If Sofía wasn't going to share, then I couldn't help her. I was done.

Chapter 7

Sofia

I can't believe Jac had stormed out like that. It was totally out of character. It shouldn't surprise me. Even though Jac had the patience of a saint. But I guess even saints had their limits. I would have gotten sick of me too. I dreaded the next phone call, knowing my brother would ask questions. But I didn't have much of a choice. I couldn't afford to take it to a repair shop. Sure, I had tons of cousins that I could bug, but my brother was by far the most reliable. My other choice was to call Diego, and he was the bastard that took out the parts to begin with. I wasn't ready to call him yet. I still didn't have the info he needed.

I took a deep breath and dialed César, "Hey big brother."

"When you start out like that, I know you're in trouble. What's up?"

I sighed. "My car's AC is broken. I know what's wrong. I just need you to put the parts back in. It should be a quick fix."

"How do you know how long it will take? And what do you mean by back in? How did they fall out?"

I pinched my brow, knowing I had phrased it wrong.

"A guess?"

"You don't know anything about cars."

He was right. Changing a tire was outside my wheelhouse, but in my defense, my brother or Jac were only ever a phone call away.

"Are you going to help me or not?" I demanded.

"Of course. You shouldn't be driving around in this heat with no AC." He sighed. "I'm home from work. Stop by my apartment."

"Thanks bro. See you soon."

Ten minutes later I pulled into his complex, dripping sweat and looking pathetic. I had already tossed the envelope and handed him a spare grocery bag with the parts. It would have looked more authentic if they were in one of the auto part bags, but I was in a hurry.

His brows lifted. Maybe he'd still assume they were new. I had wiped them off so there was no grease. He popped the hood and found where they were supposed to go almost immediately. One of these days I should try learning something about cars.

"Do you know if you got the right parts?"

I shrugged. Playing dumb sounded like the right way to avoid answering any questions.

He grumbled. "Hang on. I need to grab another tool."

He bounded up the stairs and I let out a breath.

I needed to come up with a distraction before he asked more questions, so I found a spot in the shade and messaged Mari.

'What are you doing Chica?' I texted.

'Packing up the last of my Etsy orders for the day. What's up?'

'I'm calling a girl's night.'

'Woo hoo.'

'Texting Gabriella next. Let's get silly tonight.'

I messaged my sister, and she had the night off, so she was in. Just after she replied, César was back.

"The engine has probably cooled down enough by now."

"Explain what you're doing? It would be nice to learn."

ALBUQUERQUE ALIBI

He seemed surprised, but my brother loved to talk about cars. My eyes glazed over, but I tried to remain attentive and engaged in the lecture. When we went through and tested the vents and everything seemed to be working fine, he asked the question I had been dreading.

"So, how did the part come off without a tool?" César dropped the last item back in his tool bag.

His phone chimed.

"Who is it?" I asked.

"Mari." He tilted his head after reading the message. "You guys are doing a girl's night?"

"Oh yeah. Forgot. Gotta run, big brother. You're the best. Love ya."

I waved and floored it out of the complex before he could ask me any more questions. Once I was outside of his complex, I let out a long breath. That was close. My brother was incredibly good at interrogations. I could have easily slipped up. Maybe he'd forget all about it the next time we got together. Yeah. Probably not. But a girl's gotta have hope.

Dancing with Mari and Gabriella at the club had me feeling more like my old self. The Library Bar & Grill was a dance club and sports bar all rolled into one. The outside of the building had enormous books with funny titles like Tequila Mockingbird and Gone with the Gin. The inside had wall-to-wall shelving with real books, not that many patrons would pull books from the shelves. The servers were dressed in skimpy schoolgirl outfits. One of them working tonight was a cousin. You couldn't go anywhere in this town without running into one of my relatives.

I had a nice buzz going and was letting loose. I needed something to distract me from all my worries. I had too many of them lately. I didn't want Jac anywhere near Diego. The last time Jac had gotten involved, it had almost lost him his job.

I remembered back to when Jac had texted me after the incident three years ago. He had wanted me to meet him out by the swing set in my family's backyard. Tall trees shrouded the street and porch light casting shadows across the desert landscaping. It had always been a private place for us to talk when we were kids. That night he had arrived covered in blood. It was a few days after I had broken up with Diego. I had spilled my guts to Jac. Telling him everything except for the robbery. I had been too ashamed to reveal that. What I had shared had been enough to anger Jac to do something truly stupid. When he told me that Diego wouldn't bother me anymore, my first thought was he killed him. Jac had arrived through the back gate of the property covered in blood. He didn't give me any details at the time. Jac had this wild look in his eyes, like he wanted to make sure I was safe, then he left. After the initial shock, I realized this was Jac. He was a superhero, not a villain. There was no way he'd do anything so dark. A week later I learned the truth of what happened that night. Jac had beaten Diego up badly enough that it had landed him in ICU. I learned that from posts and comments on social media. I was still friends with some of Diego's friends at the time. Luckily for Jac, Diego hadn't pressed charges.

I didn't want to put Jac in that kind of position again. I was trying to protect him for a change. That's why I needed to keep my secrets. I knew Jac was still angry with me. But he would calm down eventually, just like he always did. I just needed to give him some time and space. He'd come around. He had to. I couldn't bear losing Jac as a friend. I had so few.

The girls and I sat back at our booth with a shared sigh. The exhaustion from dancing was worth it.

A waitress approached the table. "The men at that table wanted to buy you ladies a round of drinks."

"They'll want to come over here if we accept." Mari said.

I shrugged. "Tell them thanks." I rattled off our order.

ALBUQUERQUE ALIBI

"What are you doing?" Gabriella asked.

"Having fun," I said. "Don't worry. They're not going to bother us."

I knew how to back the guys off. It was a surefire way, unless they were complete idiots.

Holding up my glass, I smiled when we got our drinks.

It encouraged them to come over to our table.

Mari sighed. Gabriella looked panicked. She hadn't dated much, but then again, she was only 22, and the youngest in our family. Mi mamá babied her. Well, to be honest, both César and I hadn't been much better. She had only been bartending at Que Pasa's for the last few months. I knew she had already gotten propositioned several times, but to my knowledge hadn't accepted a single one.

"Hello boys," I said. "Thank you for the drinks, but we're all dating cops." My grin was feral.

Two of the men's eyes went wide. The third looked too drunk for the words to register. He slid into the booth next to Gabriella and put his arm around her. Mari looked like she was ready to stab him with her fork.

"A little help here." I said to the guy's friends. "Your friend is in for some major hurt. Her brother is a Detective for the Albuquerque PD, and her uncle is a Commander. The family is quite protective."

That's when I recognized one of the guys. He had gone to my high school. "You remember César Ramirez, right?"

"Oh fuck. She's his sister?"

"We both are." I gestured to Mari. "And she's his girlfriend."

"No, no, no. Man, we are out of here."

He yanked his friend roughly by the shirt and hauled him out of the booth.

"We didn't mean any disrespect."

The three of them made a hasty retreat and I chuckled.

"César's threats still hold weight."

"My boyfriend's such a badass." Mari giggled.

Gabriella just looked relieved to be out of the octopus' arms.

"Sorry sis. I didn't think he'd use you like an armrest."

"That's ok. There are plenty that get a little handsy at my work. I just didn't have much room to maneuver." She shrugged her shoulders. "César has shown me some self-defense moves to keep me safe."

"Do you have to use them often?" I asked. If her job was dangerous, I'd encourage her to quit. It wasn't worth it. I had gotten myself into difficult situations when I was her age. I didn't want her to learn the same hard lessons the way I had.

"I've only used them a few times. Most of the customers aren't that bad. Some of them are quite nice."

"Oh. Anyone in particular?" Mari asked.

Gabriella rolled her eyes.

"Well, there was this one guy. Super cute. My age. He shows up now and again."

"What's his name?"

"Ramón."

"He doesn't speak English very well, but he's super sweet. We sometimes talk about his mom. She died a few years ago. Now, he's searching for his dad. I told him to do one of those DNA kits."

"How do you know he's a nice guy?" I asked.

"You are just like César. Paranoid."

"Take that back," I said.

"You know me, sis. I've always been a good judge of character. Plus, Ramón warned me about some sketchy guy hanging around my car. He even walked me out one night to make sure I was safe."

"So, what moves did César show you?"

She rattled off a series of pressure points and pulled out her keys. She had a kubaton hanging off her keychain.

ALBUQUERQUE ALIBI

"César gave you one too?" I asked.

Mari pulled out her keychain kubaton as well. We all burst out laughing.

"To the kubaton club." I raised a drink in a toast.

Gabriella was focused on practicing moves with her kubaton, naming off pressure points as she went. A couple of guys who had been staring at us got up and left the bar.

"Your sister is such a badass." Mari grinned.

Gabriella blushed.

"We all are," I said. Gabriella set her keys down and we all drank to that.

Diego continued to message me over the next few days. I didn't respond. His text messages were getting more frequent and violent. Early Friday morning, I got a call. I cringed until I saw the number. It was my boss.

"Hey Sofia. Sorry it's so early. But I need you to get a few things for me before my 8 am meeting."

Mitch rattled off a list of things and I wiped sleep out of my eyes and jotted it all down. My heart leapt into my throat. This was my opportunity to get Diego what he needed and finally get him off my back for good. Mitch wanted printouts of the latest shipments going out to a large pharmacy chain he was working with. He needed it for his meeting. They were going to review the list and make changes as needed before the deliveries. After printing off the copies, I made an extra copy for myself. I met Mitch at the Starbucks at 7:30. Mitch bought me a coffee, thanking me profusely and telling me to take a nice long lunch hour. I headed into the office wondering if I should reach out to Diego. But like clockwork, he messaged me instead.

'We need to meet. Lynda's Cafe. Noon.'

I sent a thumbs up emoji. I didn't even want to send that, but I knew he'd blow up my phone if I didn't.

It was a strange place to choose, further away from my office than I would normally pick to go to lunch. Not that he cared if it inconvenienced me. Luckily, I had some extra time today. I had what Diego wanted. Not that I had fully decided to give it to him. I was still debating. Maybe I could give him an excuse he'd believe. I could tell him I no longer had access to shipment details, security measures had cracked down. Anything so I didn't have to do this and betray the company that had been so good to me. What would he do if that was the case? I knew it was a risk, but the more I thought about the video of the robbery, the more I believed it was a bluff. If he shared it with anyone, wouldn't that implicate him and his crew as well? Why would he do that? It didn't make sense. Although Diego had never been known for his brains. He might be willing to take me down, just out of spite.

He was sitting at the front window of the café when I arrived. I plopped into the seat opposite him and glared. I had worked up my nerve on the drive over.

"What do you want?"

The question came out snarky as hell.

His eyebrows rose almost to his hairline.

"I asked you for information." He whispered looking around the café. "My patience is at its end."

I rolled my eyes. "An end would imply there was a beginning. You've never had patience."

He smiled, a baring of the teeth. And it made me recoil back before I could stop myself. Diego was an attractive man, but when he got vicious, he got ugly in a hurry.

"I thought you were going to be smart about this. I have other ways of getting the info."

If he didn't need me, then maybe I was off the hook. I wouldn't have to give him the paperwork sitting in my purse.

He tapped his fingers on the glass, and I watched my sister come out of Que Pasa's restaurant and walk to her car. My eyes went wide with fear. It didn't register that we were right across the street from where she worked.

"What did you do?"

I knew he had tampered with my car. What would he do to my sister's?

"It's not what I did, but what I can do to your sister, Gabriella."

He passed me a list on a piece of paper. It had locations and times. I realized it was my sister's schedule, and not just her normal work hours. He knew when she went to yoga, when she got together with her friends for book club. It had her favorite pizza place, and the grocery store she frequented. He had been stalking her.

"She's so darn predictable. It's almost too easy."

"What do you want?"

Diego rolled his eyes.

"Stop pretending you don't know."

I bit my lip and yanked the paperwork I had copied from my purse and shoved it across the table.

He opened it up and nodded his head.

"This will do."

"This is it. We're over." I waved my arms emphatically, making an X in the air. "Never contact me again."

"Yeah. Sure. Whatever you say, Sofía." He strolled out of the café.

I had given him what he wanted. The smug bastard was smiling while my world had just imploded.

Chapter 8

Jac

My phone rang. I looked at the caller ID. It was César. I didn't want to talk with him. I knew what was coming. It was Sunday. I had a standing invitation to the Ramirez almuerzo de domingo.

"Hey Jac. Are you going to be here for lunch? Mi mamá wanted me to double-check. She made tamales."

I groaned. That was cruel. I loved Irene's tamales, but I had to say no. I didn't want to be anywhere near Sofía. I was still angry with her. I had cooled a bit, but I didn't think it would change anything. Staying away was safer for everyone.

"You got someone over there, don't you?" He chuckled.

I didn't want to lie to César, but Sofía had placed me in an awkward situation. Maybe I should say I had company. That would at least make a decent excuse.

"You dog. I thought you needed to get some."

If I said nothing, he would assume, and I'd be off the hook. Still, it felt too much like a lie. In the end, I settled on a half-truth.

"My stomach's a little off today."

It had been that way since I stormed away from Sofía on Thursday.

"You must be sick if you are going to turn down mi madre's tamales."

"I thought Irene said she was making a chicken dish this week."

"Sofía convinced her that we needed to do something special. She even bought all the ingredients herself. The girls have been busy all weekend."

Maybe this was her way of apologizing. Sofía knew how much I loved tamales. It was my all-time favorite dish.

"Yeah. I'll be there."

I sat across the table from Sofía. She bit her lip as she stared at me. I wondered if Sofía thought I wouldn't show. She had texted me a few times, but I hadn't responded.

"Is everything ok?" She asked.

Her eyes were wide. I knew what she was asking, but I wasn't about to talk here in front of everyone.

"The tamales are delicious," I said.

"I, uh, well César said you weren't feeling that great."

My eyes narrowed.

"I'm fine."

It came out harsher than I wanted it to. Everyone at the table stared at me. I let out a breath. This was what I was afraid of. Everyone would see my anger and assume correctly that Sofía and I had been fighting.

"Well then eat up." Irene said. "There's plenty more."

César gave me a look, and I knew what it meant. We'd talk later. He knew I was off. I wanted to get out of there before someone in the family cornered me.

The meal was filled with awkward silence, not a common occurrence with the Ramirez lunches. Everyone usually talked over one another.

ALBUQUERQUE ALIBI

"So, Gabriella, anything exciting happen at Que Pasa's, lately?" Sofía asked.

Gabriella shook her head.

"What about that cute boy, what's his name again?"

"Ramón?" She asked.

"Has he stopped by lately?"

"Yeah. Last night." Gabriella sighed.

"La, la, la." César said, covering his ears. "I don't want to hear anything about your love life. I hear they are accepting new postulants at the Sisters of Charity."

Both Sofía and Gabriella groaned, shaking their heads at their brother.

"Postulants?" Ms. Ramirez bellowed. "Then I'll never get grandkids? Shame on you Césarito."

She started beating him with the large serving spoon that had been stuck in the rice bowl. Bits of rice flicked across the table. No one dodged it but Mari. Everyone else was used to this sort of behavior at the Ramirez Sunday lunch. It was practically a tradition.

"Stop, Mamá." He held up his hands trying to deflect the blows.

"Ignore your brother. You must bring this Ramón boy over for a visit," Irene said, setting down the spoon.

"I don't know. He's kind of shy." Gabriella shrugged. "What about you, Sofía?"

She sputtered and choked on her wine.

Sofía scowled at her sister.

"Got any hot dates on the horizon?"

"Anyone need more salsa?" Sofía said, diving into the kitchen.

Her mother stared at the full bowl of salsa sitting on the dining room table and frowned.

ZIZI HART

I felt everyone's eyes on me as I grabbed a few chips and spooned salsa onto my plate. For the rest of the meal, I gave my food intense concentration. The awkward silence continued.

After dinner, Irene asked Gabriella to clear the table, César to do the dishes, and Mari to prepare after-dinner drinks in the den. My mind churned, struggling for an excuse so I could make a quick exit without appearing rude.

"Would you be a dear and help Sofía in the attic? I wanted to move something downstairs. It's too heavy for me. She knows where it is and can point it out. It's an heirloom, so be careful."

My mouth opened to say something, but nothing came out. Not that she gave me much of a chance. She patted my chest. "You are such a good boy."

I was almost going to ask her why she hadn't assigned this little task to César instead. He would have been the logical choice to help carry some family heirloom downstairs from the attic. But I also knew that Irene was shrewd. She was forcing me and Sofía alone to resolve whatever was going on between us. But Irene didn't realize there was no fix. Not until Sofía came clean. She couldn't continue to keep me in the dark. I had to fight back and let her know I wouldn't stand for it. I knew her brother had repaired her car's AC. He had bitched about it the next day at work. I was almost positive she hadn't mentioned the envelope and what it said, otherwise I would have heard something far different from her brother.

Sofía was waiting upstairs. She had already pulled on the rope extending a set of wooden stairs that led to the attic. I followed her up watching her rear end swish in the sexy summer dress she wore. On Sunday, we usually wore nicer clothes to family lunch, but Sofía had taken extra care today. She caught me staring at her legs and pursed her lips.

I cleared my throat, "What is it I need to carry down?"

I glanced around the dusty attic. There were old pieces of furniture and plenty of boxes to choose from. How long was this search going to take?

ALBUQUERQUE ALIBI

"I'm sorry about Thursday." She came close enough to put her hands on my chest. Whatever she saw in my expression made her pull back at the last minute and turn.

"If you must know, it's an ex that's been bothering me."

I figured as much, but it was good to hear her finally admit it.

Sofía shook her head. "I'm not telling you his name."

Defiant to the last.

"What makes you think I can't figure out who it is?"

Her eyes blinked up at me. Worry and fear.

"Don't." She whispered, wringing her hands together.

"Why?"

I closed the gap between us. My arms wrapped around her. I wanted her to look at me, but she was averting my gaze. I shook her gently.

"Why?" I repeated.

"I don't want him to hurt you."

I laughed. Hard.

She glared at me.

"Sofía. Look at me." I stepped back. "What could he do?"

Her wanna-be thug ex-boyfriends couldn't do a thing. Is that what she had been worried about? She was trying to protect me. My anger from Thursday dissipated. I closed the small gap between us and kissed her. I had been wanting to do it for several weeks now, ever since I had been back here full-time. She moaned into my mouth and wrapped her arms around me, clinging to me like I was her last hope. Sofía blinked half-lidded, lust-filled eyes when we came up for air. She licked her lips.

"Why did you do that?"

I shrugged. "Because I wanted to."

"But our agreement..."

I folded my arms across my chest.

"Is over."

"What do you mean, over?"

"I'm not playing your games anymore."

"Games?"

My eyebrows rose. She wanted me to spell it out.

"This hot and cold thing you have going on."

She frowned.

"You either want me or you don't," I smirked. "And I'm pretty sure it wasn't me making those sexy moaning sounds moments ago."

"I was shocked. That's all."

"Deny all you want."

She huffed and walked toward the back of the attic, shoving boxes out of the way.

"Here." She pointed to an antique jewelry cabinet with intricate carvings. The legs were curved and spindly and barely looked able to support the large cabinet.

I picked it up with ease, and Sofía snorted.

She climbed down the steps in front of me. I had to take it down the steps backward. Slowly. The piece wasn't necessarily heavy, at least for me. However, it was awkward enough that I could understand why Irene needed help moving it.

After drinks and dessert, I left the Ramirez family home with a full belly and a light heart. I whistled as I walked to my car. I was in a good mood. Sofía hadn't said as much, but I felt like we had an understanding. Not that it had a label, but that was ok. We were headed in the right direction. I now knew that if I pushed for more, Sofía wouldn't stop me.

Chapter 9

Sofia

Flashing lights in my rearview window and a siren were the last thing I needed. I pulled over to the curb and a series of curse words flowed from my lips. My head fell forward into the steering wheel and my horn gave a pathetic noise. It sounded like a goose honking. A sick goose. Even the horn on my piece of shit car sucked. I was already running late for work.

"Do you know why I pulled you over, ma'am?"

"Were you bored?"

The officer was cute, but super young, with a high-pitched nasally voice and a snarky attitude. I might have been able to get out of the ticket if I had flirted, but instead I antagonized him. A mistake, I know, but I wasn't at my best this morning.

He frowned.

"You were speeding."

"Really?" I asked, forcing my eyes to go wide with shock.

Of course, I knew the reason. I wasn't an idiot.

"I clocked you going 11 miles over the speed limit."

I rolled my eyes.

"There are probably people going way faster right now."

ZIZI HART

I pointed at a red sports car zooming past. "Look at that one. He has to be going at least 80. If you hurry, you can catch him."

A few of the people in the cars passing were waving, or maybe giving us the finger. Possibly both. Why wasn't he pulling any of them over? Why was he picking on me?

The officer started preaching on the importance of obeying the law. The dangers of speeding. The lecture went on and on. I wondered if he was doing it on purpose, trying to teach me a lesson. I could have told him that it wasn't going to work on me. I caught myself yawning several times, but it hadn't been on purpose. I was legitimately exhausted.

"Sorry, officer. I haven't had my morning coffee. I ran out."

For a moment, he showed a bit of sympathy, but then redoubled his efforts, climbing back onto his soap box. Why did I have to get pulled over by Officer 'Chatty' Gonzales?

He finally asked for my license and registration and went to fill out all the essential paperwork back in his car.

My phone pinged a few times. I looked at the last text from my boss.

'Are you coming in?'

'I got pulled over for speeding.' I responded.

'Impossible. Your car doesn't look like it can get over 30."

'LMFAO.' I responded.

A half hour later I rolled into the employee parking lot. I grabbed a coffee from the cafeteria and hurried to my office. I was using a napkin to wipe up the bit that had dribbled down the side, when I slammed full force into someone walking the other way around the corner.

The lid popped off and nearly all the contents splashed onto some hunky guy in a black business suit. I wanted to cry. Not for myself, or even the other person, but rather for the liquid energy that I wouldn't have to power me through this miserable day. I know it was selfish, but right now I didn't care. I finally let

ALBUQUERQUE ALIBI

my eyes focus on the person I ran into. It was Nicolas, the head of building security. I wanted to crawl into a hole. He was the last person I wanted to see. I felt like he could see straight through me to the thick layer of guilt surrounding my soul. The real reason I was such a mess today.

"Sorry about that." I used some of the napkins to try to dry his soaked suit. After a few moments, I gave up and blew out a breath. "I'm having a bad day."

"Well, at least you are sharing it with others."

I stared at him. I didn't realize he had a sense of humor. We had seen each other at Biogen events over the years, but we hadn't spent much time talking. He always seemed busy or surrounded by a bevy of women. The guy was gorgeous, with dark wavy hair and golden skin. He had broad shoulders that tapered down to a trim waist. I could tell he worked out, but he also may have been blessed with wicked good genetics. His last name was Mendoza which didn't tell me diddly where he was from. Latin, obviously, but not Mexican from his accent. If I had to guess, I would think his origin was much further south. His English tutor had to be expensive. Nicolas enunciated his words too clearly to have learned in the U.S. Maybe he had a speech therapist growing up.

I shook my head realizing I had been gawking at the man, while he had been patiently letting me look my fill. Could this get any more awkward?

He held out his hand. I wasn't sure what he wanted. Was he going to whisk me away to the authorities? Had he already figured out my secret?

"The cup and napkins," he said.

I reluctantly handed them over and he turned and threw them into a nearby trash can.

"Are you all right, Sofía?"

Oh, dear lord. He knew my name.

I gulped.

He steered me into a vacant conference room and closed the door.

My heart started pounding. It was so loud I thought for sure he could hear it.

He swiped a hand over my forehead, then slid a soft palm down my cheek. He lifted my chin gently to meet his intense gaze. I saw only concern in his eyes, and the tightness in my shoulders loosened. I pressed my cheek into his hand for a moment, then I stood straight.

He took a step back, probably realizing how inappropriate it was to be touching me like that. Not that I minded. I needed some reassurance today.

He glanced down at his chest, "I should change before my next meeting."

"You keep extra clothes at the office?"

He grinned. "I always expect the unexpected." His eyes sparkled with laughter. "You never know when a beautiful woman will shower you with... her affections."

I licked my lips. I don't think he was implying coffee. I believe he was insinuating something else, and I was just sexually starved enough to catch the innuendo.

His phone vibrated. Nicolas glanced at it and swore.

"Until we run into each other again. Hopefully next time without the coffee."

He left me standing alone in the conference room with my nerves frayed. I really needed to get laid if I had thought for even a split second that an office fling was a good idea.

I arrived at my desk, ninety minutes late for work. Mitch gave me raised eyebrows, and I shook my head. I didn't want to hear it. I focused on my work, or at least tried to in between butterflies in my stomach. I had no idea when Diego would do the deed. When would his crew strike? I knew exactly what he planned. They were going to steal drugs from Biogen. Of course, I didn't know when or where. The schedule had multiple shipments over the next week. But it had to be soon. That's the only thing I knew for certain. I worked through lunch trying to redeem myself in my boss' eyes and catch up from this morning. Mitch had to leave the office in the afternoon to meet with some clients, so I had some free time to sneak downstairs for a break. I still hadn't had my caffeine fix for the day, and I was dragging despite the adrenaline.

Down in the cafeteria, I searched through the refrigerator of pre-made sandwiches, salads, and yogurts. They stopped serving hot lunch late in the afternoon, and mostly just offered snacks. I grabbed the last turkey sandwich, some fruit, and a soda. After paying, I set my tray down at an empty table. That's when I saw him. Nicolas was sitting at the table across from me. We made eye contact, and I panicked. My legs gave out and I went to sit down. I missed. My butt hit the floor, and I was stunned for a moment. I glanced over at the chair. It was one foot to my right. I was so flustered at seeing Nicolas. My eyes closed. Maybe if I stayed on the floor, he'd think I meant to do it. Sure. Sitting on the sticky floor of a cafeteria. That was the plan. I just hoped nobody else witnessed my ridiculous fall.

I opened my eyes slowly. Nicolas stood over me staring. He wasn't looking into my eyes. I glanced down. My skirt barely covered my hips. I pulled on the fabric, covering what I could. He put out his hand, and I took it, grateful that he hadn't made any comment, or worse laughed. He helped me to my feet. I glanced around the cafeteria. Luckily very few people were there. No one else had witnessed my fall or wardrobe malfunction. Nicolas held out my seat for me. I put both hands over my face and elbows on the table. I could feel heat coming off my cheeks. I was mortified. I heard the screech of a chair to my left, and the clatter of another tray hitting the table. I knew he was sitting next to me, but I was too embarrassed to open my eyes.

He still hadn't said anything. It sounded like he was eating his lunch. I peeked through my fingers and saw him grinning.

"Why are you still here?" I asked.

"I figured you might need a spotter."

My hands slapped the table. "Ha. Ha. Very funny."

"Did you hurt anything when you fell?"

"Yeah. My pride."

He snorted.

"I'm fine." I had plenty of padding. I was a curvy girl, after all. "Really. You don't have to babysit me."

"Hmm," was his response.

Nicolas popped the last bite of his sandwich into his mouth and crumpled up the wrapper.

He was so calm and collected, and I was a bundle of nerves. I took a sip of my soda with trembling hands. I stabbed a piece of fruit, and the fork tips broke off. He removed the broken fork from my hand.

"I might need to stick close. You are liable to claim workman's comp."

His words were harsh, but his eyes held warmth.

My head fell forward. Utter humiliation. Everything I did today was a disaster. So far Nicolas hadn't figured out the real reason for my worry. I gave him a sly smile and ate my sandwich. He tilted his head watching me in silence. When I was finished, he escorted me back to my desk.

"Let me know if you need anything, Sofia."

He said my name slowly, like a lover, and it warmed me. Getting the attention of such an attractive man was a welcome distraction from the worry that had been plaguing me all day.

Nicolas was in the elevator at the end of the day, and he followed me down to the lobby. We weren't alone, so we didn't make small talk, but I could feel his eyes on me as I crossed to the parking garage. I glanced back for a moment. He was talking with someone, but our eyes connected, and I took a deep breath. When I got to my car, I let out the breath I had been holding. What a fucked-up day. At least nothing had happened. No alerts. No police. I didn't know how I was going to get through the week. Maybe I should call in sick? Or would that be a sure sign that I

ALBUQUERQUE ALIBI

was involved? I put my car in drive. I kept to the speed limit, making sure I did nothing to cause myself another ticket. Concentrate, I told myself. Just get back to the apartment. My sole goal had narrowed to a single purpose, to soak in the tub and drown myself in a bottle of Rosé.

Chapter 10

Jac

I heard laughter as I turned the corner and saw César in the middle of a bunch of officers, probably just getting done telling some totally crude and inappropriate joke. I grinned. He hadn't changed much since high school. César waved me over.

"You won't believe what Gonzales was just telling me."

"Yeah?"

"Sofía got pulled over yesterday morning for speeding."

"That doesn't seem like her," I said.

"You don't know my sister like I do." César knocked me in the shoulder.

I thought I knew her far better than he did, but I didn't say that out loud.

"I bet she was pissed."

"Oh, yes. And she was feisty as hell. Gonzales asked her if she knew why he pulled her over, and she said something about him being bored. Gonzales was livid. He didn't know she was my sister, though. Right, GZ?" César glared at Officer Gonzales.

"Look man, I never would have made that comment about her rack if I had known."

My jaw dropped. This rookie was in trouble. I felt my own temper rising, but I maintained control. César on the other hand didn't have the same kind of restraint. When it came to his sisters, César was excessively protective. I didn't know much about Gonzales other than he was one of the new recruits that had joined patrol. He rolled his shoulders and made an effort to look contrite. Gonzales licked his lips and was visibly sweating.

"I just meant she was good looking, that's all." He held up his hands. "She didn't say anything about having family on the force. How was I supposed to know?"

César patted him on the back, then grabbed him by the scruff of his neck and gave a good shake while giving him a hug. It looked good-natured, nothing overtly threatening as long as you ignored César's feral grin and evil laugh. He yanked the kid's neck back, forcing him to meet his gaze.

"It's all good. You tore up the ticket. Right? No need for bodily damage."

Gonzales nodded his head rapidly up and down, then walked away. He moved as fast as he could to the other side of the office. A few of the guys watching the interaction chuckled. I didn't blame César. If the guy had made some comment about Sofía when I was here, I might have wanted to punch Gonzales too. César was clearly fighting the urge.

"You need to go to the gym?"

He shook his head. "Nah. I'm good."

We walked over to my desk. César always defended his sisters, even when they did wrong. I cared about them too, especially since we all grew up together. Now that we worked together in the same department, César and I felt more like brothers than ever before. Of course, with Sofía, there were no sister vibes. Never had been. With her, my emotions had always been complicated.

"Have you called Sofía?"

"No, not yet. Let her sweat. She needs to think about the consequences before I tell her the ticket was tossed."

ALBUQUERQUE ALIBI

So much for brotherly love.

"She was snarky as hell to GZ." César chuckled. "Sofía yawned right through his whole spiel on the dangers of speeding. He had memorized a whole speech, straight from the textbooks."

She shouldn't be driving while tired. That wasn't good. I hope her exhaustion didn't have anything to do with me. We had that amazing kiss on Sunday but hadn't talked since then. It's not like we were dating or anything. I knew she still needed to go slow, but I felt like we had made it past a huge barrier. Was she losing sleep over it? Maybe I should give her a call and make sure she was ok. I glanced at the top file on my desk, knowing it was something new. I flipped open the folder.

"I got assigned a hi-jacking in the warehouse district."

"It's better than me. I have to go hunt down some low-level dealers on the south side."

"Maybe we can swap partners at some point."

"I'm with you on that. Give it a few months. The lieutenant knows we want to work together, but you also need to learn the ropes. Different departments, different rules."

"Yeah. I know."

"Your partner is by the book. Your personalities mesh."

"I resent that. I'm nothing like him. He's like dry toast. I don't think the guy has ever cracked a smile."

"But he's been around. He knows how to kiss ass. And you are the fresh new hot shot who took down Lobo Rojo."

"You and me. We did it together."

"Yeah, but I was in the shadows. I don't get the press, and that's the way I like it."

I knew César enjoyed working undercover. He didn't need the accolades. I always had more ambition, at least in my career. We were both detectives, but I didn't see César advancing much further. He liked where he was, and didn't see the need for change. He enjoyed grunt work, being in the thick of danger. Although I wondered if that would last, given his relationship with Mari. She was domesticating him, whether he wanted or believed that to be the case.

I watched as Detective Carson made his way over to my desk. He was wearing a dark blue suit and tie, his usual attire. It's like the man only owned a single suit, but I knew that wasn't true. Carson had shared his preference for color and style and bragged about the number he owned. The only indication of his age, late forties, was the greying around the temples of his brown hair. Although I had been called a neat freak in the past, Carson was another beast entirely. The man never took off his jacket, even at the office, and didn't seem to sweat, even in the worst heat of the summer.

"Let's roll." He said, patting my shoulder.

I grabbed the suit jacket hanging on the back of my chair. I smoothed the front of my jacket and straightened my tie.

César grinned. I could tell he wanted to say something, but all that came out was, "Have fun."

I followed Carson out to the parking lot. He always drove his black Chevy Tahoe.

"I haven't read the full report yet. Where are we headed?"

"Biogen." He said after starting the car.

Great. With my luck I'd probably run into Sofía, and she would give me hell. Like I was stalking her instead of it just being a coincidence that she worked at the same place a crime I was investigating was committed.

After security checked us in, we were escorted up to the executive conference room on the fourth floor. A young woman led us into the empty room.

"Mr. Mendoza will be with you shortly."

She turned and closed the door behind us. We hadn't been offered water or coffee. Not that I was thirsty, but it seemed like

ALBUQUERQUE ALIBI

a slight. Perhaps an intentional insult. Or maybe I was reading too much into it.

We were meeting with the head of building security, Nicolas Mendoza. I hadn't found much on him while searching my phone's internet, only that he had worked for Biogen for ten years. I glanced around the conference room. It gave the feel of wealth and intimidation, from the crystal decanter of water to the large mahogany table and leather chairs. Even the accent lighting seemed to add drama to the space. Although the most stunning feature was the tinted floor-to-ceiling windows that offered a spectacular view of the city. After about fifteen minutes, a young man in a custom suit strolled in and shook our hands.

"Detective Carson. Detective Dillon. Thank you for coming in. I apologize for the wait. Please take a seat."

We both looked at one another. We had signed in at the front desk, but he had matched the correct name with the face. I saw a lot of surveillance cameras when we walked in and figured he had watched us as we entered. The wait was probably more of a tactic than tardiness. I had seen others use that strategy and expected no difference from a big corporation like Biogen.

"We have had quite the busy morning as you already know."

The man seemed a little flustered, but it could have been an act. "Where are my manners." He pressed a button on the phone. "Ginger, can you get the detectives some refreshments?"

"We don't need anything, thanks." Carson said.

I pulled out my notepad. Detective Carson always took point and I just listened in, as had been the routine so far in our partnership. It was a little one-sided if you asked me, but I was willing to take a back seat if it made things smoother between us. I had the feeling Carson felt a little threatened by me and my recent fame taking down El Lobo Rojo.

I jotted the name Mendoza and scrutinized the man in front of us. I recognized the accent. He had a similar one to Luís

Lorenzo. That probably meant the man was from Colombia. I knew there was a feud between the Mendozas and the Lorenzos, and had been for decades. They were both well-known drug families. Of course, that didn't mean that Nicolas was one of those Mendoza's. It was a common surname.

"Well, gentlemen, let's get started. I have the preliminaries, but there are still a few questions I need for insurance purposes."

Carson blinked slowly. Mendoza had surprised him.

"We haven't finished our investigation. In fact, we just started." Carson wiped a hand down his face. "Don't you want the shipment to be found? The hijackers prosecuted?"

Nicolas smiled, but it didn't reach his eyes. It was cunning and calculated.

"Speed is of the essence, Detectives. Our CEO has requested that you wrap this up quickly and quietly. He is calling your chief now. I would check with your superiors if I were you. All we need from you right now is paperwork."

Carson got up from the table to the far end of the conference room and checked his phone. He had put it on silent when we had arrived. I stared at Nicolas, who sat quietly with relaxed shoulders, leaning back in one of the comfortable boardroom chairs.

Carson came back a few minutes later and blew out a breath as he took a seat.

Nicolas slid a single sheet of paper over to him. He did it with one finger, his middle one. I don't think he liked us very much. Although he did nothing outright offensive, it was clear we were not welcome. After we answered the questions for Biogen's insurance and promised to email him a copy of the police report, Nicolas thanked us and asked an assistant to escort us to the lobby. On the way, I ran into Sofía. She was waiting for an elevator.

"Hey, can we talk?" I asked.

Sofía looked over at the assistant and back at me.

"I'm working." She whispered.

ALBUQUERQUE ALIBI

The door opened on the third floor, and she got off. I joined her, not giving her a choice.

"I'll be downstairs in a minute," I yelled to Carson.

Our escort opened her mouth to say something, but Carson hit the elevator button, and it closed before she could react.

Carson winked at me just before the doors closed. He had looked like a scolded dog up until that moment. I felt the same way. Biogen's need to close the case quickly sent up red flags. I wouldn't pass up the chance to talk with Sofía. She might have information vital to this case.

I followed her to a small desk in front of a large private office.

"I'm busy." Sofía said.

"I realize that. Hey, do you know anything about the hijacking from this morning?"

The stack of files she was holding slipped from her fingers and fell to the floor.

"Shoot."

Sofía bent down to gather them up, and I tried to help, but she slapped away my hands.

"Why are you here?" She whispered.

"Investigating. The hijacking. It's a police matter." I didn't feel like telling her we had already gotten kicked out of Biogen. Our investigation had begun and ended with a report. She didn't need to know that part.

Sofía sat down in her seat looking forlorn. Her phone rang.

"Biogen. Mr. Hammond's office."

A few seconds pause.

"Yes. Send him up."

Sofía closed her eyes. I think she was hoping I might disappear. I wasn't about to go away that easy.

"I'm sorry for the other night at your mom's."

I was not remotely sorry about the kiss.

"I don't know what you mean."

"Oh yes, you do." My eyes twinkled.
"There is nothing to discuss."
"You're deflecting."
"And you're being a pain in my ass."

We were interrupted by a man carrying a large bouquet of red roses in a glass vase.

"Ms. Sofía Ramirez?"

"Yes. That's me."

"A delivery guy dropped these off at the front desk." The man cleared his throat nervously. "Where do you want them?"

The man wore khakis and a polo. A Biogen badge dangled from his lanyard. Obviously, he wasn't an executive. More likely he worked in the mailroom. He glanced between the two of us looking like he wanted to be anywhere but here. I'm sure he felt the tension growing.

Who sent her flowers? She wasn't seeing anyone. Sofía didn't want a relationship. She had made that abundantly clear. Although she had lied to me before. The anger boiled inside me.

"Aren't you going to read the card?" I asked. My voice came out harsher than I wanted it to, almost a growl.

The mailroom guy set the flowers down on her desk and practically sprinted to the elevators.

Sofía blew out a breath, finding the card among the thorns. A small smile lit up her features as she read it to herself.

"What does it say?"

She rolled her eyes.

"Hope today is better."

"Who is it from?"

She shook her head. "I have no idea. It's not signed."

"But you must have some clue."

Sofía glared at me. "I'm not a mind reader, or a detective. I had a bad day yesterday, and people here are nice."

"Did your boss send you those?"

ALBUQUERQUE ALIBI

She threw her head back, staring at the ceiling. "I don't know. Maybe. I will have to ask him later. When he gets back from his appointments."

Nicolas Mendoza walked into the office. He stopped in his tracks when he saw me.

"Did you get lost, Detective Dillon? I assumed you left."

"Sofía and I have known each other since we were kids, so I thought I'd say hi."

He glanced at her, clearly looking for confirmation and she shrugged.

"What lovely flowers Ms. Ramirez. Almost as lovely as you."

I rolled my eyes. The guy was flirting, and cheesy as all hell.

Sofía giggled.

I gritted my teeth to keep from saying anything I might regret.

"Is Mr. Hammond back from his meeting?"

"Not yet, but I can let you know as soon as he comes in."

"Thank you."

"Detective Dillon. Your escort should not have left your side. It is Biogen's policy that visitors don't wander off. I will walk you down to the lobby myself."

Nicolas gestured for me to leave, and I didn't have much of a choice. After one more glance at Sofía, I left.

"I would appreciate it if you left Ms. Ramirez alone. She signed an NDA with Biogen, and you would not want to do something to cause the loss of her job, would you?"

"No. Of course not."

Nicolas obviously didn't care for the police, or maybe I was simply competition he wanted to remove.

"Very good. Then I don't expect to see you around here again."

Carson and I walked out the main doors.

"Please tell me you got something useful, and the detour wasn't just a booty call."

I grimaced. He was closer to the truth than I wanted to admit.

Carson made a frustrated sound, and we walked to the parking lot in silence.

He started the car and turned to me. "You've got to learn to control your hormones." Carson blew out a breath. "We have work to do."

Chapter 11

Sofia

It was almost the weekend. I sure needed a break from all the stress this past week. Maybe I would splurge and get myself a massage. I rolled my neck as I waited in line for my morning coffee. The Biogen cafeteria was slower than usual, and it gave me time to think how lucky I was. Biogen had completed their internal investigation and had sent the police report to the insurance. It didn't seem like security had been all that concerned about the hijacking. I had asked Nicolas if he thought it would affect our profit shares, and he had reassured me this was a blip on Biogen's radar. Insurance would handle this inconvenience. It made me beat myself up a little less, since it was my fault that it happened in the first place. I still felt bad, but not terrible. Since I had arrived early, I had plenty of time to unwind before the workday began. I sat down at one of the empty tables to sip my coffee and nibble on my cinnamon roll. Sugar and caffeine. My eyes closed.

"Mmm."

"I'm not sure I should interrupt."

I grinned at Nicolas.

He seemed less threatening over the last few days while he had been flirting with me. I told myself it was harmless.

"Have a seat." I gestured.

He pulled out a chair and set his own coffee down on the table.

"Maybe I should move over. We know how your coffee tends to fly off on its own."

"Ha. Ha. Nope I'm not sharing today. I'm getting every last drop."

"How about the cinnamon roll? There is no more left. It appears you snagged the last one."

"Arm wrestle for a piece?" I asked.

He chuckled. "I think I will let you savor every morsel. It is far more entertaining watching you."

I shrugged my shoulders and took another bite. I couldn't help but moan. I was a foodie. No surprise there by my figure, but cream cheese icing was my kryptonite. I couldn't say no.

Nicolas walked me up to my office and seemed to want to ask me something, but then he got an urgent call and had to step away. I promised to save him a seat for lunch, however it was not meant to be. I had no idea how horrible the day was about to get.

Just before lunch rumors spread about a second hijacking. This time the police had made an arrest. My world was spinning out of control. I let my guard down for a moment and relaxed. I knew Diego was going to take me down with him. Maybe not in the front of my brain, but deep down. I kicked myself for trusting that he would only steal one shipment. Diego was a greedy bastard. He always had been. I should have seen this coming. My phone buzzed and it was a text from Nicolas.

'Sorry, but I cannot make lunch. I will make it up to you. I promise.'

ALBUQUERQUE ALIBI

I didn't quite know how to respond. The message implied lunch was more of a date, and I didn't do dates. How could I explain that to him without sounding like a total bitch? And there was that little fact of me being involved in the theft that he was now investigating. I should be ignoring him. It would be safer.

'No worries. Completely understand.' I messaged back to him.

I wasn't about to open a can of worms over a text message. I'd explain my no dating policy in a few days when things cooled down. If they did. On the other hand, if I was arrested, I would be able to completely avoid the uncomfortable conversation explaining my non-dating policy, as it would be a moot point.

Another text had me sighing. But it wasn't Nicholas this time. It was my ex. I couldn't believe he was stupid enough to be calling me on my company phone. Why wasn't he in police custody? If the rumors were true, then he should be.

'I need to meet you for lunch. Urgent.'

I asked my boss if I could go to lunch, and he nodded his head. He was on a call, probably getting more information about the stolen shipment. It was making the company look bad, but as the sales rep that sold the drugs to large retailers, Mitch was taking the theft personally.

Diego and I met at a local taco shop. He had a drink and three tacos in front of him. My stomach was still tied in knots, so I couldn't even glance at the food without feeling queasy.

"I need your help."

"I told you not to contact me."

"You owe me."

"I don't owe you shit."

He pretended not to hear me. Typical Diego.

"If I get pulled in, you need to give me an alibi."

"I've been at work. Everyone knows I was at Biogen. An alibi's not gonna fly."

"It went down at 5am. The police probably held off on reporting it to Biogen while they were questioning the rest of my crew. They probably didn't want to get stonewalled like they did last time."

"Just tell the police I was with you. I spent the night at your place."

"I'm not going to do that."

"If you don't give me an alibi, I'll tell them you orchestrated the whole thing. I still have the screen print from the shipments that show your name at the top, and that video from your past. And if that's not enough incentive, remember I can get to your sister."

I blew out a breath. He had me cornered. I'd do almost anything to keep her safe, and the bastard knew it.

"Ok, but this is the absolute last time I will ever help you. Got that."

I arrived back at the office to find all the employees being led into the large auditorium. The President of Biogen was going to give an address to the company. I zombie walked down the steps into the theater. The regular emcee was up at the podium encouraging everyone to take their seats as quickly as possible. It was an older, stylishly dressed Hispanic woman from HR. She stood in a black and gold power suit with matching pumps. She would have looked fabulous if it wasn't for her huge 80s hair. That part of her appearance had taken a serious time warp. I was trying to remember her name when my friend from accounting waved me over to sit next to her.

"Have you heard the latest?"

"No. I just got back from lunch."

"They caught the guys that did the hijacking."

ALBUQUERQUE ALIBI

"Yeah. Mitch told me this morning before he started making calls."

"Well, one of the guys escaped."

My lips pursed. I knew exactly who that was. I felt like the floor had given out beneath me. It was only a matter of time before the others gave Diego up and I was pulled in for questioning. At least I did have a legitimate reason for printing the scheduled shipping report. Mitch had asked for it when meeting with the client. I had just made an extra copy for myself.

After everyone was seated, the President came to the podium.

"I understand that you are all concerned about the recent thefts and how that will impact your jobs. Rest assured that we are working with the police and will get to the bottom of the matter shortly. I'm not able to go into detail, since it's an ongoing investigation, but I can say that the threat has been neutralized. The fact that it happened twice raises concerns that our computer system may have been compromised."

If they thought the systems were hacked, maybe I was off the hook, and my connection wouldn't be found. Just as long as I did what Diego asked, and he hadn't given my name to his crew, telling them I was where he got the info. Although if Diego decided my usefulness had ended and talked to the police, I was screwed.

"The security team will be gathering information. Please give them your full cooperation. Over the next few weeks, we will be focused on education. This means mandatory security training to help us all recognize threats and alert the security team early if we think data might be compromised. Everyone will be receiving emails going over additional information protection protocols. These security measures will be implemented across the company at every division. Also, the security team headed by Nicolas Mendoza will be gathering information about the latest threat. Please give his team your full cooperation. With that being said, we also have folks from outside Biogen that would like to have a few words. Detectives Carson and Dillon from the Albuquerque PD." He glanced at the steps leading up to the stage.

The President's smile was guarded. He didn't look particularly excited to welcome these outsiders. The two detectives marched onto the stage. Jac stood next to the podium facing the crowd. My guess was he was watching for reactions. My heart fluttered, and I sank down in my chair. His eyes narrowed in on me, and I gave a small smile. His expression didn't change. The other detective, a shorter, older version of Jac, climbed the steps to the podium. He looked vaguely familiar, like I might have seen him on tv, most likely the news. He was an eloquent speaker. The force had chosen well. He was very non-threatening. Of course, I couldn't concentrate on what he was saying. I was too focused on Jac. He looked fabulous in a button-down blue shirt, dark pants, and a dark sports jacket. I heard the word interview and my attention snapped back to the other detective.

"The Albuquerque PD would like to thank Biogen for allowing us access to one of your conference rooms on the third floor to complete our interviews. We will try to get through these quickly and efficiently, so it doesn't impact business operations."

Everyone filed from the auditorium, talking in muted whispers.

Even though Detective Carson's words had been smooth and reassuring, it didn't matter. Dread took hold of me and sucked the air from my lungs. I found it difficult to breathe. Lying to Jac was going to be near impossible. He knew my tell. We had played strip poker in high school, and I couldn't bluff back then, and doubted my ability to do so had improved. Jac on the other hand, practiced his interrogation skills daily. He'd be able to see through my lies in an instant. I was so screwed.

Chapter 12

Sofia

It was close to the end of the day when I was finally called in. I smiled at Jac and sat down. I forced my shoulders to relax and put my hands in my lap under the conference room table.

The other Detective was seated across from me flipping through a folder.

"Ms. Ramirez. Thank you for coming in. Will you take me through what you do for the company?"

"I work as an Administrative Assistant to Mitch Hammond. I take incoming calls, schedule his appointments, and manage his day-to-day activities with clients. Basically, I get him whatever he needs to more efficiently do his job."

He flipped to another paper in the folder. "Would you say that your job duties might include printing out documents and making copies in addition to your other tasks?"

I licked my lips.

"Yes. Anything that Mitch might ask for."

"What about sensitive data?"

My eyes opened wide. "Sensitive?" I squeaked out. I glanced up at Jac who hadn't spoken a word. He was watching me carefully. I didn't like being scrutinized, especially by him. I shifted in my seat.

"I mean, Ms. Ramirez, do you print off schedules of shipments?"

Oh god. They knew. Why else would they be asking?

I refused to huddle in on myself. I heard my father's voice in my head. 'Sit up young lady.' I threw my shoulders back and sat up straighter, raising my chin.

"Yes. If he needed that information. He is in sales, after all. Sometimes a client wants to verify their shipment. Make sure they have the correct quantity or make last-minute changes. Sometimes it's as simple as checking status."

I would have patted myself on the back if I could. I had pondered what to say all afternoon and had come up with the perfect lie. It was mostly the truth.

He scribbled down my response on his notepad.

"Do you take your laptop home with you?"

My brow furrowed. I had considered this as well but was surprised all the same.

"Yes. Sometimes I work from home. I'm required to have access at all times. Just in case Mitch needs me to look up information after hours."

"Would you print documents at home?"

"Not usually, but it's possible. It all depends on the circumstances."

The document I printed for Diego came from my home printer. I printed two sheets for Mitch and copied one of them for Diego. I wondered if my print history would show that. I delivered the shipment printouts along with a key fob presentation to Mitch at a Starbucks since he needed it for his client meeting. He had been running late for his meeting. Not that I was prepared to give the police that level of detail.

"If Mitch needs a report for an early morning meeting and isn't going to stop in at the office beforehand, I might drop off

ALBUQUERQUE ALIBI

documents, promotional items, and presentation material to client sites or wherever he needs me to."

"I'm sorry Ms. Ramirez, but Mr. Hammond says differently."

I frowned. "What exactly did he say?"

Detective Carson ignored my question, and I blew out a breath. I couldn't call my boss a liar. What was Mitch up to? Why wasn't he telling the truth? Had we violated security protocol? Why was he throwing me under the bus? Not that I didn't deserve it. I realized that I was in an impossible situation. I watched the interaction between the two detectives. They were having some sort of silent communication. It ended with Jac nodding.

"I'm afraid we need you to come into the station." Detective Carson stated.

I glanced at Jac. His jaw was tense. He made no move to correct the other Detective. My shoulders slumped.

They brought me into the station. At least they didn't put me in cuffs. Luckily, most of my co-workers had already left the office, so very few witnessed my disgrace when I left Biogen with the detectives. I glanced around to those at the police station as we walked in. I recognized a few of the officers. Friends of César's. This was so embarrassing. I scanned the room for my brother, but didn't see him. I'm not sure I could face him right now anyhow.

They placed me in an interrogation room by myself and made me wait. César had mentioned that was a tactic to get people to talk. I wondered what I could possibly say to get out of this mess. Was that even possible at this point?

Jac came in and sat opposite me. I glanced over his shoulder to see if Detective Carson was going to join him, but it was just the two of us.

"The men we picked up for hijacking are known associates of Diego Ortiz."

Jac knew of my ex. Three years ago, I had reached out to him after Diego had cheated on me. That was the least of my ex's sins, but enough of a reason to get Jac to have a talk with him. Whatever they discussed ended in Jac beating him to a pulp. We never discussed the details, but I knew it had to be bad. It was the one time Jac had taken the law into his own hands. He always followed the rules, but he had broken them for me. Afterwards, Jac had told me I didn't need to worry about Diego ever again. He would leave me alone.

Jac was wrong. Diego was back in my life and causing me more trouble than ever before.

"Do you know where Diego was early this morning?"

I closed my eyes. Not only did I have to lie to Jac, this was going to hurt him immensely. I didn't want to do it, but I had no choice in order to save myself and my sister. If I didn't, I knew how vindictive Diego could be. He'd make sure I burned for this, and he'd figure out a way to take Gabriella down with us. I couldn't allow that to happen.

I blew out a breath. "He spent the night." I stared at my hands folded neatly on the table.

The sharp intake of breath made me raise my head. Our eyes met.

All I saw was pain, then it suddenly morphed into anger. He cleared his throat and his face went blank. I'm not sure what was worse, the emotion, or the deadened expression he gave me now.

"You're giving that asshole an alibi?"

"Yes."

He growled and I tilted my head.

"I need the time he arrived and left your apartment."

Diego hadn't given me an arrival time, so I wasn't sure what to say.

ALBUQUERQUE ALIBI

"He arrived sometime before dinner last night. I don't remember the exact time. He left when I went to work, around 7am."

I hoped that was enough, because I don't think I could stand to say anything else. Jac threw his notebook across the room.

"I know you're lying." He leaned over me, menacingly.

I had never seen him like this. I started shaking, not from the cold, but from fear. He had never looked at me like this. I knew he was capable of it. It went with the job. I tried to calm myself, using some of my woo-woo spiritual crap as my brother called it. I focused on my breathing. In and out. In and out. I was trying to slow down my pulse rate. Finding control. I blinked my eyes open. Meditating wasn't working. I stared at the door. César was probably throwing a fit right now. He had to be. I needed him. He'd save me. I was sure of it. With no clock, I counted the seconds. It wouldn't be much longer, I convinced myself. Just hold out. My body gave a violent shake, and the door pounded. I heard yelling on the other side. My brother. The door shot open, and Nicolas Mendoza marched in with a pair of lawyers. That was the last person I expected to see.

My mouth would have dropped if it weren't for the cold that had chilled me down to my bones.

Oh no. They found out that I was behind it all. My life was over. I was going to jail. He was here to make sure.

"You have one of our employees." He frowned at me. "That was not part of our agreement."

I was huddled in on myself, body shaking.

"Biogen takes care of its own."

Wait. What?

Nicolas took off his jacket and threw it around my shoulders. He knelt by my side.

"Are you all right?" He asked softly.

I nodded, worried that my voice would come out as a squeak. Relief flooded my body. He didn't know. They hadn't figured it out. I was still safe. I breathed in the warmth of his jacket and wrapped myself up tighter, not minding the whiff of cologne and scent of cigars. My brother hadn't been the one to save me after all. It had been the head of security for a company I had deeply wronged. My eyes teared up and my lip trembled. I had to find a way to make it up to them somehow. The guilt was eating me up from the inside.

"Are you arresting Sofía Ramirez?" One of the lawyers asked Jac.

"I need clarification on her statement."

"You didn't answer the question." The other lawyer said.

"No. She's not under arrest."

"Then Ms. Ramirez will be leaving now."

Nicolas held me while I walked out of the police station. It was humiliating. I knew several of the officers and I probably looked like a wreck. I was shaking and crying. I curled into Nicolas' side and sobbed. I just wanted out of this situation. Nicolas escorted me to a silver BMW with dark windows and opened the passenger door. I took a seat and watched through the tinted windows as my brother pulled up and sprinted into the station. He hadn't seen me. Thank goodness. Once Nicolas finished his conversation with the lawyers, he turned back to the car.

"Why don't we get you home." He said after getting in.

"Yes, please," I said.

My eyes closed and I leaned back. A sob burst free, but I bit my lip, swallowing back the tears. I had already cried enough, and I didn't want Nicolas to see me lose it. I needed to stay strong, now more than ever.

Nicolas drove with confidence, turn after turn. My eyes drifted closed and I concentrated on breathing. The car stopped, and my eyes blinked open. We were already at my apartment complex. It was only then that I realized I had never given him my address.

"How did you know where I lived?"

"Employee records."

I tilted my head. I didn't remember updating my address from my mom's house. I had only moved into the apartment with Mari two months ago.

My paychecks were auto deposited, and I didn't think my mail forwarding would have notified Biogen for another four months. But what did I know? Nicolas was head of security. He probably punched a few buttons into the computer and got every address I ever lived at.

He parked the car and turned to me. Nicolas was waiting for me to speak.

"Thank you for everything."

I tried to sit up straighter.

"I would have been fine."

He did that gentle cheek touch again that he had done at the office. I'm not sure I minded it this time.

"It was no trouble at all. The police should not have brought you in."

If only he knew.

"I supplied an alibi for someone. They thought I was lying."

"Were you?"

I licked my lips. I didn't want to lie to him. I was pretty sure he would know.

"I'm loyal to my friends."

That was the truth. He didn't need to know that Diego wasn't my friend. Far from it, in fact.

"I get that. Loyalty is very important to me. Well, my family too."

He stared out the window lost in thought. I found it odd, but then again, I didn't know Nicolas very well.

He reached out to me. My fingers were freezing. I let him cup both my hands, warming them as he gazed into my eyes.

"I know this is not the right time, but can I take you to dinner tomorrow night?"

My jaw dropped.

This sexy man wanted to ask me out after I had done nothing but cause him grief. I cost his company thousands, spilled coffee on him, and been a thorn in his side for the past week.

"Yes." I blurted out.

What was I doing? This was madness. I blamed my response on my frazzled nerves. My emotions were a jumble. Nicolas had been there for me when no one else had. And I was furious with Jac. The anger had been boiling beneath the surface on the drive home, replacing my distress. Jac was the reason I was at the station. He could have easily questioned me elsewhere, but he had chosen to bring me in and make me sweat. He wasn't the man I remembered. And now I would do something I had avoided for three long years. I was going on a date. And with a co-worker no less.

Chapter 13

Jac

César burst into the station. He looked like a rodeo bull that had just jumped the fence.

"Where is she?" He demanded.

I got in his way. He tried to push past me to the interrogation rooms.

"You've got to calm down."

"I'm so pissed at you right now." He huffed. "You should have called me."

I hadn't been thinking clearly myself. Although I knew that César would be like this. In the front of my brain, I knew and had delayed on purpose. It was the right thing to do for the investigation.

Detective Carson stood by my side. He was half a foot shorter than I was, and over a decade older. It was comical how he was trying to defend me against César.

"Back off, Ramirez. Everything was done by the book."

"She's my sister," César yelled.

The lieutenant hollered out his office door. The whole room was staring at us.

"Ramirez, Dillon, Carson. In my office now."

I took a deep breath and followed Carson. The lieutenant closed the door and took a seat behind his large oak desk.

"I don't need yelling out in the bullpen. What's going on?"

"My sister was brought in. I wanted to talk with her."

"Now Ramirez, you know better than this." He shook his head. "There's a clear conflict of interest."

César gritted his teeth but kept his mouth shut. You could almost see the steam coming out of his ears.

He glared at me like I had somehow caused this mess. He should have known better. I didn't have a choice in the matter.

"Is Ms. Ramirez still here?" The Lieutenant asked.

"No. She's not." Carson said calmly. "Biogen's lawyers showed up and more or less forced us to let her go." He shrugged. "She was never under arrest. We just needed to ask a few questions. If we are going to pursue this investigation, we need all the information we can get."

"We don't want to piss off a large corporation like Biogen. You remember the last time. The chief called and chewed my ass."

"There are some discrepancies with the facts." Carson said. "Stories don't line up."

"If you have something, fine. Do it quickly and quietly."

The lieutenant turned his attention back to me.

"Dillon, why were you in the interrogation room alone with Ms. Ramirez?"

I didn't realize anyone had noticed.

I glanced at Carson. His face was blank. It was him. He had told the lieutenant. He knew something was going on between us.

"I thought I'd have a better chance of getting her to answer truthfully. I'm practically family."

"If you're that close, we might need to pull you off the case." He blew out a breath. ""What is your relationship with Ms. Ramirez?"

ALBUQUERQUE ALIBI

That was the real question. I wasn't sure how to answer, since it wasn't clear to me either.

"We are friends. I grew up with César. You know that. So, I know Sofía through him."

"Is she a person of interest?"

"She's the alibi to one," I said.

"Do you think she's lying?"

I glanced over at César. "I'm not sure."

"Is your judgment compromised? Are you too close to this, Dillon?"

I knew the answer in my head. Not only yes, but hell yes. But I wasn't about to tell the lieutenant that. I didn't want off the case.

"No sir."

"All right. Carson and Dillon stay on the case. You can go. Ramirez, stay here a minute."

I left the office after Carson had closed the door. I wondered what the lieutenant and César were talking about. It couldn't be anything good. César stormed past me a few minutes later.

"I'm going to the gym." He said to no one in particular.

I knew that was code for me to join him. Whether we worked out on the machines or if he wanted to spar was the only question.

"You mind if I take a break?"

Carson nodded. "Go ahead."

I marched downstairs to the fitness center on the first floor dreading the story I would have to share. César was already pissed at me and was going to be even angrier. It was my own fault for keeping secrets from him for so long.

He was already on the treadmill when I got down to the gym. I jumped on the row machine until he was finished. When he went to the cooler for a drink, I joined him.

"Talk to me," he said.

"Three years ago, Sofía was dating this loser. His name is Diego Ortiz. Total bastard."

"Why am I just finding out about this now?"

I cracked my neck.

"You were undercover at the time. And Sofía didn't want me to tell you."

He raised his eyebrows. "And you took her side over mine?"

"It wasn't about sides." I shrugged. "She needed me, and I helped."

"How?"

This was the sticky part. What I was about to admit made me look pretty bad. Whenever I recalled what had happened it felt like a dream, or rather a nightmare. I had stepped over the line. It had been easy, because it was Sofía. I'm not sure what that said about me. I always followed the rules, up until that day. I looked around the gym. No one else was listening in.

"Sofía called crying. Her boyfriend had cheated on her. But she was worried if she broke up with him, there would be repercussions."

"That's the word she used?"

"Yeah."

César's eyes turned molten.

"What did you do?"

"I looked into Diego's background. He had a record, mostly low-level stuff. Convicted for possession, and petty theft. He also had a gambling problem. The thing that stuck out was an arrest for assault. A domestic abuse situation where the charges were dropped."

"Fuck. And Sofía?"

ALBUQUERQUE ALIBI

"When I saw her, she didn't look physically hurt, but it didn't matter. I lost it. Tracked the guy down and beat the shit out of him."

"I would have done the same."

"I know. That's why I tried to protect you. To keep you from doing anything stupid."

"What happened?"

"I ended up doing the same thing you would do in that situation."

"So what, you punched him a few times? No big deal."

"He was in the ICU for a week."

"Damn." César gave me a look of respect.

It didn't make me feel any better about what I had done. I had been impulsive. It was reckless and so unlike me, but I had snapped. Sofía was family. She had always been, but to me it was more.

"He could have pressed charges."

"I made things clear to him that it would be a bad idea if he tried something like that."

The anger on my face must have shown. César gave me a long glance and nodded.

"I still think you need to back off. I don't know what's going on with the two of you, but I can feel the tension when you two are together. I'll talk to Sofía. She is my sister. I'll get her to revise her statement. Say that she was confused or something." He shoved my shoulder. "Don't worry. I'll handle it."

I wondered if César knew his sister like I did. Sure, he had grown up with her, but she kept a lot of secrets. We both did. But I wasn't ready to open up that can of worms on top of everything else.

Chapter 14

Sofia

"Wow." Nicolas said when I swung open my apartment door.

I couldn't help the smile that lit up my features. That was the exact reaction I wanted. I decided if I finally agreed to a date after a 3-year hiatus, I was going all out.

The plum-colored sleeveless dress I wore was designer. I found it at a consignment shop a few years ago and never had the chance to wear it. Most designer brands didn't carry my size. I wasn't built like a stick figure model. My Latina body had curves. But I had been in luck, and even though the price was higher than I wanted to spend at the time, I splurged on myself as a gift for getting the job at Biogen. Over the last two years, I had added to the outfit. Designer stilettos in a deep purple. A silk wrap in an abstract floral with various shades of plum, purple, and violet. A vintage necklace and earrings of amethyst completed the outfit. Up until now, it had been hanging in my closet, taunting me.

Nicolas arrived wearing a black suit that fit him like a glove. It didn't look like one of those off the rack ones either. This one looked like a custom fit Brioni. Even his shoes were expensive. Santoni red leather oxfords. I might not be able to afford fancy clothes on the regular, but I knew all the designers and could drool over them in magazines. Nicolas had dressed up for me too. I felt a little giddy, like when I had gone to prom back in high school. That made me ponder how little I had dated decent guys in the past decade.

"Hang on just a second. I just need to grab my purse." I ran back to the bedroom and reapplied my lipstick. There. Perfect. Even my wild curls had been tamed for the night. When I got back into the living room, I caught him looking around. I wondered what he thought of the apartment. It was on the small side, but then again Mari and I didn't need much. At least it was clean. Well clean-ish.

"You didn't sit on the sofa, did you?" I asked with concern.

"No." He eyed the piece of furniture. "Do you think it would crumble under my weight?" He smirked.

"Very funny. I just didn't want you covered in cat hair."

I grabbed the roller we kept by the front door. "Otherwise, I'd have to take this to your backside."

"Ms. Ramirez. You don't need an excuse. Feel free to touch wherever you like."

A nervous giggle slipped out. Nicolas was smooth, but even better, he had a great sense of humor. We walked out the door and I locked up. He held out his arm, and I was grateful for the help down the stairs, plus he smelled divine. I don't know what cologne he was wearing, but I bet it was expensive, like the rest of him.

He scanned the parking lot while we walked down the stairs slowly. It was probably routine for him to be cautious working in security. Nicolas escorted me to a silver BMW and opened my door. When he had offered me a ride from the police station, I thought he had borrowed a company car, but it appeared to be his. I slid onto the supple leather seat, flashing a little leg from the high slit in my dress. Nicholas didn't seem to mind a bit.

"Quite lovely, Ms. Ramirez."

ALBUQUERQUE ALIBI

I had no idea why he was being so formal. He called me Sofía at the office, but I'd play along.

"You aren't too shabby yourself, Mr. Mendoza."

I buckled in, getting cozy. I hadn't fully appreciated the luxury on my last ride. I had no idea that security personnel made quite this much money. I knew Biogen was generous to their employees, but it still seemed over the top. Maybe I was paranoid, because of past boyfriends, always questioning motives and zeroing in on red flags. Nicolas was a nice guy, I reminded myself. He had a job and a car. He wasn't like my asshole criminal ex that was blackmailing me. Why did I have to jump to the worst possible assumption the moment I met a nice guy who treated me well? I rolled my shoulders, sinking back into the seat, forcing myself to relax. We drove over to the Antiquity Restaurant. Another surprise.

"I wasn't expecting something quite so fancy, but I'm glad I dressed up. Don't you need reservations far in advance for this place?"

"I know the owner." He said simply.

Of course he did.

We walked in and got seated immediately. I looked at the menu and my eyes nearly popped out of my head. The entrée prices were ridiculous. Why was this guy trying to impress me so much? Don't get me wrong. I appreciated it, but I would have been totally fine with something much simpler. If I were honest, I would have been perfectly fine with burgers and fries.

Nicolas ordered a special bottle of wine that wasn't on the menu. It had to be pricey.

"I want to get to know you better. Tell me about yourself."

He leaned his elbows on the table, staring at me.

The scrutiny left me feeling a little naked. I pulled the wrap a little tighter around my shoulders. There was a lot I needed to hide from this man. But he also had come to my rescue at the police station, and I owed him for that.

"I'm not all that interesting." I shrugged. The wrap fell off one shoulder.

"You are wrong." He grinned. "Everything about you is fascinating."

I got hung up on those words. I guess everyone wants to feel special, but this man seemed gifted in his ability to make me feel that way. It was a heady thing to be under his attention.

"Did you ever figure out who sent you the flowers?"

"My secret admirer? No. It's still a mystery."

His eyebrow quirked. "No guesses at all?"

I pondered for a moment, going through the possibilities. "You?" I asked.

He grinned. "I knew you were smart."

I chuckled. "Why didn't you sign your name?"

"I thought you liked secrets."

I inhaled a sharp breath. He was right, but that didn't mean I wanted him to discover them. I was in enough trouble as it was.

"I'm an open book." I smirked, raising my glass.

"A game then?" His mouth twisted. "Challenge accepted." Nicolas raised his glass. "To unveiling your secrets, Ms. Ramirez."

"Best of luck, Mr. Mendoza."

The banter back and forth made me smile. It had been so long since I had enjoyed the simple pleasure of flirting.

I sipped the cabernet. It was smooth and velvety and warmed me from the inside.

We ordered filets and lobster tails, and the chef promised us something special for dessert.

He continued to ask me questions over dinner, and we danced around topics.

Nicolas was good at plying me with compliments and keeping my wine glass filled. For some reason, I felt like this man was on my side. It seemed like he wanted to know the real me. Other than Jac, no one had spent that much time asking what I wanted out of life. The guys I usually dated were narcissistic in the extreme. Conversations tended to revolve around themselves.

"How on earth are you still single?" I asked.

"Family." He said frowning.

He didn't elaborate, just focused on finishing his steak.

It seemed even in that, we were similar. That's why I hid my dating and why I chose men that didn't have my best interests at heart. With no family scrutiny, I tended to go for looks with little substance. I also had a serious flaw. I loved the bad boys. Tattoos and danger turned me on. The only exception was Jac. He was a good guy through and through but had abandoned me to go to college. It was years before he reached out again. At the time, I felt betrayed. I think I looked for guys that would do the same. Maybe I felt like I didn't deserve better.

"Quite the somber expression, you have there, Sofía. You want to share what's going on in that mind of yours?"

We were back to first names. I grinned. Jac wasn't the only good guy I dated. Maybe my luck with men had changed. I could offer him a truth without compromising myself.

"I've dated some real losers."

"I hope you are not including me on that list."

"Of course not. You have been wonderful. It's been so long since I've gone to a fancy restaurant and had a reason to get dressed up. I could get used to this."

"Then I need to keep it up, if for no other reason than for you to continue gracing me with those dazzling smiles."

I grinned. A genuine smile for the man providing me with a respite from all my worries.

After a decadent chocolate dessert that had me practically licking my plate, he took me to a private party at a mansion. They were mostly upper-class, musicians, actors, and politicians. I wanted to ask him a ton of questions, especially just how he knew everyone there including the servants. But for every question I would ask he would do the same. We had an unspoken rule, and we shared whispered secrets with one another throughout the evening. I was opening up to him slowly, bit by bit. I didn't trust easily, but it felt so easy to talk with him. He seemed different somehow. Safe. Like maybe he was the key to fixing all my problems. He certainly had a thing for being my white knight in shining armor. The party had gotten a little wild at the end. A fight had broken out. Two girls trashed out of their minds had gotten in a heated argument. The fight involved a lot of hair pulling and slurred swear words. It resulted in a glass coffee table shattering and a few knick-knacks being hurled through the air. One narrowly missed me before Nicolas whisked me away.

"My savior." I said as he got me buckled into the car.

I let my head roll back, sighing. He must have known I was tipsy, but that didn't stop him from kissing me. I wanted him to, but it was still a surprise. He had been such a gentleman all night. I was waiting for fireworks, but there weren't any. I frowned as he walked around the car to the driver's side.

What was wrong with me? He had wined and dined me and rescued me yet again. Nicolas was good looking, and apparently rich, charming, witty, and had a mysterious edge that fed my wild side. By the end of the night, I should have been swept off my feet. But I wasn't. My mind kept wandering back to Jac.

He slid into the driver's seat grinning. Nicolas lifted my arm gently. It had fallen onto the middle console at some point. His thumb circled my pulse point, tickling. I couldn't help the shiver that traveled down my body. He laid a gentle kiss to my inner wrist, and I mustered up a smile.

"Let's get you home." He said and put the car in gear.

I spent the ride contemplating why I couldn't be won over by Nicolas. He said all the right things and treated me like a princess. My life would be so much simpler and right now, I needed uncomplicated. I sighed. It was no use. I couldn't make myself fall for him. I had never been one for easy relationships. We pulled into my apartment complex, and I dreaded the

ALBUQUERQUE ALIBI

conversation I was about to have with him, wondering how on earth I was going to let this incredible man down easy.

Chapter 15

Jac

César had told me to give Sofía some space. The lieutenant and Carson didn't feel the same way. César had tried to get more information out of her but had been unsuccessful. I knew Sofía was hiding things from me. So, I was going to try again, despite her brother's warnings. Driving to her apartment, I thought about the alibi she had provided for her ex-boyfriend. She had lied at the police station. I just didn't know why. I hoped to convince Sofía to revise her statement. I knew Diego was involved and my hunches usually paid off. When I pulled into the lot it was late and the lights were off in her apartment. I turned off the car, wondering if she had gone to bed already. Sofía was usually a night owl, but plenty of things had been going on lately. I debated knocking on her door. Or maybe just text first, to see if she was even awake. I knew I needed to apologize for bringing her into the station. Not that it had been solely my decision. Detective Carson was the lead on the case. But it's true, I hadn't stopped him. Sofía was angry with me over that. I didn't want that fury to fester one more day. I knew how hot her temper burned. She was a lot like her brother. Not that she'd ever appreciate the comparison.

Before I made up my mind, a silver BMW pulled into the lot. It was a bit unusual. Most of the people in her complex couldn't afford high-end cars. And one arriving so late in the evening had me on high alert. A suave dark-haired gentleman got out of the driver's seat. He went around the front of the car. The man scanned the lot, and I ducked down in my seat. I wasn't under a streetlight, and I had turned off the car, so there was little chance that he would see me. My reaction was second nature, built from years of stake outs. There was something about the guy I just didn't like. I couldn't quite put my finger on it. Maybe it was the way he moved. It was clear he hid a powerful body under that sleek suit. The man opened the passenger door and held out his hand. A dark-haired beauty in a purple dress and stiletto heels stepped out onto the pavement. My eyes bulged and my hands gripped the steering wheel. The woman was Sofía, and the way the man held her against his side as they climbed the steps to her apartment made me grit my teeth. Sofía was on a date. What the fuck? She had been complaining that she didn't want to be in a serious relationship. And now I catch her with some guy, clearly on a date. And it wasn't even her ex. This was some other dude.

I jumped out of my car and was moving up the steps two at a time before I could think clearly. The man pressed Sofía behind him and his chest puffed out.

"Get your keys out Sofía. In your apartment now." He ordered.

This guy was trying to protect her from me. That made me laugh. Yeah, I was steaming mad, but I'd never hurt her. Even if she had lied to me. This guy, on the other hand, I'd pummel without thinking twice. He was touching my girl. My Sofía. I cracked my knuckles and gave him an evil grin. Sofía's head popped around his shoulder.

"Jac?"

ALBUQUERQUE ALIBI

The guy leaned into the light. Now that I could see the guy's face clearer, I recognized him. He was the head of security at Biogen.

"I think you're taking your security job way too seriously."

I saw the recognition on his face. He knew who I was too.

The guy rocked back on his heels. I had seen a bulge at the side of his jacket when he had walked up the stairs. I knew he was carrying.

"I am off the clock."

"Are you now?"

He put up his hands, and I turned him around roughly and removed the Glock from an inside holster.

"Do you have a permit for this?"

He pulled a card from his wallet and handed it to me. Everything looked in order. I handed him back the card and his weapon.

I turned my gaze on Sofía who looked stricken with guilt.

"Are you all right?" He asked her with concern.

She nodded.

"I think it's time you left, Nicolas." I said with a smirk.

He hesitated, clearly thinking through his options. His eyes flashed with fury. He nodded but was clearly pissed.

"I hope you enjoyed yourself tonight." He said to Sofía.

"I did. It was just amazing." She said sweetly back to him. "Thank you for a lovely evening."

"We will have to continue our date some other time."

I thought I was going to hurl.

She went towards him, probably to give him a hug. That was her norm. But the stern expression from me had her freezing in her tracks.

Sofía reconsidered whatever she was going to do, twisting her hands in front of her.

"I'll see you at the office on Monday."

He walked down the steps slowly and got into his vehicle and drove away.

At least I had ended Sofía's date early. I got a small amount of satisfaction from that.

"So, a no dating policy, huh?"

Sofía still hadn't opened up the door to her apartment.

She took that opportunity to turn away from me. Sofía was grumbling. Probably swear words in Spanish under her breath. I would get that frequently after I had riled her up. She went to slam the door behind me, but I got my body in the way, and it bounced back. She huffed with frustration, but went further into the apartment, flipping on the light switch and slamming her keys on the kitchen table. There were no sweet welcome meows which meant that Mari and Miles were away for the evening, most likely at César's. That meant we were alone. I wanted to yell at Sofía, berate her for lying to me, but instead I closed the door and locked it.

Sofía's brows rose as she watched me cautiously.

I crossed the living room in three long strides. She backed up against the kitchen counter, and I didn't stop the momentum. I crashed into her, my lips finding hers, pressing her body up against the counter and grinding myself against her. She moaned into my mouth, clearly on board with everything I was doing. I released all my anger into that brutal kiss. All the pent-up emotions that were clouding my thoughts. My focus was singular. Make her pay. I stepped back slightly. My calloused hands skimmed up her dress, revealing black silk panties. She had worn these for him. If I hadn't been here to stop them, Nicolas might be standing right where I was. I stared at her, giving ample time for her to say something and stop me if she wanted. I wouldn't do anything to force her, no matter how angry I was. I looked into her half-lidded eyes and saw only need. My knuckle ran up the inside of her thigh slowly.

She shivered and parted her legs wider. My thumb circled her clit. Her panties were already damp. I pushed the miniscule satin fabric out of the way and slid a finger inside, burying it deep. She threw her head back and almost hit her head on the cabinets. This wouldn't do. I needed more room to do what I wanted, and as angry as I was, I didn't want to hurt her. My body was still vibrating with fury.

"Bedroom?" I managed to ask. My voice came out hoarse. She nodded.

I picked her up and she wrapped her legs around me. We kissed as I walked her to the bedroom, grateful I knew the layout of her apartment by heart. I opened her bedroom door and glanced at the bed, nicely rumpled sheets. Just like my Sofía at this moment, with her hair wild, and makeup smudged. I tossed her onto the bed, and she had the nerve to glare at me.

"I'm furious with you right now," I said.

I didn't give her a chance to respond. I was on top of her and kissing her swear words away. I positioned our bodies and thrust myself against her, rubbing at the juncture of her thighs, feeling as the moisture grew. I couldn't pull away. I didn't give a damn how damp my slacks were becoming. I only wanted to hear more of Sofía's soft moans. They were like music to my ears.

"I want you."

She bit her lip. Hesitating. Clearly trying to analyze the situation. I was giving her a chance to back out, even though I hated it. I knew she would do it. I could see it in her expression. I crawled off the bed. The look she gave me was astonishment. My brow quirked. Maybe she didn't want me to stop after all. I took her ankle and yanked her to the bottom of the bed. She yelped but stared at me with heavy lids. I ripped off her panties and knelt at the edge of the bed. I gently kissed her, and she undulated beneath my mouth, her hips rising off the bed. She was panting. I swiped my tongue along her seam, tasting her. I sucked her clit and she grabbed my head to hold on. I pressed her legs wider to get a better angle. She was becoming unglued, rattling off things in Spanish I didn't understand. They could have been praises or curses. At this point, I don't think even Sofía knew what she was saying. When she finally came, it was like my whole world narrowed down to this single moment.

"Condom?" I asked.

This was it. If she said no, I would walk away, even though it would leave me with blue balls. I'd be cursing her to high heaven if she turned me away now, but I'd never do anything she didn't want. I'd never force myself on a woman, especially not Sofía. She was still for a moment and then flopped her hand over, pointing to the nightstand.

The relief flowed over me. My breath whooshed out and I opened the drawer. The condom package was sealed, so it took a minute to open it up, and grab a few packets. One time would not be enough. I had waited too long. She pulled her dress over her head and tossed it across the room. It had been fitted enough that she hadn't worn a bra. Damn she looked fine. My mouth watered. I wanted to taste those dark nipples until she screamed my name. I quickly undressed as she watched, tossing my clothes to the same pile as hers. I slid on the condom and crawled up the bed. Her smooth caramel skin demanded to be worshiped, and I obeyed, offering kisses up her thighs. Feather light kisses that made her squirm beneath me.

"Jac." She groaned.

I grinned. Normally she was a chatterbox. Having her all but mute was a novelty that I wanted to explore, but I couldn't wait any longer. I slid myself over her opening, back and forth, until she was vibrating with need.

"Please." She begged.

I thrust in, and she gasped. I gave her a moment to adjust to my size then I couldn't hold myself back any longer. My needs took over and it was like I had been possessed. On straight arms I plunged into her over and over, then repositioned, leaning down to capture her moans with my mouth. She wrapped her legs tighter around my hips. I swore at the sensation of being buried deep within Sofía. I wanted to make it last, but I was losing my rhythm.

ALBUQUERQUE ALIBI

It was just too good. She was too tight. Too perfect. I came with a shout, and she let out a deep groan coming with me. I gave myself a few seconds before separating, not wanting to leave the warmth of her body. I quickly disposed of the condom and came back to the bed. I pulled Sofía on top, and she sprawled over my chest. I managed to untangle the comforter and cover us both. Her skin was cool to the touch, so I knew she was chilly. My body was still on fire, but I wanted her comfortable for round two.

Chapter 16

Sofia

I stretched my sore body and grinned. What had gotten into Jac last night? He lay sprawled out on my bed softly snoring. One bent arm covered his face, and his leg hung off the bed. He looked amazing, as always, with his square jaw, perfect hair, and even more perfect body. He looked like a fallen angel. The comforter and pillows had shifted. They framed his body, making it look as if he was resting on big white fluffy clouds. The sunlight streamed through the blinds illuminating him like a spotlight. Jac's chest was a sculpted masterpiece. Broad shoulders and hard pecs leading down to chiseled abs. I knew he worked out for his job, but he had also been well and truly blessed by genetics. My fingertips tingled with the need to touch him. I just couldn't get enough. I felt almost giddy with anticipation. Even though we had spent a wild night together doing plenty of exploring, this was the first time I had seen him in the daylight, fully unclothed, or almost. The sheet barely covered his hips. Just that one tiny barrier to remove. Would he notice if I just whipped the sheet away? So I could see him in all his glory.

"Are you going to stare all day?"

My breath hitched.

"I didn't know you were awake."

"Not that I mind your gawking, but I was hoping you might do something instead."

"Are you daring me?"

"Call it what you like. I just didn't realize you were so shy."

I grinned, remembering he had said something similar when we were teenagers.

"You and I both know I've never been shy."

Being dared to do things over the years had gotten me into trouble, because I rarely backed down from a challenge. It was a personality flaw; one I had never fixed.

"Your expression got way too serious." Jac pulled me into his arms. "Bringing up the past wasn't supposed to make you sad."

I buried my face into his neck. "It had nothing to do with you. I've never regretted anything we've done together."

"Stop spending time thinking about other men, especially while naked in bed with me. You'll give me a complex."

I chuckled. "You're the most confident man I know. I believe you've told me insecurities are for the weak."

"Most of the time that's true, but not when it comes to you." He rubbed his calloused thumb along my spine. "You make me vulnerable. And sometimes it scares the shit out of me."

He adjusted me on top of him, and I felt how hard he was beneath the sheet. I needed to feel him fully skin to skin.

"You have me at your mercy." He grinned. "What are you going to do about it?"

My eyes must have lit up. Jac wiggled his eyebrows. I felt my mischievous streak kick into high gear. I rolled off and flung the sheet to the floor. I stopped to stare at his magnificent body for only a moment, before jumping back on top of him. I wanted this. Him. And not just for the weekend. And not just because he had been jealous and pushed past my ridiculous walls. I wanted it just as much as Jac, if not more. I unlocked that piece of myself I kept hidden from others. Jac would never hurt me. I was safe.

Hours later, when exhaustion had overtaken us both, we collapsed onto the couch laughing. It was late afternoon, nearing dinner time, and neither of us had stopped to eat. I didn't have the energy to cook anything, so we ate cereal straight out of the box and watched tv. I was cuddled into his side with one leg over his lap, and it felt darn near perfect.

"Why did you give Diego an alibi?"

Way to ruin the moment. I scowled at him. In moments everything came flooding back. The reason I needed to keep up my walls. I couldn't allow Jac to find out the truth. My sister was in danger, and I knew what Diego was capable of. He could easily turn his sights on Jac. Working for the police didn't make him invincible, despite wanting to believe Jac was my personal superhero.

"Must we discuss this?"

"I won't tolerate lies. Not after what the two of us just shared."

"Just let the past go." I swallowed. "Please."

"Less than 72 hours ago, you slept with Diego."

My jaw dropped.

"That's what you think?"

I extracted myself from the comfort of his arms. I missed his warmth immediately, but I couldn't have this conversation without some distance between us. I paced back and forth in front of the tv.

"Just because I said he spent the night, doesn't mean I slept with him."

"He implied as much."

"Is that what this is about? You wanted what you thought he had? Is this some kind of competition?"

"Then tell me what happened."

"He needed a place to crash." I twisted my fingers in my hair. "I was trying to be a good Christian, and I offered him my couch."

"That's not what you said in your statement."

"I said he spent the night. Why should I go into details? It's nobody's business but my own. My father always taught me when dealing with the authorities to give as little information as possible."

"Your father was a criminal."

"He was an entrepreneur."

"You're delusional."

"Don't taint the memory of the dead. I can remember him however I want to. I was only ten when he died."

I had spent time with my father at the bar with his buddies. He always made me feel special. I didn't care what he did for a living. He loved me. That's all that mattered.

"I still know you are lying about Diego."

"That's your jealousy talking."

"Maybe, I just can't believe you'd do it. You're too intelligent to do something so stupid."

I bit my lip. I wanted to tell him the truth, to convince Jac to trust me, that I was worth it. This felt like a turning point for us.

"You are right about being jealous. First finding out about Diego, imagining him touching you after all these years, after what he did to you. And then two days later Nicolas was minutes away from doing the same. I couldn't help it. I snapped."

Jac's competitive nature had surfaced. It was as simple as that. I had witnessed it years ago, how he played sports in high school like nothing else mattered. I didn't want to be some prize to be won.

I had always thought that it would be César who tore us apart, but perhaps I had been deceiving myself all along. Until I could come clean and tell Jac everything, our relationship was doomed.

ALBUQUERQUE ALIBI

My mouth opened and closed. I couldn't tell him anything without fear of what would happen, so I said nothing. The frustration and anger on his face was too much to bear. I couldn't hold eye contact anymore and turned away. Jac left in a rush after that. Grabbing his clothes in a hurry, barely getting dressed like he couldn't stand the sight of me anymore. I curled up on the couch, sobbing into a giant pillow, clenching it to my stomach. Everything ached like he had torn a piece of my insides and taken it with when he had slammed the front door.

After my sobbing had subsided, I went to clean up the mess in my bedroom. Pillows, sheets, and bedspread were tossed on the floor, along with various articles of clothing. Sifting through the items filled me with sorrow for what might have been.

My phone pinged and I lunged for it across the bed, sliding across the slick sheets I had just put back on. I had hoped it would be Jac, apologizing for leaving like that. I desperately needed to see him again. But of course, it wasn't. Instead, César was messaging me.

'Why have I never heard about this Diego guy before now?'

'I had to learn about this cheating pendejo from Jac. WTF?'

'And now you're sleeping with the guy????'

'Call me back ASAP or I'm disowning you.'

Great. Just what I needed. César thought I was sleeping with the bastard too. I crawled into bed hoping that sleep would come and take it all away. This morning had started out perfectly. I had actually been happy, an emotion that was fleeting for me at best. Where was the redo button? My mind spun through the possibilities, but too many if only's jumbled in my head. I couldn't go back in time to undo the damage. I had to move forward. The only fix was to get Diego out of my life permanently. But how was that possible? I wish I had the answer.

Chapter 17

Jac

"Let's hit the street, partner." Carson stood over my desk.

My eyebrows raised.

"You seem in a good mood today."

"Got laid this weekend." He grinned.

"Me too."

I thought about how Sofía and I had left things. We spent most of Saturday together, and she wouldn't discuss the situation with Diego. I didn't understand why she was covering for him. I assumed sex would have broken down that barrier, but apparently not. She was still holding back.

We pulled into the Biogen parking lot and my gut clenched.

"Who are we here to see?"

"The head of building security."

This was not going to go well. Maybe he'd be civil and wouldn't bring up Friday night. As much as I tried to convince myself, I knew it was going to be a shit show.

"Detectives Carson and Dillon here to see Nicolas Mendoza."

We waited in the lobby, checking out the modern furniture that looked unusually small and uncomfortable. Carson took a seat, but I chose to stand. I didn't think my body would fit on the abstract pieces of art they called sofas. It was only a few minutes before I saw Nicolas. His eyes met mine, and I knew I was in trouble.

"He is not welcome here." Nicolas pointed at me.

I should have told Carson on the way in, but I had been distracted thinking about Sofía.

"What is this about?"

I sighed.

"We had an altercation Friday night."

"He ruined my date."

"It was already over when I stepped in."

"You ended it early."

"Sofía wouldn't have put out for the likes of you."

That's when Sofía walked into the lobby heading over to the cafeteria. She had heard her name and turned in our direction. Sofía stood there frozen in shock. Her cheeks flushed. And she turned heel and ran back toward the elevators.

Nicholas squared off to the men at the front desk. "I am not accepting any visitors today. If these two do not leave peaceably, you can remove them by force."

"But the shipment manifest?" Carson asked.

"Will be emailed to you, once I resolve other more important issues."

He stormed off after Sofía.

I wanted to follow, but I'd have to wait until later to apologize to her. I hadn't realized how loud our conversation had gotten or how well the voices echoed in the atrium-like lobby.

We got back into Carson's Tahoe. He didn't say a word. Carson started the SUV and headed back to the police station. His jaw was tight. I think he was trying not to let the anger boil over, at least not yet. It felt a little like a ticking time bomb. Carson was

ALBUQUERQUE ALIBI

usually so calm and reserved. I knew I fucked up. I sent Sofía a couple of text messages.

Back at the station, I followed him in, waiting for the shoe to drop.

He flopped into his chair and rubbed his eyes.

I put my hands on his desk and leaned in, hovering. "Get it out."

The last thing I needed was a partner that couldn't trust me or was so pissed he wouldn't talk with me. We couldn't work like that.

"You don't want to do this now." His eyes narrowed.

My anger had been simmering since the interaction with Nicolas. I wanted a fight, that's probably why I felt like poking the bear.

"Yes," I gritted my teeth. "I do."

"Fine." He stood and circled the desk. Even though he was short, Carson seemed to fill the space.

"You've screwed this case. The one contact we absolutely needed was Nicolas Mendoza, and you managed to piss him off to the point where he doesn't want to work with us. He could have been the key to solving a nationwide hijacking problem, and instead he'll more than likely file harassment charges against you."

"He's an asshole." I crossed my arms.

"It doesn't matter. Did you forget that Biogen execs are tight with the chief?" He growled. "The chief knows how valuable that company is to the city. We depend on those tax dollars." He threw his hands in the air. "Why were you there Friday night, anyhow?"

"You were the one that pushed me to contact Sofía." I said through gritted teeth. "Pump her for answers, you said."

"Yeah. For information. I didn't ask you to fuck her."

"You did what?" César yelled.

He had just walked in.

This was not my day.

I sighed. It would have come out eventually. I just didn't mean for it to happen in the middle of the bullpen.

César's biceps bulged despite holding his arms straight at his sides. His fists were tight, knuckles white. His jaw ticked. I knew we were going to have words.

He walked past me toward the break room and bumped his shoulder into mine. César did it on purpose, but I didn't say a word.

I blew out a breath.

"Office. Now." The lieutenant yelled, waving Carson and I to the door.

Carson did the talking. That was fine by me. He explained the whole mess. The lieutenant gave a lofty sigh and pinched the bridge of his nose.

"Is Sofía Ramirez a suspect?"

"Possibly," Carson said.

"Not a chance," I said.

"You're biased." The lieutenant said.

He grabbed the Tums bottle he kept on his desk next to his stapler and shook a few into his mouth. Crunching them like hard candy, he handed some paperwork to Carson.

"I'll issue an apology to Nicolas Mendoza."

He turned his gaze on me. "For now, you are not allowed to initiate contact with anyone from Biogen."

My eyes bulged. I had to see Sofía after this weekend. Things were finally falling into place between the two of us. Surely, that didn't include her.

He shook his head. "No one."

I nodded even though I was unhappy. "Yes, Sir."

"Get to the courthouse, then after that, you're on desk duty."

I opened my mouth to complain, but he cut me off.

"I don't want to hear your excuses. You can work the case behind the scenes. You're lucky that's all I'm doing."

ALBUQUERQUE ALIBI

I didn't see César when I walked out of the office. The looks from the other detectives were bad enough. A few shook their heads. César must be somewhere close, otherwise they'd already be razzing me.

After stopping to get the rest of the file, we headed downstairs in silence. I followed behind Carson and into his SUV. He handed me the file. The bail hearing was to take place today for the three men arrested for the Biogen hijacking. They had multiple priors and current charges including aggravated assault with a deadly weapon, attempted theft, and resisting arrest. We were going to the courthouse to make sure bail was set high enough that there was little chance those men could be out on the street. They were dangerous to the community and far too much of a flight risk.

We walked into the courtroom and sat behind the prosecution. Another lawyer in an expensive suit, Armani by the looks of it, strolled into the courtroom after us and beelined to the court-appointed defense. Carson and I gave each other a look. The counsel for the defense nodded rapidly and went over to the bailiff. I sat up a little straighter in my seat. What the hell was going on?

Mr. Armani whispered to the three men at the defense table. He opened his briefcase and slid a sheet of paper and pen to each. They read through the document briefly and signed while grinning.

"What do you think he's doing?"

"I would say some sort of plea deal from the expression of excitement on their faces, but I know the prosecutor hasn't agreed to anything. Not at this stage."

The prosecution looked just as puzzled as we were.

The court-appointed defense lawyer was nowhere to be seen. I wondered if he was with the judge.

A few minutes later, the bailiff announced, "All rise. The Second Judicial Court District, Division Nine is now in session, the Honorable Judge Flores presiding."

"Everyone may be seated."

The three yahoos were first on the docket. From the looks of things, Mr. Armani had taken over their case. How they could afford him was a mystery.

"It appears there has been a last-minute change to counsel in The State of New Mexico vs. Perez, Otero, and Chavez." Judge Flores looked over at the defendants. "Are the defendants satisfied with their new counsel, Mr. Perez?"

"Yes, your honor." They all said.

Of course, they did. No big surprise. But who had paid for this high-priced lawyer? They certainly couldn't afford him. Did we miss something when we researched their finances?

"You are being charged with attempted cargo theft, aggravated assault with a deadly weapon, and resisting arrest. Do you understand the charges you are being accused of?"

"Yes, your honor." They agreed.

"I've read through the reports and if no one has anything to add, I'm ready to set bail."

"May I have a word, your honor?" Mr. Perez asked.

"Counselors approach the bench."

Both lawyers spoke quietly, conversing with the judge. They covered the microphones so no one else could hear the discussion. The prosecutor's voice rose, clearly upset about the situation. He turned abruptly and walked back to the table. Plopping down in his seat, he looked all but defeated.

Mr. Perez on the other hand, had a sly smile upon his face that had me squirming in my seat. I hated those sleazy lawyers that knew just how to poke and prod the system to their advantage.

The judge called out the names of the defendants. "Your counselor, Mr. Perez has indicated that you have agreed to a pretrial work-release program to complete a construction project for Habitat Homes. You will be ankle monitored during this six-

ALBUQUERQUE ALIBI

week project. This will be in lieu of posting a cash bond. Note that if you complete this project with no problems, it will more than likely result in a reduced sentence when it comes to trial. Do you understand the paperwork you have signed?"

The three defendants all said Yes.

"A pretrial services officer will install the ankle monitors, after which you will be free to go on your own recognizance until your trial date which has been set for October 29th."

"I can't believe they are doing work-release. Doesn't the Judge realize they pose a flight risk? The prosecutor didn't even get a chance to talk. Those guys are dangerous." I blew out a breath. "They assaulted the driver. He's still in the hospital."

Carson shook his head, "Perez has friends. I've seen him do stuff like this before."

"Fucking lawyers."

We got back to the station, and I finished up paperwork. It sucked. We could be interviewing others for the case, but I had messed that up. My shoulders hunched. I looked at my phone. I wanted to try Sofía again, but the lieutenant's words sounded again in my head. 'No contact with anyone working at Biogen.' And now I couldn't even get a message to her through César. Maybe I could leave one with Gabriella or Mari. I closed my eyes and stared at the clock. Time was going in slow motion. The end of the day couldn't come soon enough.

César was waiting for me at my car when my shift was over. I knew what was coming. His fist slammed into my face. Even prepared, it still knocked me back two steps. His punches always packed a wallop. I wanted César to do it. I wasn't going to fight back. I couldn't contact Sofía and I felt like shit. I had fucked up her work life. But as much as I hated myself, if I had to do it all over again, I wouldn't have changed a thing. That's probably what caused the most guilt. I wasn't remotely sorry for my actions.

"You bastard. How could you do that to my sister?"

"It was mutual attraction. I assure you."

"That makes it better?" César's eyes were wild. "She's off limits. Period."

I shrugged. "That's what the lieutenant told me, because of the case."

"Screw the case. You should stay away from her because you are my best friend. Or were."

"Don't say that, man."

"Fuck you." He waved his hand in the air, cutting through it like a karate chop. "I can't talk to you right now."

César stormed away.

Detective Carson stood off to the side. He had witnessed my shame.

"Damn." He said watching the blood drip down my nose and chin onto the pavement. "César doesn't pull his punches."

Not ever. He got that right.

Chapter 18

Sofia

I had been avoiding Nicolas for most of the day. Overhearing what Jac had said this morning down in the lobby was humiliating. It wasn't like him to say something so rude, despite that it hadn't been meant for my ears. I just wanted the day to be over, so I could crawl into a hole somewhere. At least my work had been light Friday and today. Mitch hadn't been in the office much. He was out smoothing things over with clients, making sure we didn't lose them over the hijacking. We had already scheduled new shipments to replace the lost inventory. Everything seemed to be going smooth-ish. We still hadn't talked about being questioned by the police, or the fact that we had given opposing reports. Each of us avoided that subject like the plague. I know eventually we'd have to discuss it, but I was fine with the delay. The only pestering I received today was from my brother. César had been blowing up my phone all day. He had sent a ridiculous amount of text messages. That meant Jac had told him about us. So much for keeping it a secret. There were no messages from Jac. I would have picked up if he had called. More to blast him with my fury than anything else. I overheard some women talking about the incident in the bathroom while I had been stuck in one of the stalls. Slut and whore were the least of the insults. I knew that many co-workers also thought I was sleeping with my boss. Mitch hadn't exactly dispelled the rumors. I tried not to let it bother me. It was my own fault for keeping people at a distance. My coworkers didn't really know me. Ever since Diego, I was reluctant for people to get close. They never failed to disappoint me. That's why I had so few friends.

I figured the reason Jac had been so vulgar this morning was jealousy. It was clear from the interaction on Friday night, but it was still strange to see him lose it like that. He was normally so calm and collected. There was just something about Nicolas that set him off. My stomach was in knots. I knew that sooner or later I would run into Nicolas. Avoidance only worked for so long, and being head of building security meant it was only a matter of time.

Mitch left for the day around 4 o'clock, and I headed to Biogen's mailroom. With nothing to do, I spent the last hour of my day listening to the mailroom clerk. He had just filled me in on his latest Dungeon & Dragons campaign. I pretended to be enthralled, but after 60 minutes my enthusiasm had waned. I spun a pen I had grabbed from the supply cabinet like a pinwheel on the counter. It was my excuse for coming down to the dreary windowless basement of Biogen in case anyone asked. I had a whole box of pens and several stacks of Post-it notes. I glanced at the clock. Just a few more minutes to 5. My pen fell to the floor. I bent over to pick it up and noticed designer shoes in the doorway. My eyes slowly climbed up his body, but I knew who it was. With my luck, there was only one person it could be. Nicolas had found me. He leaned against the entry with arms crossed. How long had he been standing there?

"Uh. Hi," I said.

The mailroom clerk cleared his throat. "Mr. Mendoza. Sir." He quickly started putting away supplies and made himself scarce, leaving me alone with Mr. Grumpy.

"You have been avoiding me."

ALBUQUERQUE ALIBI

It was the truth, but I still didn't like the fact that he was calling me out.

I licked my lips.

"I've just been busy."

"Obviously." He smirked. "I did not know you were into D&D."

I wasn't. Not that I wanted to admit that I had been hanging out down here for a whole hour just to avoid him. I knew I was being a coward, trying to escape a confrontation.

Shrugging, I said, "There's a lot you don't know about me."

I regretted saying it the moment the words left my lips. I was being defensive, and that's the last thing I wanted to do. Nicolas had been kind to me, and I was being a jerk. He didn't deserve that.

"Come with me." He said and walked toward the elevators.

I followed along. His knuckle hit the button for the fourth floor. Most of the people were going home, so after the lobby we were by ourselves.

He exited the elevator, and I was a few steps behind him. Nicolas was not slowing, and I had to walk faster to catch up. He knew I was wearing heels, and I thought he might be doing it on purpose. Nicolas turned into a small conference room. He held the door open and gestured for me to take a seat.

"I am waiting for an explanation."

I gulped. His expression was like stone.

"That was rude of Jac to say that in the lobby this morning."

He shook his head with disbelief.

"I'm sorry. Jac and I have known each other for years. He's a friend of the family. And well, things sort of spiraled out of control on Friday night." I closed my eyes. "I didn't want to hurt you."

"The two of you had sex?"

I blinked. "Yes." I covered my face with my hands. "We have a history, the two of us." This was beyond embarrassing.

"That is not what I'm talking about."

I stopped hiding and stared at him. "What do you mean?"

"I have been researching the hijacking."

My eyes went wild with fear. The thing I had been dreading had happened. He discovered my involvement. I tried to school my face, but he had already witnessed my distress.

"I thought the police were handling that."

"Biogen has decided this needs to be an internal investigation." His eyes narrowed. "We believe it's an inside job."

My pulse just jumped in my throat. "Really?" I asked. My voice came out like a squeak, and I would have kicked myself if I could have.

"I am a very good judge of character." He stared at me. "Usually."

I bit my lip.

"Apparently, I have a blind spot. Most people do. But before now, I would not believe I could be deceived so easily."

Was he referring to me? What would he do? I felt like fainting or throwing up. Maybe I'd do both. I had to figure a way out, something to distract him.

"I don't understand what that has to do with us?"

"You mean our date?" He asked.

I nodded.

"It does not," he said.

"I'm confused."

It was the truth. I needed him to spell it out for me. Was he taking me to the police? I needed to know.

"I have not pieced together everything. But I will."

"Ok?"

He sighed. "So, the two of you are dating?"

"Maybe. I guess." I crossed my arms on the table and flopped my head forward. "Honestly, I have no idea."

ALBUQUERQUE ALIBI

"Does that mean I still have a chance?"

Despite all the turmoil in my tummy, that made me laugh. "Why on earth would you want all my drama?"

He shrugged. "Maybe I crave conflict?"

I had no idea what to say to that. If Nicolas was trying to uncover the inside man, he wouldn't need to dig very far. I needed to play this smart. If I refused Nicolas' advances, it would cast more doubt on my character, and I knew I was in serious trouble right now. If I said nothing to clarify the situation, it would feel like a lie, but then it might have him focusing elsewhere. Nicolas was obviously frustrated. I'm sure he felt betrayed, and I didn't blame him. Would it be so bad to string him along a little longer, until I figured things out?

"Am I free to go?"

His phone beeped and he looked at it and groaned.

"Your brother is at the front desk, demanding to see you."

I blew out a breath. César was like a rottweiler.

"I kicked the police out of here this morning. I do not want them sniffing around. This is none of their business."

"I'll take care of him," I said, wondering if he believed me. "He's been messaging me all day, and it has nothing to do with the hijacking or Biogen. My brother is not even working the case."

Nicolas tilted his head. "How do you know?"

"His girlfriend is my roommate." I shrugged. "We talk."

"You have signed an NDA. I hope you know as far as Biogen is concerned..."

"My lips are sealed. Got it." I patted his chest. "Don't worry. My brother is a pain, but I know how to handle him."

He grinned. "I think you know how to handle a lot of things, Ms. Ramirez."

"Back to last names, huh?" The banter made me feel a little safer. If we could keep that up, I might be able to steer him away from looking in my direction for any connection to the hijacking. "Thank you for understanding. But you should be grateful, Mr. Mendoza."

"And why is that, Ms. Ramirez?"

"The way I see it, you dodged a bullet. My life is pretty much like a Spanish soap opera. And I'm far more trouble than I'm worth."

"I do not think you give yourself enough credit, Ms. Ramirez."

And with that he left. I let out a whoosh of breath grateful for the disaster I managed to avoid. Now, I just needed to grab my purse and get to the front desk before César caused more trouble than he already had.

"I can't believe you didn't tell me about you and Jac." César complained.

"Keep your voice down." I said as I walked him out the front door of Biogen.

"Why did I have to learn about it from Carson?"

I blinked rapidly. "Who?"

"Jac's partner. The two of them were going at each other in the bullpen, and it slipped out."

"What exactly did he say?"

"It doesn't matter."

"Yes. It matters to me."

César frowned. "I'm not going to repeat it. Suffice to say, everyone at the station knows you and Jac slept together."

"Wow. And I thought women gossiped."

"You should have called me."

I shook my head.

"It just happened this weekend. I've hardly had time to process it."

"But he's my best friend. Why would you go and do something like that?"

"It's not like I did it on purpose to hurt you." I shrugged. "It just happened."

"You can't pretend like you slipped and fell on his dick."

I stuck my tongue out at him. "Sometimes César, you can be so crude."

I stormed away from him toward my car.

"I have to get to my night class. Fall session just started at UNM."

It was the truth, but also a good excuse to escape this conversation.

"How's your AC?"

I bit my lip, and my footsteps faltered. He had been there for me when I needed him.

"Thanks for helping me with that the other day."

"Those parts just don't fall out. I know you are keeping things from me."

My mouth dropped. I thought I had been so careful.

"You realize I'm a detective, right?"

"Yeah. Whatever. I'm late. Love ya," I said hopping in my car.

As I drove to campus, I thought about everything going on in my life. Where had it all gone wrong? With everyone seeing right through my lies, it was only a matter of time before my world collapsed and took me with it.

Chapter 19

Jac

Desk duty sucked. César hadn't been able to talk with Sofía about Diego and her alibi. He had been side-tracked by the whole relationship. It had sent him down a rabbit hole. Now that I was stuck with no way of contacting her until this investigation was over, I needed something to occupy my time. After finishing all my paperwork, I took a drive to one of the bars Diego frequented and parked out front. I wanted to track down the loser to determine his innocence, or rather his guilt. My gut told me he was involved in the hijacking. His crew was caught, and we knew that one man had escaped. Logic dictated that he was our fourth, but without any evidence, I couldn't do a damn thing.

I tried to make myself inconspicuous which was difficult given my size. A ball cap and sunglasses were the extent of my disguise. I needed some pointers from César. Undercover had never been my thing. I couldn't act worth a damn. Not that I needed those skills watching from my car, but if he showed up, I'd have to get closer. Diego showed up with glazed eyes. He stumbled his way into the bar.

Only a few minutes after Diego arrived, he was escorted out by two burly men. It didn't look like he was traveling under his own free will. His feet barely touched the ground. They took him into an alley. I got out of my car and crossed the street, bumming a cigarette from a man smoking just outside the bar. I walked to the edge of the building and stopped a foot from the alley entrance, just close enough to hear their conversation. Unfortunately for Diego, they weren't talking. Grunts and groans followed thuds and cracking. These tough guys were beating the shit out of him.

"You owe our boss money. We are done waiting."

Diego coughed and it sounded liquid. "I'm having trouble selling some stuff." He whined. "But I'll get it. Soon. I swear."

Needing a reason to be so close to the alley, I leaned back against the wall and lit my blunt. A stale menthol that left a nasty aftertaste. I hadn't smoked in years. I wasn't sure if it was the cigarette or the next words that caused the burrito from lunch to curdle in my stomach.

"It won't just be you who gets hurt. Your girlfriend looks like a real piece of ass. It'd be a shame to see anything happen to her."

"Leave Sofía out of this," Diego said.

One of the goons must have hit him again.

"She's not even my girlfriend," Diego wheezed. "Sofía's my ex."

"You know who our boss works for, right?"

"Yeah. The Mendoza's."

"You got until Friday."

One more thud, and I moved farther away from the alley entrance. I let my limbs go loose as I concentrated on making myself look invisible. Quite a hard thing for a guy 6'4 and 220 lbs to do.

The thugs glared at me for a few moments. I lowered my chin, focusing on the long puffs of my cigarette. They must have decided I wasn't a threat, because they finally marched over to a

ALBUQUERQUE ALIBI

black GMC Yukon Denali with dark-tinted windows. After they peeled from the curb, Diego slowly made his way out of the alley and down the block. He was a bloody mess, limping and clutching his ribs. I didn't want to see anyone in pain, but for him, I'd make an exception. He had put Sofia's life in danger. He deserved every kick and punch he got. I followed Diego into the bar a few minutes later. I grabbed a beer and found a booth at the back. It had a good view of most of the bar. After cleaning up in the bathroom, Diego sat at the bar chatting with some regulars. A few of them bought him drinks after he told a ridiculous tale of getting robbed in the alley. Diego was a charismatic criminal. I understood how Sofia could have fallen for the guy once, but what I didn't understand was why she was still covering for him. She knew he was full of shit. Every other word out of his mouth was a lie. I thought she was smarter than this.

Diego ended up leaving the bar with some trashy-looking blonde in a crop top, mini-skirt, clear acrylic heels, and too much makeup. She drove back to her apartment, and I tailed them.

Carson messaged me, 'Get back here, ASAP.'

I groaned. Just when I had Diego pinned down. The guy didn't own a car or have a job or apartment that I was aware of. It seemed like he relied heavily on others. I hoped his booty call would last a few hours, so I could finish my shift and return, otherwise I'd have to start up the whole process again. I needed to see where he was staying.

Back at the station, Carson waved me over.

"Where have you been?"

"I had an appointment."

"Mm hmm. Not investigating anything Biogen related, right?"

"Of course not."

"Well, I thought you'd find this interesting, even though you are supposed to be on desk duty." He handed me a note. "This was from one of my contacts that I put on the three guys arrested in the hijacking."

Unfolding the slip of paper, I read the details.

"They've gone missing?" I asked.

"Yep. And interestingly enough, the GPS trackers haven't alerted Pretrial Services."

"So as far as everyone else knows, these guys have reported where they need to be and are not outside their designated zones?"

"Exactly."

"Do you think they skipped town?"

"My hunch is whoever hired them is pissed they got caught, or Biogen has their people taking care of business."

"You don't think Biogen is the reason they went missing?"

"It wouldn't be the first time I've seen a corporate clean-up."

"Are you telling Pretrial Services they're in the wind?"

"I can't."

"What do you mean?"

"My contact isn't exactly above board."

"And everyone told me you were by the book."

"That's because I am, at least on my reports. Tips on the other hand, sometimes come at a cost."

"So, we have this information, but we can't share it?"

"Not until something triggers the alert. It can't come from us. There will be too many questions. And that's one thing we never want to do, encourage others to investigate us. It opens them up to discover things we need to keep secret."

"I notice you are using 'we' and 'us' a lot."

"That's because we're in this together. We're partners."

In Santa Fe, I had been flying solo working the Lorenzo case. I was in charge of my team, but no one directly had my back. It would be nice to have someone to count on now. My last case in Santa Fe was a joint task force with various agencies. PD and the Feds tended to clash more than cooperate. When I first moved

ALBUQUERQUE ALIBI

back to Albuquerque, I hoped that César and I would team up, but the lieutenant had quashed that dream. It was disappointing at first, but after working with Carson for several weeks, I realized there was a lot I could learn from the man, and he seemed more trustworthy than I had originally assumed. I wondered if I should tell Carson the truth that I was following Diego. Maybe the guy could help. The fact that he was still involving me in the case meant something.

"Do you think they'll reach out to their fourth?" I asked.

"You mean if part of the shipment is missing?"

I nodded. That's exactly what I meant. "Did we get a copy of the manifest?"

"Nope."

I felt like crap. It was my fault that Nicolas refused to work with us.

"Don't beat yourself up too bad. I think it was a convenient excuse, a reason to tell us no." He shrugged. "They would have come up with something else. I doubt they were going to give us any details. I know how these companies operate."

I went back and forth debating if I should involve Carson. In the end, I decided not to tell him about my investigation of Diego. It wasn't because I didn't trust him. It had more to do with plausible deniability. Now that I knew that Carson wasn't as squeaky clean as everyone thought he was, he seemed more real. More down to earth. That was a very good thing under the circumstances. Especially since I was working outside the confines of the straight and narrow myself.

Chapter 20

Sofia

I was in a miserable mood and taking it out on customers. Irritable and jumpy were my default lately. Mitch had noticed but kept his mouth shut. I had wanted him to yell at me. I deserved it.

My phone rang as I was heading to the cafeteria. There were some quiet rooms off the main lobby with just a single chair and a desk. I ducked into one and answered, not bothering to look at the caller ID.

"Hello?"

"Miss me?"

Ugh. It was Diego.

"About as much as I miss cockroaches. What do you want?"

"Why is someone following me?"

"Maybe you pissed someone off? Hmm. Didn't pay off your debts? Or maybe cheated with a married woman? How the hell would I know?"

"Stop being a smartass. I recognize the guy. He's a detective. The same guy who pulled me in for questioning. In fact, he's the same one who put me in the hospital three years ago."

"Hospital? What are you talking about?"

He chuckled. "I guess he never told you. Three years ago, I ended up in the ICU. Your cop friend is a thug. Beat the shit out of me and left me for dead."

I knew what happened, but not from Jac. I had read about it from social media posts. When Jac had stopped by promising that Diego would leave me alone for good, I had assumed Jac had been responsible for Diego's hospital stay. At the time I had been grateful. Did that make me a horrible person?

"Did you change your statement?" He asked.

"What? To the police? No. Of course not."

"Well, you better tell your friend to back off. I still have ways of getting to your sister."

He hung up.

My lip quivered. Diego could uncover somebody's weakness with ease. He had a knack for knowing just what to say or how to apply the exact amount of pressure to get what he wanted. That's why I stayed with him as long as I did. Gabriella was innocent. I didn't need to get her any more involved than she already was. We hadn't talked much since she had watched my video of shame. I knew it was a shock to see me committing a crime, even though I had been tricked into it. Recalling her expression of deep disappointment, I started crying. She used to look up to me. I was the big sister. It fell to me to protect her. Bang-up job I was doing. After my emotional breakdown, I pulled myself together. I found the compact in my purse and checked out the damage. After fixing my mascara and reapplying lipstick, I stared in the mirror. My eyes still looked way too wide and puffy. I couldn't stay in this room forever.

I stepped out and Nicolas was watching me from the front desk. I couldn't believe my luck. I must be cursed. We made eye contact, and I looked around for an escape, but he was coming directly my way with no sign of stopping.

"Come with me." He said escorting me by the elbow, not giving me much of a choice. Nicolas moved me to the far side of the front desk. I wondered what it looked like to the others in the lobby staring in our direction. I smiled and pretended that I wasn't being treated like a reluctant ragdoll.

"Fine," I said, glaring at him. I shook my elbow loose and fell into step beside him. "Where to?"

He swiped a badge, and we went through a door marked security. Nicolas led me down a corridor I had never traveled. He held open another door to a small conference room. Or at least I think that's what it was. It had four uncomfortable-looking folding chairs and a steel table. The room looked sterile. The walls were a dull putty. There were no paintings or artwork to make the room appear welcoming. I took a seat for a lack of anything to do.

"What happened?"

I shrugged. I wasn't going to give him details. It wasn't his business.

"Give me your phone."

My mouth hung open.

"No." I clenched my purse tighter to my chest.

"It is company property."

He had me there. Why didn't I opt out of the employee-provided phone option? Oh yeah, because it was expensive, and I loved having one less bill to pay out of pocket.

I pulled out my phone and grumbled, slapping it in his outstretched palm.

"Password?"

I rattled off the code and scowled at him.

He went through my call history. Nosy bastard.

"Who is Pendejo?"

"That would be my ex?"

"Did you already break up with the detective?"

I rolled my eyes.

"He's my ex from three years ago."

"And what is his real name? I am assuming Pendejo is a lovingly bestowed nickname."

I snorted. How did Nicolas manage to make me laugh amid the chaos I called my life?

I bit my lip wondering how I could avoid giving him the information. It wouldn't take him much to figure out my involvement. In fact, it was a horrible idea, but what alternative did I have?

"I have his phone number." He transferred the digits to his phone. "It would not take much to find out the name it goes with. Are you going to make me work for it, Ms. Ramirez?"

I blew out a breath. "Diego Ortiz."

"Diego Ortiz, aka Pendejo." He said out loud while typing the contact into his phone with a smirk. "What exactly did he do to upset you?"

There was no way I was sharing that my ex was blackmailing me, and that I was worried for the safety of my sister. That would be giving away too much. He leaned against the wall staring at me. I shifted uncomfortably in the metal chair.

"You know I could take care of him for you."

My eyes went wide. Was he serious? Why would you help me?

"If I were your boyfriend. No one would dare to bother you. I could protect you."

I knew there was a catch. Nicolas wouldn't do something for nothing. I should have known better.

"I'm fine. I appreciate the offer."

He handed me my phone and escorted me back to the lobby.

"Let me know if you change your mind."

His expression changed to something downright sinister. I had never seen that sort of look cross Nicolas' face before. A shiver ran up my spine. I knew he had an edge, but his scowl went far beyond that. I would hate to be on the receiving end of all that menace.

After I got back to my desk, my mind wandered to Jac. Why was he following Diego anyhow? I had given the police an

ALBUQUERQUE ALIBI

alibi. They should have backed off. How was I going to stop him, especially since Jac was ghosting me? A tear slid down my cheek. Another quickly followed, and I wiped them away. The passion-filled weekend had meant the world to me. I had wanted it to happen for over a decade, ever since we were teenagers. Despite all my bluster about saying we should remain strictly friends; I had wanted him with every fiber of my being. It had only been a few days, but he should have texted by now. I knew it was selfish. I was crying because my boyfriend didn't text me after epic sex, and my sister was in danger. Regret and rage battled within me. Anger won, but despite everything, I wasn't as enraged at Diego as I was at myself.

Chapter 21

Jac

"Carson told me you were taking a sick day," César said.

"Do you think the lieutenant bought it?"

"You're a horrible liar." César shook his head. "He knows you are up to something, but as long as you aren't actively antagonizing Biogen execs, you should be ok. Just make sure there is no blowback from anything you are doing. The lieutenant thinks you walk on water most days."

"Not right now."

"True. But you've been the golden child since you moved from Santa Fe. On the other hand, I am usually treated like the town leper."

"It's just your temper."

"You and I both know that's not true. The guy has it in for me."

It was more likely César's constant battle against authority. It started when we were kids. César's father, Rafael, ran a bookmaking business out of a bar. His dad died when he was 13. A hit and run. They never found the truck driver responsible. César was a rebellious little shit back then, but then his mother's brother, a Commander on the Albuquerque PD started hanging around more often. By the time César was 18, he joined the police force. Normally you have to be 21, but his uncle had pulled some strings and gotten him in early. It had probably saved him from following in his father's footsteps.

"You're lucky the lieutenant likes you."

I didn't feel fortunate. I had this gut feeling that danger was circling Sofía. I needed to figure it all out before it was too late.

"How's your sister?"

"Sofía? I haven't talked to her much. She's been dodging my calls. Every time I try to pin her down, she slips away."

"It shouldn't be that hard. Your girlfriend and her are roommates."

He shook his head. "Mari's been helping her."

"Really?" I grinned.

"Shut up."

"Not saying a word."

It made me feel good knowing that Sofía had such a close friend. She needed that. I know she had separated herself from others after breaking up with Diego, but I hadn't quite realized how lonely she was until I had moved back from Santa Fe.

"Well, I appreciate your help with this."

"Of course. You know I always have your back. So, what do you need? Your message was cryptic."

"I've tracked down Diego Ortiz."

"The slimy dude that used to date my sister?"

"Yep."

"What do you want with him?"

"I know Sofía was lying when she gave him an alibi. I believe he was the fourth guy in the crew."

"Why do you assume she's lying?" He asked.

"She twirled her hair during the interrogation."

"Yeah?"

"Sofía does that when she's bluffing."

ALBUQUERQUE ALIBI

"Maybe she was just nervous."

"It's possible, but why can't you just trust my gut?"

"All right, say that she was. There's a problem with your theory. One of the patrol officers that initially made the arrest is now questioning if they saw a fourth man escape."

"Fuck. Did someone get to them?"

"It's not always a conspiracy. Sometimes people make mistakes, especially rookies. He now believes it might have been a witness running from the scene."

I still didn't believe it. Diego was a troublemaker. He was involving Sofía somehow. I just didn't know how everything fit together. I needed him caught and thrown in jail. That was the only way to keep her safe. I hadn't wanted to involve César, but working undercover, he had critical knowledge of the city that I didn't have.

"So, what do you need from me?"

"I'm wondering if I can borrow a few of your contacts?"

"That's why you called me here? You want to use one of my CI's?"

He groaned.

"Fine. But I'm going with you. I've got a few hours before my shift starts. I'll see who's willing to talk, but if this doesn't yield anything, you have to stop before it tanks your career. I hate Diego's guts too, especially for what he did to my sister, but being a complete dick doesn't mean he committed the crime."

I knew what everyone thought, and because I had a history with the guy, maybe I saw things that weren't there. But I couldn't let this go, not until I exhausted all possibilities.

César and I found one of his contacts at a pool hall.

"Let me do the talking," César said as he messed up my hair.

ZIZI HART

I tried to keep from fixing it, but it was driving me crazy as I followed César over to a guy playing pool. It didn't take long before the short vaquero in a cowboy hat and boots crushed his opponent. The other guy moped off to the other side of the room, while the vaquero collected his cash at the end of the table.

"Hey Pepe, what's up?" César asked.

The man squinted at me. I was maybe a foot taller than Pepe, but he didn't look scared, just intrigued. I was still sporting a cut on my lip from César's swing, so I didn't look as put together as I usually did. It might have helped me look less like law enforcement.

"Who's this guy?" He asked.

"A cousin." César stated.

"He doesn't look Mexicano."

César laughed, a full belly one that loosened the tension.

"Don't tell his papa." He whispered. "His mamá will have some explaining to do."

He chuckled and shook my hand. "I'm Pepe."

I took the lead from César and answered with a Spanish name. "Jacabo. Qué tal?"

"Pagar para jugar." Pepe said, nodding to the table.

Pay to play I translated in my head. I pulled out a twenty and set it on the rim of the table.

Pepe racked the balls as I chalked the tip of my cue stick.

I continued my questions in Spanish, asking him if he knew Diego Ortiz. He must have realized I was struggling with Spanish and switched to English.

"Yeah. I know the guy. He's always needing money. Diego's got gambling debts. He said he was in big trouble last I talked to him."

That didn't surprise me. Diego had asked Sofía for money over the years as well. She had told me about his gambling problem. That's another reason I had wanted her to stay clear of him.

"You know where he hangs out?"

ALBUQUERQUE ALIBI

Pepe cleared the balls, snagging my cash. He put his hands on his hips, clearly wanting another twenty. I slapped another on the edge.

"You rack this time," he said.

While doing that, he rubbed his chin in thought. "He hangs out at the Sandia Casino quite a bit. Or the horse track. There are a few bars as well."

"Do you have the location names?" I asked.

Pepe cleared the table and tilted his head at me. I slapped my last twenty on the table, flashing my now empty wallet.

He rattled off business names and cross-streets. A few I had never heard of. Pepe had laughed and said, there was a reason for that. Hole-in-the-wall bars didn't have signs for a reason. After he won, again, César and I left. I was pretty good at billiards, but I wasn't anywhere near as talented as Pepe.

"He is quite a character," I said walking César back to his car.

"Go ahead and say it. He's a hustler. But his information is accurate." César shrugged. "People talk around him, and he's a really good listener." César shook his head. "The amount of information he retains is incredible." He gave a knock to his temple. "The guy is a genius."

"I appreciate you letting me use your CI."

"Anytime man," he said. "I'll drop you off at your place, then I gotta get to work." César smiled. "We can't all play hooky."

"Ha. Ha."

A couple of bars and a cheap motel yielded nothing, so I went to the Sandia Resort and Casino. That's where I got lucky, and not from gambling. Diego was playing blackjack with a few of his buddies. I was surprised he could afford to play given the rumors about his financial troubles. I sat at a slot machine and watched him from across the casino. After following him back to a cheap motel, I wondered if César was right. Maybe this guy didn't have anything to do with the hijacking. I still thought he was a royal prick and shouldn't be anywhere near Sofía, but that didn't mean he was involved in the crime. Since the guys who were arrested had gone missing, I didn't have anyone to question. I needed to go back to work tomorrow and face the fact that I couldn't pin this on Diego, no matter how much I wanted to.

Chapter 22

Sofia

"Can we give Clara her gift early?" Mari asked.

She had designed a magnificent piece for her Quinceañera. Georgia O'Keefe's 1920 flower paintings inspired Mari's latest line of jewelry. She had decided to do a whole line of flowers made of wrapped metal and stones. Our museum and art gallery tour in Albuquerque and Santa Fe resulted in massive amounts of Etsy orders from her new collection.

"Let me just text to see where they are," I said, grabbing my phone. A few minutes later, I had my answer. "The hairdresser just left. She's putting on makeup and then slipping into her dress. Her court isn't due to arrive for another hour."

"It's like going behind the scenes for a queen's coronation."

"That's closer to the truth than you realize. It's all about her journey from child to adult. During the reception, she will be given a crown, and she will feel like a queen."

I ran to finish primping my hair and threw on my dress for the evening.

"Why are we doing this now?" Mari asked.

"I know it's only eleven in the morning, but you'll understand when we get there. It's a bit of a whirlwind. Someone will need us to run a last-minute errand, and we will have zero time to do much else."

"Should I tell César to meet us there?" She asked.

"No. Mi mamá told me he was rehearsing with some out-of-town guests, showing them dances he had choreographed for the event."

"He is an amazing dancer. Well, he is pretty good at everything." Mari blushed.

"I'm glad he makes you happy. Now let's hit it before the hoard arrives."

"You call Clara's court a hoard?"

"Well, there are twenty-eight of them. But they usually come with aunts, uncles, and cousins, not to mention the grandparents. The massive quantity of relatives that will be traipsing through the house and surrounding her all day is insane. There is no better word for them. Trust me, when you see and hear them, you'll understand."

I drove over with Mari practically vibrating in her seat.

"You might be even more excited about this Quinceañera than I am."

"It's my first one. I can't wait to see everything. César told me a little bit, but then we got distracted."

"Yeah. That sounds like my brother." I chuckled.

We pulled into the circular drive of my uncle's house, making sure we were furthest away, so I had an escape path. I knew it would soon become jam-packed with cars.

"Clara's papa has money, and since she is the youngest, the family is going all out."

When we arrived, there was a flurry of activity at the doorway. The photographer was taking pictures as Clara made her way down the staircase.

Mari gasped at the gown my cousin wore. Clara looked gorgeous in her white ballgown with flouncy tulle and so many sparkling gold sequins it was almost blinding. She wore a simple rhinestone tiara, but I knew that would be swapped out during the coronation. There was a special crown that all the Ramirez girls wore for their Quinceañera.

After the pictures, she sat in the living room while Mari presented her with a gold and ivory-wrapped present. The ribbon had gold sparkles and complimented her dress.

"Can I open it now, Mamá?" She asked.

Her mother sighed. "Go ahead. But we need to be quick before the others arrive."

She untied the bow, and Clara's eyes sparkled. She squealed with delight.

"I'm wearing this today." She announced with authority. "Mamá, help me put it on."

"Tan hermoso." She agreed.

"Mari made it. Isn't she amazing?" I grinned.

That caused a series of gushing compliments.

While I had only bought the supplies, I was still pleased to play a small part in the creation of such a unique piece of jewelry. Mari had designed the necklace with thin gold wire, pearls, and citrine gemstones. It looked as if delicate flowers encircled and dangled from Clara's neck. It was stunning, a true masterpiece. Mari grinned with pride.

"I thought it would be perfect when you told me her colors." She whispered.

Soon after, the hoard arrived.

"Like I said before, there are twenty-eight in her court of honor. Fourteen chambelánes that will be escorting fourteen damas." I explained to Mari as she got shoved out of the way when the girls wanted to give each other hugs.

"I didn't realize it could be quite this violent."

"Too many bodies in too little space. You learn to sharpen your elbows and hold your ground."

We found a place to sit so we could watch the show. The chambelánes were all dressed in traditional black tuxedos with vests and gold bowties. Her damas wore gold off-the-shoulder satin cocktail gowns. Everyone looked beautiful, but the aunts started fussing and then someone cried out that there was an issue with the florist.

"That's our cue," I said, running over to help.

After getting the instructions and swearing that all would be well, we took off.

Mari breathed a deep breath when we got to the car.

"Are you ok?" I asked.

"Yeah. I'm fine. Just not used to so many people."

"That's why I'm here. We can look like heroes and get a break from the hoard. Win. Win."

She giggled.

We took care of the florist disaster and stopped over at the park to watch the photographer, while we ate a small lunch trying not to get anything on our evening gowns. At four o'clock, there was a small ceremony at our local church.

"I need to speak with you." César pointed at me.

"Someone's waving at you for pictures." I gestured to the altar as I ducked into the bathroom.

Mari and I snuck out early and headed to the banquet hall. She texted César that she'd meet him there.

"It looks like a fairy-tale dream," Mari said, staring at the soft creams and gold tulle swaths of fabric that draped over the walls and ceilings. Twinkling fairy lights dangled behind a throne at the center, and a series of candles filled the hall. Pink and cream roses were arranged on tall pedestal centerpieces on the banquet tables covered in gold and ivory tablecloths. Several balloon arches were set up. I was particularly impressed by the dessert tables as we walked around the hall taking in all the details.

"That's my downfall. Sweets." I said, gesturing to the tables.

"Check out the cake." Mari gasped.

ALBUQUERQUE ALIBI

The five-tier cake with white frosting, gold beading, and gold-tipped flowers looked incredible. My aunt and uncle had outdone themselves.

Mari found every aspect of the Quinceañera fascinating. It was a joy to watch her excitement.

Clara and her father walked into the banquet hall to oohs and aahs as a soft ballad played in the background. But when they made it over to the dance floor, her father was shoved out of the way by her Chambelán de honor. He was a cousin. She had specifically picked him because of how well he could dance. César and a few from her court jumped onto the stage. They gave a spirited choreographed performance to one of Clara's favorite pop-rock songs.

"This is unusual. It's called a baile sopresa, a surprise dance. They don't usually do that until later in the evening. Typically, the baile de entrada is a more serious conservative dance, but this fits Clara's style."

It led to both her parents and grandparents and her entire court joining her on the dance floor like a flash mob.

Everyone cheered when it was over. César had been working with her family and friends the past few months helping them with all the dance moves. Clara thanked him in a moving speech, saying he was one of her favorite cousins, to equal parts cheers and boos. Our family was competitive. Then she made sure to thank her parents, grandparents, court of honor, and everyone else for attending her fiesta.

After dinner, the throne was moved forward onto the dance floor. Clara sat on the throne while her father approached with a pair of gold sequined heels on a white satin pillow.

"It really is like Cinderella," Mari said.

I grinned. "This is called the cambio de zapatillas." I explained, as her father removed Clara's white sneakers and replaced them with heels. "Every tradition is about the Quince's journey into womanhood."

During La Coronación, her mother had been so overwhelmed with tears, and shaking hands that a few of Clara's sisters had run up to help pin the gorgeous crown to Clara's hair. The crown was a hand-made heirloom with Swarovski crystals that glittered under the ballroom lighting.

"Screw Cinderella." Mari gasped. "Clara's a frickin' queen."

"That's the point. Isn't the crown to die for? I was able to wear it for my Quinceañera, like a million years ago."

The song changed to a sweet melody, and a doll was then presented to Clara by her mother.

"It's La Ultima Muñeca. The last doll." I whispered to Mari. Clara waltzed around the dance floor holding the doll high in the air and hugging it. When a cute little six-year-old in a gold tea-length gown stepped onto the dance floor and waved, Clara stopped. Looking between the doll and the little girl, she handed it over in a dramatic flourish. The little girl waved to everyone as she ran back to her mother.

"Look what I got Mamá."

Everyone chuckled and cheered.

Then began the series of formal dances. First with her father, then her mother and grandparents until her whole court of honor took the dance floor. Finally, they started grabbing others, officially opening the dance floor up to anyone.

César had been so preoccupied for the first half of the evening making sure everything ran smoothly, I was able to sit next to Mari and not worry about him pestering me with questions.

"We need to talk." He said as he approached our table.

I grabbed a nearby cousin and dragged him out onto the dance floor. "Go ask Mari to dance, she's feeling neglected," I said as I started dancing.

Whew. I needed help if I was going to avoid him. As many people as there were at Clara's Quinceañera, it would only be a matter of time before he tracked me down and I couldn't get away. I'd have to stop dancing at some point.

ALBUQUERQUE ALIBI

The Quinceañera was a smashing success, and by smashed, I meant me and about eighty percent of the guests. My family knew how to party.

"You've been avoiding me," César said.

I had been hiding out in the corner behind a series of balloon arches leading to the dessert tables.

Where were my blockers? I looked around frantically. I had recruited a few of my cousins to keep César preoccupied, but unfortunately, my brother was persistent. I frowned at the closest one, who would not make eye contact.

"Let's not do this here," I said.

"I'm not falling for that. If I don't question you here, I'll never get answers."

"That's the problem, isn't it? You approach everything like an interrogation. It's never just a conversation with you. Besides, if you wanted to talk, you could see me at Mamá's for Sunday lunch."

"You know with my work schedule, that's not always possible."

I knew that, and it's exactly why I suggested it, plus Gabriella and Mari would be there. They were the perfect buffers.

"Plus, Mamá doesn't want us to fight at the house, so that's no place for this kind of discussion."

I moved toward the bar for another drink I didn't need. But it had more to do with getting away from this conversation. César prevented me, blocking me with his body, and I growled at him. Since I was in heels, I couldn't easily maneuver around him. Damn these designer shoes. He had a hold of my arm now and wasn't letting go. I had no choice but to follow along, in between tables and out toward the lobby. I could no longer use the excuse that I couldn't hear him over the blaring DJ. The distinctive clacking of my heels echoed off the vaulted ceiling of the venue. I heard the sounds of the party and wished I could be back inside.

"Why had you never told me about Diego?"

My eyes went wide. That was not the question I thought would come out of his mouth. I expected him to be more concerned about me and Jac.

"I dated him years ago. And besides, you always get crazy whenever Gabriella or I mention boys."

"But you kept me in the dark."

For good reason.

"I think you've indicated that Gabriella and I should both be nuns."

"It was only a suggestion."

My eyebrow rose.

"Really César? That's your attitude."

"I know that you broke up with that guy three years ago because he cheated on you."

Among other things I didn't want to mention.

"Yes?" I asked, feeling like whatever he was going to say would cause my temper to rise.

"So why the hell were you sleeping with Diego after all he's done to you?"

Mari walked into the lobby. "Wait, what?" She asked.

The back of my hand covered my forehead. It was starting to get hot in here. What could I say? I couldn't tell them the truth that I had falsified my statement. The police would be furious with me and may charge me with something, but that wasn't my biggest concern. If I didn't supply Diego with an alibi, he could tell Biogen of my involvement, he could release the video showing I had participated in a robbery, and he could potentially hurt Gabriella. I couldn't allow any of that to happen.

César turned to Mari. "Yeah just a few days ago. Diego spent the night at her place."

"You let that asshole into our apartment?"

ALBUQUERQUE ALIBI

Great. Now Mari was mad at me. And I couldn't tell her the truth until I could get her alone.

"Please, Mari. You have to understand."

"I've been by your side since day one. I know you want to see the good in people, but some people don't deserve it."

"Trust me. I know."

Gabriella walked out to the lobby. "What are you guys talking about? You all look so serious."

"Sofía slept with Diego last week."

"The dangerous one?"

I rolled my eyes.

Gabriella knew a little of our history and had seen the video of the robbery. She knew after breaking up with Diego, I severed the relationships with most of my friends. I didn't want to have any connection with that part of my life. Most of them were toxic, so I hadn't missed them, but trust these days was still hard. Diego had caused more psychological damage to me than I wanted to admit.

"I can't believe you would do that after all he's done to you," Gabriella said with hands on her hips.

"You knew about him?" César yelled.

"Of course, I'm her sister." Gabriella shrugged.

"What does that make me?" César asked.

"Overprotective." All three of us responded. We giggled despite the tension of the situation; it lightened the mood.

"And then you go and sleep with my best friend." César let out a breath of air. "How could you?"

"You and Jac?" Gabriella asked.

"Yeah," I said.

"Finally." She high-fived me.

"You knew about that too?" He asked her.

"So obvious, it was ridiculous." Gabriella shook her head. "And you call yourself a detective." She rolled her eyes. "Anyhow, I hate to break this up, but they are doing speeches."

She gestured with a thumb over her shoulder, "We all need to head back in."

I was grateful for the distraction.

"This conversation isn't over." César shook his finger at me and stormed back into the hall.

I breathed a sigh of relief.

Gabriella rubbed my shoulder and followed him in. Mari stayed by my side.

"Are you ok?"

"Yeah."

"Sorry for my reaction. I know there has to be a good reason. It was just a shock. I thought you liked Jac."

"I do."

"Then why on earth would you sleep with Diego? How come I'm just finding out about this now?" She shook her head. "When did this happen?"

"Wednesday night last week."

The expression she gave me was utter disbelief. I couldn't bear to lie to her. My family, yes. To keep them safe, but Mari meant too much. What friends I made now meant the world to me, especially since I had so few. Mari was just such a person. Even though we had only known each other for a few months, I considered her more than just a roommate. She was one of my best friends. That's why I had confided in her about Jac and how I felt about him. And after watching the video, she had been unwavering in her support, even though she had no reason to.

"I promise you. Diego never set foot in the apartment. But you can't share that with anyone else just yet. Can you keep my secret?"

"From your brother, you mean?"

I nodded and squeezed her hand. "Especially him. I'll tell you everything as soon as I can."

"Okay. He probably won't ask me anyhow, as I was just as confused as everyone else, but you owe me an explanation. All of it. You know I'm here for you."

ALBUQUERQUE ALIBI

I gave her a huge hug, and we headed back into the hall. "I don't know what I'd do without you."

Chapter 23

Jac

A sleazy hole-in-the-wall bar was not where I wanted to spend my Saturday night. I had yet to see anything suspicious from Diego, besides his lack of taste in women and sporadic beat-downs from a certain loan shark with ties to the Mendoza family. César's CIs didn't yield much info on Diego. He was low-level. Rumors were that he had committed some robberies with his crew over the years, but it wasn't clear if he was involved in the most recent hijacking. Once the name Mendoza came up, the CIs clammed up. It had them spooked. All I had learned was that the Mendoza family was not to be fucked with. My research told me very little. They were a wealthy Colombian family with suspected ties to an international drug trade. I heard the name while working the Lorenzo case in Santa Fe. The Mendoza's and Lorenzo's were rivals. Other than the name, which was common enough, it wasn't clear if any of the Mendoza's currently residing in the city were part of an elusive drug trafficking operation. If they were, their PR team was working overtime.

My cell phone vibrated, and I looked at the number. It was Sofía. We hadn't talked for a week. I made my way out of the bar and answered. A series of swear words in Spanish came over the speaker.

"Sofía?"

"Yes. It's me. You're such an asshole."

"Wow. Good to hear from you too."

"I want to hate you." She said with a hiccup. "But it's impossible. You haunt my dreams. Why are you so damn sexy? It should be a crime."

Sofía was drunk dialing me. I chuckled. It reminded me of a time long ago when we were in high school. I had rescued her from a teen party gone wrong. She had been drinking back then too.

"Are you in trouble? Do you need something?" I asked, suddenly concerned.

"You, Jac. I need you." Sofía sighed. "Ya know. I thought detectives were supposed to be smart. Wasn't last weekend a glowing example of how good we are together."

I heard music and laughter in the background.

"Where are you?"

"At my cousin's Quinceañera. There's an open bar."

I figured as much. It took quite a while to get Sofía tipsy, and she sounded well beyond that point.

"Total ghost after epic sex. What the hell, Jac?"

Epic sex? I grinned. I felt the same way.

"Didn't your brother tell you?" I asked.

"I've been avoiding César. It's been incredibly hard to do that tonight, but I've enlisted some of my favorite cousins as blockers."

That would have been fun to see. Sofía's family was crazy, but the extended family was even more so.

"I've missed you." She said, giving a little sniff.

Was she crying?

"I'm sorry Sofía. I had no idea César hadn't told you. The lieutenant pulled me off the case. I've had desk duty this week,

ALBUQUERQUE ALIBI

and I wasn't allowed to initiate contact with anyone from Biogen. That's why I haven't called."

"You wanted to call me, but your job wouldn't let you?" She snorted. "That's the lamest excuse I've ever heard of."

"It's the truth. Go ask your brother."

She hung up on me.

Damn that woman. She didn't believe me. That grated on my nerves. She didn't have a reason not to believe me. What was I supposed to do? Following orders was part of the job, even if you didn't like them. I sighed, deciding to head home. Diego might have noticed me rush out of the bar earlier. I had been watching him for the better part of a week. If Diego hadn't done anything to incriminate himself by now, he probably wasn't going to. He might have been a piece of shit scumbag, but that didn't mean he had been part of the hijacking. Maybe I was too close to this case. The lieutenant was right. I wanted Diego to be involved because otherwise, I'd have to acknowledge the truth. Sofía had spent the night with this asshole. She had given him an alibi. That's the part I couldn't get past. I wanted to punish Diego, but not for his crimes. It's because he had touched My Sofía.

I had just turned out the lights and crawled into bed when Sofía called again.

"I'm an idiot." She cleared her throat. "I talked to César."

"What? No swearing at me in Spanish?"

"Ha. Ha. I've calmed down."

"Are you sober?"

"Getting there, but I could sure use a ride if you aren't still mad at me."

I should tell her no. I sat up in bed.

"Why would you assume the worst of me?"

"You know why. My past boyfriends. I haven't had the best track record with men."

"But I'm not them. You know that. Over the years, you always called me to clean up whatever disaster comes your way. I've done everything you've asked and still you doubt me."

"I'm messed up. I know that. But I… care for you more than you could ever imagine. Please Jac. I need to see you."

Her voice had gotten that vulnerable quiver at the end. It would be the death of me.

"Give me the address," I mumbled.

Sofía stood at the curb looking like a hedonistic goddess in a green fitted gown that flared at the hips. Her hair was a tousled mess and her makeup was a little smeared. She held her heels by the straps. They dangled on one finger. Sofía waved and walked over to the car in bare feet. I jumped out and opened her door. She planted a kiss on my cheek and giggled. I couldn't help but smile. It was worth it to see her so happy.

"Thank you for picking me up. César took Mari back to his apartment, but they were going to stop by and pick up Miles first. I swear that cat acts more and more like a dog every day. He loves his car rides."

"So, let me get this straight. You called me in the middle of the night, got me out of bed so I could race across town and pick you up even though César was going to the same address?"

"He's been on my last nerve all evening."

"Not a big surprise. Didn't you say you had been avoiding him?"

"Yeah, I have. But it wasn't just that. César also left early. Mari wasn't feeling well. That girl can't hold her liquor."

"That's because she weighs practically nothing."

ALBUQUERQUE ALIBI

She grinned. "Mari is a tiny little thing. Let me check and see if she's ok."

Sofía's fingers typed into her phone at inhuman speed. A minute later, her phone pinged.

"We need to re-route. There's been a change of plans. I'm crashing at your place."

"What?"

"César is staying at the apartment with Mari. She's been worshiping the porcelain god since they got there."

A thrill ran through me. Sofía had never asked to see my place. I could see her uncertain expression at the traffic light. She was waiting for me to reject the idea. But now that it was out there, I didn't want to back down.

I cleared my throat. "Do you need anything from your apartment, first?"

"And go through the drama with my brother? No, thank you. I'll just text Mari to let her know I'm staying with you. I'll deal with César tomorrow."

"She'll tell him where you are."

She nodded. "I know."

"No more secrets Sofía. We are either doing this or not. I don't want to lie to your family. Not anymore."

"You mean dating for real? Publicly?" She asked.

I nodded.

"Will that mess things up for you at work?" She asked, clearly concerned.

"It's a gray area. You were a person of interest in the hijacking case. I was too close. That's the reason the lieutenant wanted me to keep my distance. But Biogen isn't cooperating with the investigation, even without me, so it might not matter. We'll see what next week brings."

"Jac Dillon is going against his lieutenant's orders. Let me mark it on my calendar. It's a momentous occasion."

Technically I was still following orders. I hadn't initiated contact. However, if the lieutenant knew, he wouldn't be pleased.

"I had no idea you were such a rebel."

"Just make it worth my while."

"Count on it." She said in a sultry voice.

My speed increased. I wanted to get to my townhouse before she changed her mind. I focused on driving and not crashing my car thinking of all the things going on in that mischievous mind of hers. She wouldn't regret taking this step with me. I'd make sure of it.

Chapter 24

Sofia

I yawned and stretched in what I was convinced were the softest sheets in the universe. All the stress I usually held in my neck and shoulders had eased. After last night's workout, my body felt amazing. Well, so did Jac's. I snuggled back into his powerfully muscled body and sighed, feeling his warmth envelop me. It earned a grunt for my efforts, and his arm wrapped tight around my waist, pulling me close. Even asleep, Jac didn't want me to slip away. I grinned, feeling more content than I had any right to be with all the turmoil in my life, but I didn't care. I was going to enjoy the moment fully. All my worries had been officially kicked to the curb until I woke up enough to deal with them all over again.

My phone pinged and I reached for the side table. Jac grumbled in his sleep when I separated from his arms to stare at the text from mi mamá.

The Ramirez Sunday lunch had been canceled. It said she had a headache. The message implied she had a hangover, which was nearly impossible with Mamá's tolerance for alcohol. I knew better. Her excuse was pitiful. So, I sent a message to Gabriella. A response came back a few minutes later.

'It's too early.' She complained.

'Mamá just canceled lunch. WTF?'

'Oh. That. Yeah. She went home with that guy she had been dancing with all night.'

I remembered a very suave gentleman she had been dancing with at the Quinceañera. He was a family friend, but I couldn't recall his name.

Normally, I would rather cover my ears and close my eyes to the fact that mi mamá was capable of a sex drive, but today I was grateful for the extra time with Jac. Lazing around in bed and exploring his body at leisure sounded like a perfect Sunday. When we finally rolled out of bed, he gave me a tour of his townhouse. We had been far too distracted the night before and pretty much all day. The sheer number of orgasms proved that. It's why I was still floating on air. Everything in Jac's home was perfectly coordinated, from furniture and pillows to rugs and wall décor. The color palette was soft blues, browns, and tans, masculine but not overly so. It fit Jac's personality. The rooms flowed together seamlessly with unique accent pieces and a massive amount of family photos captured throughout the years. Some were formal, but I appreciated the spontaneous ones the most. Jac was, of course, equally handsome and adorable in all of them, no matter his age. He was very photogenic with a smile that could light up my world. I even saw a few photos of Jac and my brother standing together. In one, they were in football gear. I could make out myself in the crowd staring at them, awestruck. I wondered how many times I had been captured doing that over the years.

Jac decided to prepare dinner, an Italian dish that had been passed down from his grandmother. The chicken parmesan with pepperoni was divine. Every piece melted in my mouth, and I couldn't help but moan with each bite. He had even whipped up a salad with homemade dressing.

"Is there anything you can't do?" I asked.

He grinned. "I'm horrible at sewing and I don't like enclosed places."

ALBUQUERQUE ALIBI

"Finally. Some flaws. I was beginning to think you were too perfect."

"I have another surprise for you." He said while leading me upstairs to the loft which doubled for the library.

We had breezed past it on our tour earlier. He went over the large floor-to-ceiling bookcase filled with classics and clicked one of the shelves. A door slid open to reveal a hidden staircase.

"No way," I said grinning.

He knew I loved anything mysterious, and a secret passage was something that you witnessed in old movies but never got to see in real life.

A giggle slipped out before I could stop it.

"I knew you'd like it. But it's too hot up here during the day, so I wanted to wait until evening to show you."

We climbed the spiral staircase to the roof and all the breath left my body.

I had witnessed the incredible view of the Sandia Mountains from Jac's bedroom, but this was something else entirely. After watching the sunset, we strolled around the rest of the terrace. The garden looked straight out of a fairy tale. The space was surrounded by a privacy trellis on three sides. The fourth side in the east was open for a view of the mountains.

"All the trees and plants up here are set on drip lines. Everything is completely automated."

We walked on cobblestone paths between plants. Each grouping of plush patio furniture had a view of the mountains. I walked further in and found a gourmet grill and a bar.

"You could have some amazing parties up here."

"I believe that was the point. My mother worked with an interior designer on the whole place. Since you spent the weekend with her, you probably know how much she enjoys entertaining."

Yep. That fit Faye.

He poured me a glass of wine from the bar, and we drank while relaxing on the oversized chaise lounge staring into the night sky. It was completely peaceful. I needed this in my life right now, especially when every other part of it was pure pandemonium. Wrapped in Jac's arms, leaning back against his chest, I felt protected.

"Do the other townhouse owners ever come up here too?"

"My mother bought the whole building. There are no other owners."

I inhaled a sharp breath. I needed privacy for what I was proposing.

"No one can see us up here?" I asked.

"Especially if I turn out the lights."

Jac pulled a remote from his pocket and touched a button. The multi-colored patio lights strung up on the trellis died out.

"Then we can do things up here without anyone knowing."

"What do you have in mind?" His voice had deepened.

I bit my lip and stripped off my dress. There was still enough light from the moon to see what we were doing.

"Sofía." He whispered, running his hands across my hips. "So silky soft."

"Pants off Jac," I said, desperate for him to be inside me.

"Not yet. I need to explore you."

"Haven't you been doing that all last night and today?" I grinned.

"Not nearly as much as I want to."

I felt the same. We switched places on the lounge chair and Jac took his time. Light touches that had me stretching and undulating like a cat in heat.

"I don't know if I can take more of this anticipation. Please," I said.

"You are so impatient."

"Sí. Quítate la ropa ahora antes de que explote."

"Did you say you were going to explode?"

"Yes. If you don't get your clothes off now."

He chuckled.

ALBUQUERQUE ALIBI

I heard the sounds of his belt buckle and his jeans being chucked and flung to the side. His shirt came next. His body was framed by the light of the moon, and I felt my mouth go dry. This man was too much. Broad shoulders, sculpted pecs, and taut abs, with zero body fat. A honed hero, and he was all mine. I felt a little giddy. Not that Jac gave me much time to stare. Before I knew it, he was on top of me, covering me with his large, muscled body. He captured my lips with his own. We moaned into each other's mouths. I felt him hard against my stomach and I squirmed beneath him.

"Do you have a condom?" I asked.

"Damn. It's downstairs."

"I've been careful up to now, at least where sex was concerned."

"So have I."

"I don't want any barriers between us. Is that ok with you?"

He only waited a few moments. Jac answered my question by thrusting inside me. I was so wet, and slick. He buried himself up to the hilt and we both gasped for breath. Jac didn't move for a moment, always careful and worried about hurting me. I started rocking my hips, impatient as always. He was right about me. I heard him swear under his breath, then we found our rhythm.

Before long we both came long and loud. Jac collapsed on top of me, and I wrapped my legs tighter around him. When I could focus once again, I blinked up into the night sky now filled with stars and felt a peace I hadn't felt in a long time

"Have you become an exhibitionist?" He asked.

I giggled. "No one can see us, right?"

"Nope, but they can hear us. My mom only bought one building. There are still other townhomes behind us."

I wasn't particularly embarrassed. Our exploits in the park back when we were teenagers should have given Jac a clue. I guess I hadn't changed much in that regard.

"Any law against that?" I asked.

"Not that I'm aware of. It's indecent exposure, not indecent acoustics."

I threw back my head and gave a full-body laugh. "Were we that loud?"

"I'll see if the neighbors complain tomorrow." He said against my lips. He was smiling. I could hear it in his voice. He rolled to the side and reached into an ottoman. He pulled out a sheet and a blanket. Jac covered the two of us, and I snuggled in close, leaning back into the soft cushions. The sheet was Egyptian cotton and luxurious. The Dillon's never skimped on thread count. I didn't want to move a muscle. Jac must have felt the same way. I wondered if we could sleep up here all night under the stars. He took one of my hands, intertwining our fingers together. Jac pressed a soft kiss to my knuckle. I didn't want to think about the future, so I forced my worries to the back of my mind. Right now, I was here with Jac, and there wasn't a place in the world I would rather be. Everything would work out. Somehow. Before long, sleep overtook me. I felt safe in his arms and more protected than I had in far too long.

Chapter 25

Sofia

Monday rolled around far too soon. I had to leave Jac's house before sunrise so I could get home and change before work. I got an Uber back to my apartment. Jac had offered, but I refused to have him chauffeur me around once again. Mari was still in bed when I arrived, so I quietly moved about the apartment, getting ready. With no one to talk with, dread crept up and took hold despite every effort to stay positive. When I got to the office, the tension was high. Mitch was in a particularly nasty mood. He had gotten progressively more irritated with me over the past week and a half. I could do nothing right in his eyes. I sighed when he started berating me for failing to use the correct font in an email.

"Tahoma. Ms. Ramirez." Mitch's nostrils flared. "I've told you time and again. Times New Roman. That's the only font we use here at Biogen."

I rolled my eyes.

"Yes, Mr. Hammond," I said through gritted teeth, trying to sound contrite, but failing.

"And I don't appreciate what you said to the police."

Now we were getting to the root of the problem. The real reason he was angry. He had lied, and I hadn't covered for him.

"I only told them the truth."

Or at least most of it.

"Biogen employees back each other up. We are all team players here."

Toward the end of the day, Mitch told me about a last-minute meeting. I grabbed my purse and notepad and followed him to a conference room on the fourth floor.

I took a seat at the large table and got out my pen. Mitch liked having handwritten notes before they were typed into the computer. It was double work, but I didn't mind. Up until recently, I would have said he was a great boss, but the last few weeks had become increasingly difficult. Most days I felt like quitting, but my finances wouldn't allow me that sort of freedom, so I put up with the emotional abuse.

"No one's here," I said.

"Not yet. They should arrive any minute."

"Will we be working overtime this evening?" I asked.

He shook his head. "The meeting will be quick." Mitch kept glancing at his watch.

At a quarter to five, he couldn't sit still anymore and started pacing.

"I filed a report." He said, glancing back at me.

"Should I start taking notes?" I asked.

"What? No. I don't give a fuck." He waved his hand in the air with a dramatic flourish.

My jaw dropped. Mitch didn't swear. Appearance meant everything to him. I remember him stating that swearing was unprofessional.

ALBUQUERQUE ALIBI

"I filed a report with HR and Security. You are about to get fired Ms. Ramirez for violating Biogen's security protocols."

My eyes widened. How had Mitch realized I gave the shipping schedules to Diego? Or was he bluffing, hoping I'd react? I felt like he had been setting me up to fail this past week. Maybe if I played dumb, it would give me enough time to figure a way out of this mess.

"What do you mean by that?" I asked.

"You are not allowed to print secure documents outside the office."

Wait. That's what he was upset about? Just the printing. "But," I complained, "I only did that because you asked me to."

He shook his head like he pitied me.

Nicolas strolled into the conference room.

"Where is HR?" Mitch asked.

"They will not be coming."

Nicolas looked between the two of us.

"Sit down," Nicolas said. It was an order.

Mitch's mouth opened and closed like he wanted to say something, but nothing came out. He took a seat three chairs over from me. Like he wanted to distance himself from whatever was coming.

Nicolas asked us a series of questions. It was far more intense than the police station. I tried to answer as honestly as I could.

"Where were you this weekend?" Nicolas asked. "I require a timeline."

I wondered why that was his concern. I wanted to tell him it was none of his business, but I bit my tongue.

"My cousin had her Quinceañera on Saturday." I went through the details leading up to the party, wondering why he needed all this information. "After the party, my brother and roommate went back to our apartment because she wasn't feeling well. Since she wanted privacy, I stayed with a friend."

"At Jac's place?" He asked.

I swallowed. How did he know? Was he following me?

"Yes," I admitted.

Mitch scrutinized both of us. "What's going on here? Are you two fucking?"

"That is completely inappropriate," Nicolas said through gritted teeth.

"It was one date." I sputtered.

Nicolas glanced at me. Maybe I shouldn't have shared that information. I bit my lip.

He turned back to stare at Mitch. Nicolas' demeanor had changed. I had seen it before. That edge I found so attractive a few weeks back was now threatening. At least he was no longer focused on me. The intimidation was directed at my boss.

Mitch adjusted his tie like he could feel the heat from Nicolas' stare. "I meant no disrespect if that's the case." He cleared his throat. "But that means you're biased. Another reason we should have HR here."

"That is not going to happen." Nicolas sneered. "I know you are sleeping with the HR director. I sent her home."

My eyebrows rose. That was a surprise. I thought I knew everything about Mitch, but apparently, he was just as good at keeping secrets as I was.

"I have been investigating the hijackings and have narrowed it down to the two of you. One of you was involved in the theft."

I swallowed hard. Biogen had found out.

"I know it was an inside job. Both of you had access to the shipment details of both thefts. Talk now, and I will try to make it painless."

I tilted my head. Painless? Why would he use that word? Nicolas was careful with everything he said. In the short time I spent getting to know him I witnessed his need for precise language. Nicolas had never looked more dangerous. I shivered and he turned in my direction. Mitch took that opportunity to run

ALBUQUERQUE ALIBI

for the door. Nicolas moved with a speed I didn't know he was capable of. He slammed Mitch's face against the wall. Mitch slumped to the floor, out cold. Nicolas ripped open my boss' shirt and rifled through his pockets and jacket. I didn't know exactly what he was looking for, but he seemed almost disappointed. He turned his gaze on me and I'm sure I looked like a deer in the headlights. I sat up a little straighter in my seat and refused to be intimidated by him, even though my pulse was racing.

"Up, Ms. Ramirez." He demanded.

I raised my eyebrows, but I wasn't about to say anything to cause a reaction. I didn't think he'd hit me, but I apparently didn't know Nicolas as well as I thought I did.

"Face the wall," he said.

I assumed the position. Palms above my head touching the wall and my legs spread. This was not my first time being searched. I was becoming an expert.

Nicolas patted me down, and he was thorough. At least he didn't rip open my shirt like he did Mitch's. He unbuttoned it slowly.

"I liked that green dress you wore on Saturday. Very sexy" Nicolas whispered in my ear.

He was stalking me. I knew it. But what was I supposed to say to that comment? I bit my lip.

Nicolas sighed. "Sit." He waved to one of the boardroom chairs.

I re-buttoned my shirt and tucked it back in, adjusting my skirt before taking a seat.

He radioed for some additional men who removed Mitch and dragged him away. How was I going to get out of this?

"Your purse."

I handed it over, not having much of a choice. He dumped it on the conference table rifling through the contents briefly. My gaze lingered on the DVD. The reason I had gotten into this mess in the first place. I had never gotten rid of it. I wanted to say something, but I bit my tongue.

"Now Ms. Ramirez. It's just the two of us." He leaned in close. "I will give you one chance to tell me everything you know about the hijacking. If you lie, I will know. No more games, or I will make things very unpleasant."

Chapter 26

12 Hours Earlier

Jac

I knew two things for certain. Sofía was still hiding things from me, and she was in trouble. My valiant efforts to get her to call in sick this morning had yielded multiple orgasms, but not the results I expected. She promised to meet me for dinner tonight but refused to miss work. Shortly after she left, I came up with a plan. I drove to César's apartment, bounded up the stairs, and pounded on his door. It was early morning before our shift started and I needed his help or I'd never look undercover enough to get even close to Biogen.

He yanked open the door.

"What the fuck? Do you know what time it is?"

I grinned and walked past him into the apartment. I knew it was still dark, and César had never been a morning person, while I on the other hand was the opposite.

"I know she's in trouble," I said. "I've got this gut feeling."

"Sofía?" César asked as he closed the door.

I nodded, anxious to get through this conversation as quickly as possible.

"You really have it bad for my sister."

"I have since high school. She had a crush on me, and honestly, I had a crush on her too. It just took me a while to admit it."

"High school? How old were you?"

"Seventeen," I admitted.

I could see his Adam's apple bob up and down as he did the math. His face heated, and his jaw ticked. César's fist tightened and loosened repeatedly like he was getting ready to punch me. Again. We didn't have time for this, but I stood straighter and stuck out my chin. I'd take whatever he dished out.

"Then my sister would have been fourteen."

I gave him direct eye contact. "Yeah."

"Fuck." César paced back and forth in his living room.

"We spent plenty of time together when you first went to work for your uncle."

César had been a wild teenager, angry at his father for dying. He got into fights whenever and wherever he could. César's mother had asked her brother, Jesus Garcia to take him under his wing. Commander Garcia worked for the Albuquerque PD and still did. His uncle had been instrumental in his training, and the reason he joined the force.

"I would have killed you back then if I had known."

I nodded. "That's why we didn't say a word."

"But that was fourteen years ago. You had plenty of opportunities to tell me over the years. I've mellowed out."

I raised my eyebrows.

"Ok. Maybe not mellowed, but I'm not nearly as bloodthirsty as I was in my teens."

"We only dated that one summer. When I moved away and started college, it was over. I thought about telling you, but it never seemed like the right time. Finally, it felt like too much time had passed. And besides, Sofía swore me to secrecy."

ALBUQUERQUE ALIBI

César sighed. "My sister and her damn secrets. She had told me to mind my own business on multiple occasions, especially when it came to her dating."

"I'm worried about her."

"You believe she's in danger?"

"Yes. You might think I'm paranoid, but I want to keep an eye on her. I need surveillance equipment to get close to Biogen without being noticed. I've already called in sick."

"Again?" He shook his head. "I never thought I'd see the day. Mr. By the Book is going against the lieutenant's orders."

"Shut up." I shoved his shoulder.

I blew out a breath. If he could joke, that meant we were ok.

"Yeah. I got something I can loan you." He opened a drawer and grabbed a key ring with a remote.

I followed him down the apartment steps over to a set of garages. He opened up the third one.

"Your car will stick out, so you can borrow the van. It's got everything you'll need inside."

I glanced at the white van. It seemed innocuous like it could be in any neighborhood or business and not look out of place.

"Is this registered to the PD?"

"No. My uncle acquired it for my temporary use. You need it to be off the books, right?"

I nodded.

César dangled a set of keys in front of me.

"I use it for undercover work, but I won't need it for today's assignment, so it's yours for 24 hours. It's an impound vehicle seized in a drug smuggling case, but the owner is in jail. The plates have been swapped and it ties to an organization that contracts to several businesses including the city, just in case someone checks. There is a bag of clothes in the back, along with various workmen's shirts that should allow you to blend in if you have to get out of the van. It also has the appropriate gear, badges, and fake work orders if anyone comes asking. You'll need a pair of dark work pants since you are quite a bit taller than me. Choose simple, nothing that will stick out or be remembered."

He took a deep breath and stared at me.

"Call me if you need me, and Jac?"

"Yeah."

"Don't get caught."

An hour later I followed Sofía from her apartment to the office. I found a spot up on the hill overlooking the Biogen parking lot. I watched her and several employees arrive to start their day. I made notes of movements just like I would on any stakeout, even though it wasn't official. I noticed Nicolas' car was already in the lot. Mitch, Sofía's boss arrived around 9. Nicolas had personally wandered over to my van at lunchtime, jotting down the license number. I hoped whatever plates César used would hold up under scrutiny. I was monitoring from inside the van at the time, utilizing the hidden cameras installed in the van's trim. The day dragged on. Not being able to risk leaving the van sucked. At least there was some airflow from the battery-powered air conditioning, although not enough to keep me from sweating. When five o'clock rolled around, most of Biogen's employees left for the day. By 5:30, only a handful of cars were still in the lot, including those of Sofía, Mitch, and Nicolas. I knew she would work late if Mitch did, but that feeling in my gut intensified. Something was wrong.

At 6:15, two men, clearly building security from their uniforms, escorted Mitch to a black van. They weren't exactly gentle when they shoved him in the back. One jumped in after him, and the other went to the driver's seat. They started the van, and I got ready to follow them, but they just sat there. Forty minutes later, Nicolas strolled out of the building with Sofía pressed to his side. It didn't look overly aggressive, but it did look intimate. I zoomed in on her expression with the binoculars, she was panicked. I called César, but he didn't answer. I couldn't call the station for backup, since I was supposed to be home sick. There was also that matter of violating a direct order from my superior. I wasn't supposed to be investigating Biogen, including its employees. Not that I was about to leave, not with Sofía in potential danger.

  I followed the black van to a dark warehouse a few miles away. Nicolas had a key. I looked up the address, and it didn't appear to be owned by Biogen, but they had multiple holdings under various subsidiaries. I found very little online, other than the building was owned by a company with an address in the Cayman Islands and appeared to be vacant. After scoping out the surrounding area, I parked in a nearby lot. César had yet to respond, so I texted him the address and the details in case things went south. I checked my weapons and sprinted to the building. There was a fire escape on the opposite end from where Nicolas and the others had entered. It led me to a metal door. I wasn't sure if the building had an alarm, so I climbed onto the roof, looking for another way in. The grimy skylight allowed me a view inside. It offered a general layout of the building. My suspicions were confirmed. It looked like the building hadn't been used in quite some time. Empty shelving filled the majority of the space, with offices on the far end. Since I wasn't doing this remotely by the books, I utilized a few borrowed tools from César's van to open a maintenance hatch. The metal ladder creaked as I climbed down. Luckily the wind whistling through a few broken windows made enough racket to cover up the noise. Creeping between the rusted shelves I followed the sound of voices. Nicolas was saying something to a man tied to a metal chair. I didn't recognize him at first. The man's lip was swollen, and there were cuts on his cheek and forehead. Blood dripped from his nose onto a white shirt.

Other than the blood, his suit was immaculate. It was Mitch. Sofía's boss.

"Why am I here?" Mitch asked. His voice quavered. "I did nothing wrong."

"I thought a change of venues was in order, so you could appreciate the seriousness of the situation."

Nicolas cracked his knuckles.

"I know you are lying. The pharmacy tech talked. He told me how he retrieved the additional product stored in the delivery trucks. Ingenious. I was impressed. I did not realize you were quite so creative."

Mitch's eye twitched.

"Now that you are sufficiently softened up, we can begin again." Nicolas struck the man in the face. His head jerked to the right and blood sprayed in an arc. The brass knuckles gleamed, lit by thin beams of light streaming from the skylight.

Nicolas grabbed the guy's shirt, practically nose-to-nose with the man. "I need names. Your partners. You did not do this on your own."

"I had no part in the hijacking."

"I never said you did."

My gut churned. The guy was a jerk, but I didn't want to see anyone hurt. I'd have to step in and help, but first I needed to know that Sofía was safe. There were at least two other security guards unaccounted for. I couldn't jump in without fully assessing the situation, otherwise, I'd end up right next to Mitch tied up in a chair of my own. There were three offices with lights on the far side of the warehouse. I had to cross 10 meters of empty floor to reach the offices. There was no way I could get to them unnoticed. I either stayed put or risked going outside to find another entrance.

An outer door opened, and a man in his late fifties entered. He was dressed in a designer suit, wearing sunglasses and smoking a cigar. The man wasn't quite as tall as Nicolas, but he had similar features that made me think they were related. He carried himself with authority. The thin scar on his cheek gave him a sinister edge. Although I had never met the man before, he somehow seemed familiar.

"Did you get anything?" The older man asked with a thick Colombian accent.

"We just started."

"I want faster results. We need this over, and a message sent. Am I clear?"

"Yes Padre," Nicolas said.

The pieces were falling into place. They were both Mendoza's. While Nicolas' accent was difficult to identify, there was no doubt the origin of his father's. If they worked for the Colombian Mafiosa family I had researched while working on the Lorenzo case, this changed the dynamics dramatically. I needed backup. The Mendozas were equally as ruthless as the Lorenzos. The two families had been rivals for years. If the Mendoza family was connected to Biogen, no wonder those higher up didn't want me investigating, and why the feds didn't want me involved. It was all making sense. Exactly how far up in the organization was Nicolas' father? The door swung open, and two more men walked in. They looked like muscle. Thick necks and beady eyes that scanned everywhere at once. That made six against one. My odds were getting worse every minute I delayed.

The older Mendoza approached Mitch. "What have we got here?"

I couldn't see what the guy was doing, but Mitch started screaming.

"Do you know who I am?" He asked, puffing on his cigar.

Mitch started blubbering incoherently.

"I'm the one you've stolen from." He blew smoke in Mitch's face.

"It wasn't me. I swear." Mitch begged. "It was Sofía. She's the one who printed out the shipping schedule."

"I see." The man scratched his dark beard.

"Did you get anything from the other one? We need confirmation."

Did he mean Sofía?

"Not yet. He hasn't talked," Nicolas said. "Let this one stew."

My heart felt like it would jump out of my chest. I let out a breath. I needed to get Sofía out of here. Her life was in danger, and we were running out of time. I doubted anyone being interrogated was walking out of here alive.

Nicolas, his father, and one of the guards entered the office on the left. The other guard stayed behind to watch Mitch. I needed to incapacitate him without alerting the others. At least his back faced me.

As much as I hated to help Sofía's boss, especially after what he just said, I needed a distraction.

I shifted my position so Mitch could see me. He glanced over briefly. I pointed at the guard and made a talking sign with my hand hoping Mitch took the hint.

"So, what's your name?" Mitch said to the guard.

The muscled guy just grunted.

"No comment huh? Or maybe I should call you Estúpido. That's a good name for you. Or do you not understand English?"

"Cállate."

"Shut up?" He shook his head. "Make me." Mitch taunted.

I launched from my hiding spot, striking hard and fast with a metal pipe that I found on one of the shelves. The grunt collapsed to the floor with a thud. I used my knife to cut Mitch free from the ropes.

"Do you know which office Sofía is in?"

Torture sounds started coming from the office where Nicolas and his father had entered.

Mitch shook his head and ran for the door.

Coward. Although I didn't expect much from him after he threw Sofía under the bus the first chance he got. I knew his type, only out for himself. I removed the weapons from the bodyguard and ran across the open floor. I chose one of the two remaining offices, hoping to get lucky.

Chapter 27

Sofía

Thumps and cracks with intermittent screams from the office next door made me ponder all the mistakes I had made in my life. I thought I had poor judgment with men, but I hadn't realized the extent of my flaw until I was tied to a chair in a vacant warehouse. I was late for my statistics class at UNM. I estimated my probability of walking out of here alive at one percent. I made my peace with dying relatively quickly. I should be screaming. They hadn't gagged me. What did it say about me, that I could give up so easily? Or was I just being practical? I wondered how my body would be found, or if I would be added to unsolved cases of missing women. Would my brother and Jac search for me? I wasn't sure how long I had been waiting in the office, only that my arms were numb from the position I was in. The tight ropes cutting off my circulation didn't help matters.

Nicolas walked in from the adjoining office, and I blew out a breath. Was my time finally up? A man twice his age and almost twice as wide shoved him out of the way.

"Is this Sofía?" He asked.

I didn't appreciate how he leered at my body, but it's not like I had much of a choice. I couldn't very well cover myself in my current position.

"She's Mitch's assistant."

His eyebrows rose. "Does she know what he did?"

"No."

My brows furrowed. I had listened in the van, learning what Mitch had done. Nicolas knew this. Mitch had some side deal going on with the pharmacy shipments. He added packages to Biogen's delivery trucks in exchange for cash. Something illegal. That's why he had met with them privately to discuss terms. He had been doing it for some time under my nose and the company's.

The older gentleman ran a calloused thumb over my cheek. "I'm sorry my dear, but your boss stole from the company."

My eyes went wide. Did I have an out? The man was waiting for me to say something. Did they think Mitch and Diego were in on it together?

Nicolas was trying to say something with his eyes, but I couldn't figure out what it was.

"Should we call the police?" I asked.

Nicolas closed his eyes. From his stance that was the wrong thing to say.

"No. That would be a bad idea. This is company business. It's an in-house problem."

"You work for Biogen?" I asked.

The fact that the man was talking, maybe I could figure out what was going on and find a way to smooth things over. As an administrative assistant, that's what I did.

"I. Am. Biogen." He said smiling.

ALBUQUERQUE ALIBI

That didn't exactly clarify things. Maybe it meant he owned stock or was an executive. I had met several Biogen board members. They occasionally showed up at company parties, but I don't remember this man. He was someone you wouldn't forget.

"Well, then you would know best what's good for the company," I said, trying to look appropriately respectful.

"Cut the ropes." He demanded.

Nicolas walked behind me and suddenly my numb arms were free. The older gentleman picked up one of my limp hands and placed a kiss on my knuckle. I forced myself to smile. He let go of my arm and it flopped to my lap.

"My name is Mario Mendoza."

"A pleasure," I said. "I can see where Nicolas gets his good looks and charm." I smiled.

I didn't mean a word of it, but I could schmooze with the best of them. I had been dealing with a smarmy salesman for three years. And my experience dating criminal ex-boyfriends meant I could lie with ease. I probably should have felt guilty about that, but it might keep me alive.

"Weren't you at my son's party?"

"Yes. I was."

"He was quite taken with you and now I can see why. You've got spirit. Most women in your situation would be sobbing or hysterical."

I swallowed hard. "What good would that do?"

"None." He agreed. "But it tells you a lot about a person, in their final moments." He turned to Nicolas. "Bring her into the next room."

Mario strolled into the adjoining office and lit a cigar.

Nicolas held out a hand and shook his head. What was going on? Why did they want me to go into the room where I had heard screams? This wasn't good. I hadn't witnessed anything yet. I needed hope that I could escape. I wanted to cling to that possibility. I climbed up on unsteady feet and joined them.

The scene that greeted me was worse than a horror film. Streaks of blood slashed across the floor and an old, rusted utility cabinet. The man sitting tied to the metal chair was hunched over. At first, I thought it was Mitch, but he wasn't wearing the same thing as earlier. A blood-soaked t-shirt, jeans, and sneakers. Mitch wouldn't be caught dead in an outfit like that. Then the bloody body moved. The man's head lifted and my eyes went wide with fear. It was my ex, Diego. A man well-versed in lies. What had he told them?

"You know him," Mario said.

It wasn't a question, but I still nodded, too dumbstruck to do anything else.

"He's told us quite the story." Mario paced. "You were playing the model employee while plotting against us."

Diego stared at me grinning. Blood dripped from his teeth.

"That man is a no-good cheat and a liar," I said.

Mario grinned. "Oh, I know that. I just found the whole thing funny. What's his name again?"

"Diego Ortiz," Nicolas said.

"Yes. Yes. This Diego tried to tell us that you had masterminded the theft. That it had all been your idea. Can you imagine?"

It didn't surprise me that he would stoop to something so low.

I licked my lips. "You were too smart to believe his lies."

"You're not going to defend him?"

I laughed.

"Isn't he your boyfriend?"

"He's my ex." I seethed.

"Tsk. Tsk. Poor choices, Sofía."

I knew. Oh, I knew. That was my life. Filled with bad men and bad choices. And now I was going to pay the ultimate price.

"As amusing as it's been, I'll let my son take things from here." He turned to Nicolas and whispered something into his ear. Nicolas just nodded and wouldn't meet my eyes. Mario Mendoza snapped his fingers, and his bodyguard opened the door for him. He strolled out into the dark warehouse. His bodyguard followed him and closed the door.

"I'm sorry." Nicolas said as he pulled out his gun and pointed it at me. I closed my eyes, waiting for it all to end. My body jerked with the sound of the loud crack, and I crumpled to the floor. I felt my chest and face for the bullet wound, but I hadn't been hit. My legs had just given out. Jac and Nicolas were wrestling for the gun. I glanced at the adjoining office door behind me, the one he must have just burst through. The third office door was open as well. He must have been hiding in there, waiting for his chance to rescue me. My heart filled with so much emotion. I wanted to kiss him. He gave me hope when I had all but lost it on my ride over here, what seemed like hours ago. I needed to snap out of it and help him. I gathered my nerve and got to my feet, stepping around Diego's chair. It must have crashed to the floor. Diego was out cold. He must have been knocked out in the shuffle. I kicked at the gun and managed to knock it into the corner under a rusty cabinet.

Jac pulled out another gun and pointed it at Nicolas.

He put his hands up.

"Do you think you can get away? My father is right outside."

Nicolas' phone vibrated. Jac yanked it out of his pocket and glanced at the message.

"Are you sure about that?"

He showed Nicolas his phone.

"What's happening Jac?" I asked.

"Mario Mendoza left with his bodyguard, probably after discovering his other guard unconscious. The two Biogen security guards are tied up in the third office."

"But that's not all," Nicolas said. "It also says hora de limpiar."

"Time to clean?" Jac asked.

"You don't understand the message, do you?" Nicolas smirked. "The clean-up crew is on their way. They won't leave anyone here alive unless you do exactly what I say."

"I'm not listening to you."

I wobbled over to Jac on shaky legs and clung to his side. "Trust him," I said.

"He just had a gun pointed at you."

"I know. But I still believe him. He's not bluffing."

"Mario ordered Sofía to be eliminated. Didn't he?" Jac asked.

Nicolas shrugged.

"If we leave, is she still in danger?"

"Only if she talks. Her NDA still applies, and the company has deep pockets. We would bury her with our lawyers." He sighed. "I can make it clear to my father that it would be a bad idea to pursue the matter. That's all I can offer you. With a boyfriend, brother, and uncle working for the police, I can get him to let this go. We don't have much time. Once the cleaners are here, my ability to do anything dies with me."

"Mario wouldn't kill his own son, would he?"

"If I'm a risk, then I'm weak. He doesn't tolerate weakness."

"What about him?" Jac asked, pointing at Diego.

"He's ours. There are still questions we need answered. Besides, he doesn't deserve to be rescued."

"We aren't leaving without him."

"You don't have much of a choice. Either take Sofía and leave now, or none of us survive."

"Please Jac. Get me out of here."

Chapter 28

Jac

"Corbata Colombiana." César rocked back on his heels as he stared at the heavily beat-up body propped against the dumpster.

"Subtle," I said. Diego's tongue was sticking out of the deep slit in his throat. I had never seen a real Colombian necktie until today. The message was clear. He had wronged an old-school Colombian family. I was sure it was the Mendoza's, not that I could prove anything, or even tell César. Nicolas had mentioned that he could only keep us safe if we told no one what happened. I hated to keep this from César, but I didn't have a choice. The Mendoza's were far too well protected, and I doubted any evidence would point back to them directly. My FBI friends had told me to steer clear of the family, along with my lieutenant. The FBI was handling their own inquiry and didn't want the local police disrupting their investigation. I didn't have much of a choice. I had wanted Diego out of Sofía's life for good, but I never pictured it happening like this. I wanted him to go to jail.

"Why were we called in?" I asked.

"We weren't." César shrugged. "Not officially. Diego still had his wallet in his back pocket. Whoever did this was not trying to hide his identity. This was a professional hit. The case was assigned to a friend of mine in homicide. When they checked, his name popped up on a recent case, and since my sister's name also came up on that same case, he called me. I needed to see it for myself, and I figured you would as well."

Normally Narcotics was not pulled into a homicide investigation, but César had developed quite a few friends on the force. Maybe he thought I needed closure to ensure he would never trouble her again.

"Have you told Sofía?" I asked.

"Not yet. I'll leave that to you."

"Thanks a lot."

My gut was already churning. I didn't know what kind of reaction she would have. I wasn't quite sure how to feel about it myself. On one hand, I wanted the bastard to pay for what he did to her, but on the other, it didn't feel like justice had been served.

My phone rang. "Dillon here."

"Are you staying clear of the Mendoza's?" Carson asked.

I laughed. "I'm actively ignoring them."

"Good." He sighed. "Then I can give you an interesting update on our case. You remember the three guys arrested in the Biogen hijacking?"

"The ones that went missing?"

"They've been found."

"We've got them back in custody?" I asked.

"Not exactly. They are with OMI."

If they were with the office of the medical investigator, then they were dead. Seemed like a pattern. I knew exactly who was behind it too.

"How did they die?"

"In a fire over the weekend. Arson had ruled it suspicious but hadn't been able to identify the bodies. After the autopsies, OMI was able to confirm their identities from dental records."

"What about the ankle monitors?"

"They were destroyed during the fire."

"Why didn't they send out an alert?"

"They did. But since it happened over the weekend, the report didn't come over until Monday. By then, all we knew was that the men were missing. The last known GPS coordinates didn't yield anything of interest."

"Finding out 48 hours after the fact doesn't help."

"You are preaching to the choir. The company handling the pretrial ankle monitoring is a joke. But they won the bid."

"It always comes down to money, doesn't it." I sighed. "Did you hear about Diego?"

"Yeah. I got a call from Homicide. They wanted our file and his interview for their case."

"I'm at the scene now."

"Is it as grizzly as they say?"

"Pretty much. So where does that leave us?" I asked, even though I already knew.

"Case officially closed. It's not going to trial if our suspects are all dead. Biogen sent their claims through to insurance. I finally got a note back from some admin thanking us for our service. The Chief has been pressuring the Lieutenant to close cases. Something to do with this month's numbers. As long as you aren't pursuing Biogen or the Mendoza's, you are off desk duty. I could use your help with some of my other cases. They've been piling up."

Even though I knew the Mendoza's were involved, I had no way of proving it. The family managed to eliminate the threats while making a public point to others who might be tempted to steal from them in the future. I wondered if Mitch, Sofía's boss, had left town or if he met a similar fate to Diego and the others. Would we find his body in the coming weeks? All those involved in the hijackings were dead. Diego's murder would be investigated, but how much effort would homicide give to a low-life like him? Plus the fact that a lot of people wanted the man dead. The suspect list would be extensive. The debt collectors alone would keep homicide busy for weeks. Not that any of them would have gone to so much trouble or staged it in such a way. With pressure to close cases, I figured the higher-ups would soon force homicide to close Diego's case or pass it on to the FBI. My buddy at the Bureau made it clear that Biogen was off-limits. They had moles in the organization that were trying to gather evidence against the family. I was just grateful that Sofía was no longer under Diego's thumb. He could never hurt her again. I had promised her that three years ago but had failed to deliver. It grated my nerves that Nicolas had done the one thing I couldn't. Not that he was in her life anymore. Luckily, she had been fired from Biogen. I knew she was sore about her dismissal, but I think she got off easy. She could have ended up like Diego. I shuddered at the thought. I took one last look at the body and texted Sofía to meet me at our favorite restaurant for lunch.

She was waiting for me at our regular table in the back. Even though we didn't need to hide our relationship anymore, I didn't mind a little privacy after the day I'd had.

"Jac. It's good to see you."

I smiled. "Same here," I said, sliding into the booth.

I grabbed her hands across the table.

She tilted her head. "What happened?"

I debated on whether I should tell her, but I didn't want to lie. She deserved to know the truth.

"Diego was found today."

She inhaled sharply.

"Did he give a statement?" Her voice quivered.

I shook my head. "He's dead."

A slow breath leaked from her lips.

"Has his place been searched?" She asked.

I frowned, narrowing my eyes. "I'm not sure. The case is with Homicide."

Sofía's eyes shifted, glancing around and then down at the table. She took a long drink of water and set the glass down. She was hyper-focused on the condensation ring left by her water glass. She rubbed the drops back and forth in circles. Sofía finally lifted her eyes and met mine.

"I have to tell you something."

I knew by her expression that I wasn't going to like what I was about to hear.

Her phone rang.

"I'm sorry but I have to take this."

Sofía sprinted from the table before answering the phone. I gritted my teeth, wondering why she was hesitating. Hadn't we already gotten through all our trust issues? What could she possibly still be keeping from me?

Chapter 29

Sofia

Glancing at the phone, I saw it was my sister. I raced from the table, heading to the restroom. Not that I needed privacy for the conversation. It was more that I needed to work up the nerve to tell Jac something I was reluctant to share.

"You are a lifesaver," I said.

Gabriella laughed, "I do my best."

"What's up?"

"Mari and I wanted to know if you could go to Zozobra tomorrow night. We just got tickets."

"How many did you get?"

"Six. So, you can invite Jac if you want. Mari is already inviting César, and I'm still working on my date."

"Are we finally going to meet Ramón?"

"Maybe, if I can get him to commit."

"What about Mamá?"

"She's off with that boyfriend of hers."

"I still can't believe she is dating. Isn't she too old for that?"

"I guess you are never too old for some things." She hinted.

I almost gagged. "Don't you dare say another word. I can't even begin to think along those lines. There is not enough bleach to wipe the images from my brain."

Gabriella snorted. "Mom is not that old."

"Again. TMI. So, what time do you want to leave? My schedule has been pretty open since I lost my job."

"It's probably going to depend on the guys. I took the night off. And now that both your and Mari's schedules are flexible-"

"That's a nice way of putting it."

"I'll check with Jac and get back to you."

I needed to talk with Jac about several things, but this was a wonderful distraction, and I was just cowardly enough to take it. Maybe it would give me a reprieve for an hour or so, just enough time to get through lunch. When I got back to the table, I didn't allow him to ask questions. Instead, I launched into conversation.

"That was Gabriella on the phone. I thought it might be an emergency, but she got tickets to Zozobra. Do you want to go with us tomorrow night?"

Jac grinned. "Yeah. That would be great. I haven't been to Zozobra in years."

"It will be the six of us. Mari, César, you, me, Gabriella and her date."

Zozobra was the perfect diversion. It got him talking and we steered the conversation away from the giant elephant in the room. Maybe he realized what I was doing, but didn't call me out on it. We both ordered Jac's favorite, fish and chips, and talked about our plans for the weekend. By the end of the meal, I grew nervous again. I wrung my hands together after the server took away my empty plate.

"Are you ever going to get back to that thing you had to tell me?"

I bit my lip. "I was hoping you might have forgotten."

"I was giving you time. You seemed like you needed it."

ALBUQUERQUE ALIBI

I sighed. He knew me too well.

"Come on. There is nothing you can't tell me. This is a judgment-free zone. Remember."

A giggle burst from my lips. It was something he used to say when we were teenagers. I thought about the meaning behind the burning of the effigy called Zozobra. He was called Old Man Gloom. The burning was a way of letting go of the worries from the past year. It was a way to start fresh. I needed to do that with Jac. He deserved the truth, but I realized I didn't want to do it here, in a public place where others might hear.

"Do we have time to go to your place?"

"You want to fool around?" He grinned.

"No."

His face fell. I didn't mean for it to sound like that.

"Well, that's not true, but I need to show you something first."

His eyebrows rose. I could almost see the gears grinding in Jac's brain. He was trying to puzzle it out.

He took out his phone and typed a few messages. "We have two hours before I need to be back at the station."

When we arrived at Jac's townhouse my nerve had nearly left me. My pulse was in my throat and my mouth felt desert dry. How was I going to say what my conscience demanded? Then I realized, I didn't need my voice after all. I still had the DVD in my purse. Even though I had originally wanted to burn it, for some reason I had kept it. Maybe I didn't want to forgive myself, at least not yet. Not until Jac knew the truth. It was somehow easier to play the video than try to explain. I slid the DVD into the player and sat down on the couch about a foot away from Jac. He went to put an arm around my shoulder, but I shook my head. I didn't want his comfort. At least not yet. I kept my distance, folding my feet beneath me, and crossing my arms over my chest. I had already seen the video, so I didn't pay attention to the TV. I concentrated all my focus on Jac as he watched it. He seemed to understand the importance of my distance and directed his attention to the screen. He watched it until the end. Other than a tick in his jaw, he didn't say or do anything. When the recording ended, I bit my lip. I was still staring at him, or rather his chest when he turned in my direction. At some point, I had lowered my gaze not wanting to meet his eyes. He lifted my chin with his finger.

"Is this how he blackmailed you?"

My eyes widened and I nodded. "How did you know it was blackmail?"

He shook his head. "It's clear from how things went down. Now I understand why you did the things you did."

I let out a deep breath. Jac wasn't judging me. I thought he would let me have it or at the very least point out my stupidity. Over the years, I had managed to get myself into horrible situations time and again. Jac would always come in and save the day.

"But the evidence. What if someone else saw this?"

"Don't get me wrong. It doesn't look good. Especially if people who don't know you saw this. But I know you, Sofia. You blame yourself for things you can't control. You've always done that."

I guess I did tend to beat myself up worse than anyone else. I was my own worst critic.

"The video doesn't show you carrying a gun or taking any money. From your expression, it looks like you were ill."

"You're right about that. After the robbery, I holed myself up in a fast-food bathroom sick to my stomach. I refused to come out. Diego and his friends were so pissed at me, but they also didn't want to cause a scene. They ended up leaving without me."

"When did this happen?"

"Two nights before I called you. Three years ago."

"Did Diego sleep with that woman?"

I groaned. "I didn't lie about his cheating. He did that on many occasions, too numerous to count. Of course, I hadn't known the sheer volume of women until after we broke up. But that night I hadn't told you everything. The main reason I was upset was because of the robbery."

"Who else has this tape?"

"Only Diego as far as I know."

"But someone else recorded it."

We played the video again. I counted the number of people. I recognized the guys and myself, but someone was missing. Then I saw the edge of a woman's hand on the screen. She had hot pink nail polish. I thought back to that time, and then it hit me. The woman was a girlfriend of one of the guys in Diego's crew. She was also the one I had walked in on with Diego. She must have been the one recording the whole thing. She could still have a copy. The woman hadn't been in any of the scenes on the film, because she had always been behind the camera.

"You figured out who it was?"

"Yeah." I licked my lips. "It was the woman Diego had been sleeping with. The one I had walked in on. She was the girlfriend of one of his crew."

"Do you know her name? Her address?"

I shook my head. "I only know where she worked and her first name. Candy. But I doubt that was her real name. She worked at one of the strip clubs Diego's crew used to frequent." I stuck my tongue out in disgust more at myself and the situation than because of her profession. "I've tried to put her out of my mind. And it's not like we kept in touch."

"It's ok," Jac said. "We'll figure everything out. Come here."

I let him hold me in his arms while I sobbed. Jac understood. Somehow, he didn't condemn me for my actions. How did I ever get so lucky? I swallowed back tears and gulped in breaths of air. Relief filled my body as I buried my face into his chest, holding him tighter. I was so damn grateful.

The next afternoon, Jac had come over early. I answered the door, surprised to see him. We weren't supposed to get together for a few more hours.

"I found Candy."

"Do I want to know?" I asked.

"Probably not, but you also need closure."

I nodded.

"She died about a year ago. Complications from an infection. They think maybe from a needle."

"Candy used drugs back then too. She was a big heroin user. That's why I didn't blame her for cheating. I figured she was too high to know what she was doing at the time. Not that I stuck around to ask her questions." I bit my lip. "Since it was a year ago, did she have someone collect her things? You know, a relative? Someone who might have kept her phone or a computer that might have the video?"

Jac shrugged. "If someone did, it's not on record. Her stuff was probably tossed or donated to a thrift store after she died. Candy didn't list any next of kin on her lease. If she had a phone or computer, it's probably long gone."

I felt bad for the woman. She didn't deserve to die like that. No one did. Was it awful of me to feel relief despite the circumstances?

"I have a surprise for you."

I tilted my head. He smiled at me and led me down the steps to his car.

Jac drove to a convenience store. It was one of Mr. Torres'. He now had a string of them despite the robbery.

ALBUQUERQUE ALIBI

Mr. Torres waved when we walked in. One of his clerks took over the register. We walked to the break room in the back. My face heated. Had Jac told him what I had done? Or was I supposed to confess? I'm not sure I could bear the humiliation if that's what he wanted me to do.

"Detective Dillon told me you've been having a rough time lately." Mr. Torres stared at me. His eyes were filled with compassion. He gave me a giant hug, and I felt my limbs go liquid. I cried in earnest.

"Hush now child. You didn't do anything wrong."

I shook harder in his arms.

"If you only knew," I whispered.

"But I do know. I always knew it was you behind the mask."

My eyes bulged and I pulled back from the embrace. "How could you know? "Did Jac tell you?"

He chuckled. "No. Your boyfriend didn't need to. It was your shoes."

I took a deep breath, purposely avoiding his mention of Jac as my boyfriend. I didn't want to touch that one for the moment. I concentrated on the other part. How had he known all these years that it was me?

"Wait. My shoes?"

"Yep," He grinned. "You always wore those purple and teal sneakers."

I thought back to three years ago. Yep. He was right. I had worn them until they had holes in them. They had been a gift from mi mamá.

"The fact that you came so often to the hospital and had been instrumental in raising funds to get me back on my feet showed me how much you wanted to make amends. Whatever reason you had for being there in the first place no longer mattered to me."

He gave me another quick squeeze. "The detective told me that the men who beat me up are dead. That you are the only one left."

My eyes widened. What would Mr. Torres do with this information?

"Look at her face." He said to Jac and chuckled. "Like I would ever testify against you." Mr. Torres shook his head, "Sofía, you are the reason my business is such a success. You raised more money than was stolen, plus you inspired the whole community to support local businesses. You didn't just help me. Because of your influence, the neighborhood banded together. We had a purpose and we drove out a lot of the gangs in the area."

After my initial philanthropic efforts, more to appease my guilt, I hadn't been back to check on him. Right after that, I started with Biogen, and my focus went elsewhere.

He gave me another hug, and we sat down to catch up. What a relief to realize that he wasn't going to turn me in, regardless of another DVD copy resurfacing. I hoped it didn't, but I'm not sure it mattered. Mr. Torres wouldn't press charges. He reassured me and even seemed grateful. I was so glad his business was doing so well. I left our meeting feeling lighter than I had in a long while. We headed to Santa Fe early to make sure our worry letters were added to the gloom box to burn that evening. We met his parents for lunch, and it wasn't nearly as awkward as I thought it would be. His mother was overly pleased that we were a couple. After César got off work, the rest of the gang headed up to Santa Fe to meet us at Zozobra Field at Fort Marcy Park. Gabriella's date couldn't show at the last minute, so she had taken a waiter friend from work. It was clear the guy had a thing for Gabriella, but I wasn't sure she shared the enthusiasm. I knew she was bummed that Ramón had bailed.

César glared at the guy throughout the evening, and Mari and I thought it was hilarious. My brother had finally turned his attention away from me and Jac. Did that mean he accepted our relationship? Or was that too much to hope for?

ALBUQUERQUE ALIBI

As we watched the gloomies dance around Zozobra, I felt like that had been me these past three years. I had been merely existing, walking around barely living. I didn't realize how deep of a depression I had been in until that moment. When the fire spirit came out and danced, I realized that is who Jac represented in my life. He was there to fight my sorrows, to lift me whenever I was down. He was a warrior, ready to battle against any obstacle that came in my path. He had been my savior most of my life. Anytime I needed him, Jac would come running. He'd drop everything when I called. Why hadn't I trusted him earlier and told him the whole truth about Diego and the robbery?

As the crowd all chanted to burn Zozobra and the fire spirit lit the pyre beneath him, I realized that I was ready to move forward. I could finally let my worries go. Jac would be by my side whatever came my way. He would never desert me, no matter what happened. As the crumpled papers of worries that Old Man Gloom was stuffed with caught fire, I breathed a sigh of relief for the future.

The fireworks went off. Everyone was dancing and cheering. The sky lit up with colors as the pile of Zozobra's ashes burned. Jac gave my hand a gentle squeeze. How did I ever get such an amazing man to love me?

"I'm keeping this one brother," I said to César. "So, get used to it."

He rolled his eyes, but Mari jabbed him in the ribs.

"Oof. Fine." He rubbed his torso. "I'll let him live."

"That's mighty big of you." Jac chuckled.

"I love you," I said with tears in my eyes.

He wiped them away. "I love you too. I always have."

"To everyone's worries melting away," I said grinning at Jac, holding up our entwined hands, watching as the multi-colored lights from the fireworks cast shadows over our outstretched arms.

Jac's eyes twinkled. "And to new beginnings." He said, pulling me into his arms for a kiss.

ZIZI HART

I vaguely heard my brother's groan over the noise from the crowd of people celebrating around us. My whole world narrowed down to the sexy man in front of me, lighting off his own fireworks display with his tongue. I ignited for him, groaning into the kiss. It was freeing not to worry about who might witness our PDA. I was absolutely in love with this man and didn't care who knew it.

Chapter 30

Jac

I was about to do something epically stupid or brilliant, depending on how it all turned out. Sofía and I had only been officially dating for over a month, but I didn't want her to slip through my fingers again. Recalling my conversation with César last night, I couldn't help but grin.

"Marriage? Are you nuts?" He had asked.

"Maybe." I admitted. "But I don't want to wait."

He shook his head. "You two haven't been dating that long."

"That you know of."

He took a half-hearted swing at me and missed. César chuckled. It had become a joke between us. He was no longer upset that we had kept it from him. We had explained the reasons, and César agreed that he would have reacted poorly when we were teenagers.

"And you want my blessing?"

"Of course. I need you to be ok with this."

"Would it change things if I wasn't?" César asked.

If I were honest, no. It wouldn't. Our friendship meant the world to me, but I still loved Sofía.

"I hoped it would never come to that," I said.

"Would you choose my sister over me?"

"Don't make me choose." I put my hand on his shoulder. "Would you let anyone stop you from being with Mari?"

He wouldn't meet my gaze. César didn't want to admit how much he cared for Mari. I knew he wanted to propose to her as well. Maybe he was more upset that I had beaten him to the punch. Although, I'm not sure Mari minded the wait. Their relationship had gone off like a rocket, but at her request, they were trying to take things slow, much to César's disappointment. I never thought I'd see the day when he would be the one pushing for more in a relationship. I, on the other hand, had wasted too many years apart from Sofía. It had been fourteen years, and I refused to let another year go by regretting not making my move.

"Don't try to spin this back to me." César shrugged. "It's your funeral. Not mine."

I chuckled. He was in denial.

"We've always felt more like brothers." He sighed. "I guess we can finally make it official."

I slugged him in the shoulder and then hugged him. "Thank you, Brother."

"Of course, that's only if you get her to say yes. Sofía has a mind of her own."

"Don't they all?"

He nodded, looking solemn for a moment, then a grin cracked through the serious expression. "Mi mamá will be ecstatic. She'll be bugging you about grandkids." He wiped the back of his hand across his forehead and flipped his wrist as if flicking off sweat.

"At long last, she will be off my back."

ALBUQUERQUE ALIBI

Sofía and I walked across the lawn hand-in-hand at Balloon Fiesta Park. I could sense the excitement bubbling within her. She practically vibrated with it. It was early morning before the sun came up, so I couldn't see her features clearly. I had managed to book a private balloon ride for Sofía and myself. Despite living her whole life in Albuquerque, she had yet to ride in a hot-air balloon and I was about to fix that. But there was something else I wanted to do if I had the nerve to follow through with it.

"I can't believe you managed to score tickets this late."

"I have a friend."

"Uh-huh," she said, "You have lots of friends. No doubt it's a woman." She mumbled under her breath.

"As a matter of fact, Rebecca is of the female persuasion."

"Figures." She smirked. "You are just like my brother, getting way too much attention from women." Sofía put her hands on her hips. "This Rebecca person does realize you're off the market, right?"

I frowned, trying to think if I had made things clear. I guess I hadn't talked about Sofía specifically. But Rebecca had to assume since I had asked for two VIP tickets. That would make logical sense. Although, the woman had asked me out in the past.

The exasperation on Sofía's face made me grin.

"I'm sure you will straighten her out if there is any confusion."

"You better believe it." She nodded.

I didn't realize that Sofía would show such jealousy when we started dating, but her Latina passion was intense, and I was enjoying the benefits of that in the bedroom. I guess a bit of jealousy now and again wasn't such a bad thing.

I stopped walking, pulled her close, and kissed her. She melted in my arms.

"I am yours. Only yours."

Sofía kissed me back. A quick peck on the lips and pulled away. It was far too brief, but we were trying to get across the grounds quickly. It took longer to park than I had anticipated, and we needed to arrive by our launch time. I took her hand in mine and increased our pace across the field.

There was a whirlwind of activity all around us, but we finally made it over to our designated spot. I recognized the man who worked for Rebecca. He was going over instructions with another couple. I handed him our consent forms and we listened in, as the dark skies began to lighten ever so slightly. There was something magical in the moments just before sunrise; before the earth woke to begin its day. Maybe I had a poetic soul, but I still had that sense of wonder. It had never gone away despite my line of work. I saw the worst in people on most days, but Mother Nature was consistent, and the beauty was my solace. Although staring at Sofía's face as the field lights danced across her features, I felt like maybe I'd find a new solace in her.

"Why on earth are you grinning like a maniac?" She asked.

I had been staring at her, thinking of our future together. I took a deep breath.

"Nothing you need to worry about," I said nonchalantly.

I don't think she believed me. Her eyebrow quirked in that adorable way.

We watched as several balloons got ready to launch. They were called the dawn patrol. They would test for wind directions before giving the ok for the mass ascension, which we would be a part of. The balloons glowed with an inner light; a multi-colored luminescence made more impressive in the darkness. As they floated around, the dark skies changed to a deep crimson streaked with tangerine. Gold-hued puffy clouds surrounded the flag balloon as the national anthem played across the speakers. Rebecca waved us over and I realized I hadn't had a conversation to make sure there were no misunderstandings. It turned out I didn't need to worry. The man who had given us the instructions

ALBUQUERQUE ALIBI

earlier was going to be our pilot. I sighed with relief. He gestured for us to climb into the basket. There was a small step on the outside, but I still had to give Sofía a boost. She made a graceful entrance despite the frilly peach floral dress she wore. It was completely impractical for climbing into a balloon and exactly like her to choose something so purely feminine. We waited patiently for the green flag. When it went up, our pilot hit the burner, and hot air blasted into the balloon. The rest of the crew released the tethers. Sofía covered her ears and giggled. I had forgotten how loud the thing was up close. I had ridden in one when I was younger. That's why I had wanted Sofía to experience it. Her eyes lit up and she gripped the edge of the basket as we floated higher into the sky. We didn't move fast, but it was a little unnerving the first time. She grinned at me as we watched more balloons join us in the sky. Sofía kept making comments that we could barely hear over the burner pointing to the various balloons of all shapes and sizes, trying to select which was her favorite. There were so many to choose from. The Balloon Fiesta in Albuquerque was truly a sight to behold, although all my focus had narrowed on her. When her questions finally slowed, and our altitude seemed to stabilize, I knew it was now or never. I took a deep breath and pulled out my phone to text one of the other balloons.

"Look at that one," I said, pointing at one of the balloons.

"Oh yes. I love all the hearts on it." She tilted her head. "What are they doing?"

I glanced over where she was pointing.

"Hmm. I'm not sure."

I tried to hide my grin.

"They're unrolling some kind of sign on the side of the basket."

"What do you think it says?"

"I'm not sure."

Our pilot maneuvered us around and then the sign became clear.

"It says, Will you marry me? Aww. Isn't that sweet. Someone is proposing."

She turned around to see me down on one knee holding a small jewelry box.

Sofía's eyes were huge, and she grabbed her chest like she was going to pass out.

"Will you marry me?" I asked.

Sofía let out a whoop and threw her arms around me, joining me down on her knees. "Yes." She said in between covering my face with kisses. Then she got a good look at the open Tiffany box in my hand.

"That's not a ring. That's real estate."

I grinned. Maybe an eight-carat engagement ring was a little excessive, but I had provided the jeweler with my specifications, and this had been what he delivered.

"You can always exchange it for something else."

She snagged the ring out of the box and slid it onto her finger as if I would snatch it back and return the thing if she waited a moment longer.

"I didn't say that I didn't like it." She stared at her hand, now glittering in the sun, admiring the oval cut eternity ring.

Her grin was contagious. Our pilot was smiling.

"Well done." He said to me, patting me on the back.

I agreed. It had all gone off as planned. I let out a huge sigh of relief. I texted back the other balloon. They released the second banner that said, 'She said Yes!'

A loud cheer could be heard from those on the ground. Sofía laughed as tears rolled down her cheeks.

"How did I get so lucky?"

"I'm the one that's lucky."

"I can't believe you kept this a secret."

"I've had a lot of practice."

She chuckled. "I guess you have me to blame for that."

ALBUQUERQUE ALIBI

"Or to thank."

Sofía smiled.

I held her and turned us both so we could watch as the multi-colored balloons floated through the vibrant blue sky. It felt like we were flying through some fantasy world. The weather was perfect. I couldn't have asked for a better day. Life was grand. I had the most amazing woman in my arms, and I could hardly believe she had agreed to be my wife. Sofía was beautiful and sweet, and even though she worried about her past, there wasn't a more selfless person on the planet. I knew we would be great together. My family loved her, and hers loved me. I had been a part of her family's lives since we were both young. We had been family in a way already, but now I was ready to start my own. I rubbed her flat belly and her eyebrows rose.

"Do you want kids right away?" I asked, whispering in her ear.

I knew her mother would be thrilled with the idea, but I had no idea if Sofía would be on board.

Her body tensed, and her jaw dropped. She tried to turn and look at me, but I held her in place.

"I'm not sure." She admitted. "I've been engaged for like 5 seconds."

I grinned at the sarcasm. She was as feisty as ever.

"Just something to think about." I didn't want to do anything to pressure her.

"You know the court dates have been finalized for the Lorenzo case. I'll have to fly out to St. Louis next month. Do you want to join me?"

"It's not exactly a romantic getaway, but since losing my job at Biogen, I've had a lot of free time."

"Leaving that job was a good thing. It was dangerous, and I thought you were leaving that part of your life behind."

"I'm getting good at compartmentalizing."

"Ooh that's a big word. You learned that in college?"

She elbowed me in the gut.

"I'm just showing off my vocabulary. Trying to impress you."

"No need for that. I'm always amazed by everything you do."

She wrapped my arms around her front tighter and admired her ring.

"I don't know. Mari said she might want to hire me for her Sales and Marketing. She wants to take her business to another level, maybe get into some local shops in Albuquerque and Santa Fe."

"You'd be great at that."

"We'll need to break our apartment lease early."

"Why is that?" I asked, wondering if Sofía had already picked a date for the wedding.

"Mari's pregnant."

"What?" I asked. "When did this happen?"

"You remember when she was sick after the Quinceañera?"

"Yeah."

"It wasn't the alcohol. It was morning sickness. Well, all-the-time sickness, to be honest."

"Does César know?"

She grinned. "Not yet. But since you are so good at keeping secrets, I thought I'd give you another."

"Wow. César's going to be a dad?" I shook my head.

"Yeah. I can't picture it either. She'll tell him soon."

"I guess he won't be able to drag his feet much longer."

She chuckled. "Nope. But he needs the push. Fate is giving him a swift kick. Mari's good for him. He realizes that. She's been more hesitant than him. But I think it will all work out."

"What about with us?"

"We were always going to end up together. I knew that, even back in high school."

"But you never told me."

Sofía shrugged. "You never asked. At least until now."

"What about St. Louis? We can throw in some romantic moments, in between court sessions." I raised my eyebrows. "And, if you aren't set on having kids just yet, we could always practice?"

She turned in my arms. "Really? That's where you're going with this?"

"Just a suggestion." I grinned. "Your mom would be thrilled. Could you imagine if the two of you were both pregnant at the same time?"

"Hush." She put her hand over my lips.

"Make me."

She grinned and kissed me long and deep, and I knew I had her. Sofía was mine and whether we had kids right away or not didn't matter to me. I knew she would be a great mother. When she was ready.

"Practice." She whispered.

"And lots of it."

"Maybe I should come with you." Sofía snuggled in closer. "If nothing else, just so you don't lose interest or find someone new."

"No chance of that happening," I said. "Ever." And I meant it. I'd never stray.

She grinned. "With me by your side and this rock on my hand, I'll finally be able to fend off your admirers."

"Might be assault with a deadly weapon. I'd have to arrest you."

"You already tried that," Sofía said against my lips. "And look how that turned out."

"Pretty darn perfect, if you ask me."

Book Club Questions

- What did you think about the main couple's chemistry and compatibility?
- How was the heat level in the book? Did it need more or less spice?
- Which tropes did you find in the book? Do you have specific trope favorites?
- Did the characters' sense of humor enhance or distract from the story?
- How likable and relatable were the main characters?
- Did you have a favorite or least favorite side character? How did they contribute to the story?
- Are there other side characters you wished would have been explored in more depth?
- Was the second chance love believable?
- What did you think of the villain? Was he complex and realistic?
- Did you agree with the decisions the characters made?

- What did you think of the main conflict that kept the couple apart?
- Was there enough tension in the book?
- Do you feel the book moved along at a good pace?
- Did the author balance the romance and suspense? Or do you feel it leaned one way or the other?
- How did the author explore the complexities of the character's life choices? Did you feel the mistakes and consequences were dealt with?
- Did you learn something you never knew before? If so, what?
- How were the author's descriptions of the settings? Were there locations in the book you now want to visit?
- Did the setting enhance or distract from the romance?
- How was the ending? Did it come to a satisfying conclusion, or did it leave you wanting more? Were there any unresolved issues or questions?
- What do you believe happens to the main couple after the novel ends?

Take a Sneak Peak at Zizi Hart's Next book in the Sizzling City Series

ST. LOUIS
Secrets

Prologue

Rosa

I stared down the barrel of a Glock and felt numb down to my core. The man threatening my life was my cousin, Luís Lorenzo. We held no love for one another, even though we were family. I knew I would go out like this one day. Bold and Bloody. It was inevitable. I had no illusions of how my life would turn out, but I did have regrets, plenty of them. I cringed thinking of how my body would be found. Why had I delayed changing out of my Club Cuervo uniform at the end of the night? My skin-tight next-to-nothing outfit barely contained my figure. While it might work great for tips, it sucked at providing any warmth in a vacant warehouse in the middle of the night. I shivered.

The evil grin on my cousin's face was sickening. He enjoyed my fear. I wanted to scream that I wasn't afraid, I was freezing, not that it would do any good. Luís would call me a liar. I had long ago wished for a world where good would conquer evil. Then again, good was relative, especially, if you worked for my family. The Lorenzo's were Colombian Mafiosos. Our money came from drugs. Cocaine was our bread and butter, but we had diversified over the years. Each branch of the family was involved in the process; cultivation, manufacturing, exporting, distribution, and selling. I was low-level, and a cousin of the Lorenzo Brothers on their father's side. I worked for Luís, the youngest of the three brothers.

Another cousin of mine, Ramón, fell to his knees beside me. He was only 21 and had lived a sheltered life. Ramón was the reason I was in Santa Fe. His mother, Maria Lorenzo had been my best friend growing up. On her deathbed years ago, I had sworn to protect Ramon and keep him out of this life, and away from the family business. I had failed. His uncle Luís had been trying to recruit the kid despite his sister's wishes. Luís had promised me that he would leave the kid alone if I agreed to come work at Club Cuervo in Santa Fe. He had lied. The kid arrived in town a month ago. Ramon had been hired as a barback for the club.

The kid cowered in front of his uncle.

He shook his head, sobbing.

"Nunca. Nunca. Never. Never. I swear."

"On your feet Ramón," I said, my voice low. "You're a Lorenzo."

The kid climbed to his feet, sniffing. It filled me with pride. I needed him to remain strong. Reminding Luís of the family connection might save us. It was a slim chance since he wasn't always rational. Luís knew that someone betrayed him, and needed someone to blame. Cruz stood on my other side. He was a bartender at the club. We had worked together for the past six months.

Luís pointed the gun at each of us in turn. Ramon, me, and Cruz.

"Two of you are family, and the other a trusted employee," he said. "How. To. Decide."

Luís' phone buzzed. He slipped his gun into his holster while he smiled at the message. He signaled for several guards to follow him over to another part of the warehouse. My breath hissed out when he walked away. Cruz cleared his throat, and I gave him a sidelong glance. He was trying to tell me something with his eyes. We had worked together and had developed an unspoken way of communicating. He needed a distraction. Did that mean he had a plan? At this point, I was up for anything. I scrutinized the two men left guarding us. One I had flirted with back in Columbia. I focused my attention on him. I shifted my stance and waited for Cruz's signal.

He fell to the ground like his knees had given out.

"The whole thing's a mistake. I would never do anything against the boss."

Cruz sobbed like he was falling apart. It was an act. I knew that Cruz was made of sterner stuff, but the two guards didn't. They were fresh from Colombia.

"This one is no Lorenzo." I scoffed, nodding at Cruz. The guard I didn't know well stepped closer, poking him with the tip of his gun, trying to get him to stand back up.

I took a step toward the other guard.

"Hey Pablo, can you itch my shoulder? With these ties, I can't reach it."

I wiggled my left shoulder. "This one." My breasts bounced with the movement and Pablo was more than willing to inch his way closer for a better view. Typical pendejo.

"Por favor. It's been driving me loca," I said sweetly.

The second guard swatted Pablo away and jostled me in the process. I stumbled but caught myself. Cruz suddenly did something the guard didn't like. He rushed forward and slammed Cruz against the van. In the collision, I noticed Cruz's hands were free. Neither of the guards seemed to realize. I was blocking Pablo's view, so I'd make sure he kept his focus on me.

"That was uncalled for," I said.

We heard arguing from the other side of the warehouse. It was Luís. He was not happy. The voices rose in pitch. Then a gunshot was fired. Not a big surprise. That's how he ended most arguments.

The next sound, however, was unexpected. It was an explosion. The bay doors blew inward in pieces. Floodlights blasted through several windows and the open space that used to be a door. Pablo and the other guard stared at the chaos.

"DEA. You're surrounded." I heard over a megaphone. The staccato sounds of gunfire drowned out the voice. Cruz tackled me to the floor. The impact made me gasp. My hands were still tied behind me, so my knuckles took the brunt of my fall and dug into my back. Somehow, I managed not to break anything. Either Cruz had been careful, or I had been lucky. Not something you could usually say about me. I did not live a charmed life.

Our two guards were still focused on the commotion by the trucks. Cruz knocked Pablo to the ground, grabbing his gun in the process. The other guard was shot from above and collapsed in front of Ramón. Cruz cut my zip ties and did the same for Ramón. The kid was splattered in blood and shaking violently. My poor cousin. He was not used to this kind of thing.

I watched as Luís made a run for his limo. He was limping. Blood stained his Armani slacks. La policía were everywhere. Normally that would fill me with dread, but tonight I was grateful. I'd take them over Luís pointing a gun at me any day. I watched as Luís aimed his Glock at one of the officers, and pulled the trigger. He had to realize there was no escape. Although, I didn't expect him to go quietly. That wasn't his way. Like his nickname, El Lobo Rojo, the red wolf left a path of blood in his wake. The policía fired at him, but he used one of his guards as a shield. After the barrage of bullets, Luís tossed his shield to the ground. Finally, someone tackled him to the cement. The policía issued a series of commands in Spanish demanding surrender. The whole thing was over before I knew it. Cruz appeared to be shot in the shoulder. Ramón sprinted to a corner, heaving up his last meal. I glanced down at my body. I had a few bumps, some scrapes, and a broken nail. I felt lucky.

"Jac." Cruz yelled to a large officer in a tactical vest who was cuffing Pablo.

ALBUQUERQUE ALIBI

The man grinned at Cruz. It was clear they knew one another.

"You were in on this?" I asked.

Did that mean that Cruz had been working with the police this whole time? Was he an informant?

"I was undercover," he said.

"I knew it."

Everything Cruz had done these past months. It all made sense now. Cruz had that good guy streak he just couldn't hide.

My attention focused on Luís. He was screaming promises of revenge, while one of the officers arrested him, trying to lead him away to one of the vans. Luís fought back. The man wouldn't give up. Many colorful obscenities in Spanish spewed from his lips. I couldn't help but grin at his predicament, even though I would be arrested too. But arrested was way better than dead.

Luís' eyes turned feral.

"You. I will get you!" He roared.

I shivered. I knew that look. He thought I had betrayed him. Luís was going to make me pay. Even if it wasn't true, it wouldn't matter. His mind was made up. Logic never played into his decisions. As soon as he got out of jail, it would happen. And with his political contacts, I knew that wouldn't be long. I inhaled a sharp breath.

Suddenly this huge man came out of nowhere and punched Luís in the jaw. He fell to the floor with a thud. I sighed with relief. Someone shouted a reprimand at the mysterious hero with an unrepentant grin.

"What?" He yelled. "He was swearing, and there are ladies present."

The man stared at me. I gulped. This handsome stranger started walking straight toward me. I briefly wondered what expression he saw on my face. Awe? Gratitude? Shock?

Jac blocked the man's progress.

"How the hell are you, Taz?" He asked and gave Taz a slug on the shoulder. It barely moved the behemoth of a man. Taz reached out to shake Cruz' hand. He knew them both. I stared at the three men standing together. All stunning in their own right. When had the policía started recruiting straight from Chippendales?

"Howdy ma'am." Taz nodded. Clear concern on his face. "You all right?" He said with a Texan drawl.

I nodded. My mouth was still open. There was something about this man. He pushed all my buttons. Big and protective. Ruggedly sexy.

"I don't want Rosa arrested," Cruz said. "She's been through enough."

"Ramón either." I managed to say. I finally found my voice. "I'm calling in my debt."

Days ago, I had helped Cruz rescue some girls from the club. He had promised me a favor to be named later.

"What do you think?" Cruz asked.

"I'll see what I can do," Jac said.

"What if I..." I glanced between the men. "I know things."

"She's a Lorenzo," Cruz said.

Taz was listening intently. His stance stiffened when the name was mentioned.

"Luís already thinks I betrayed him. As soon as he lawyers up." I crossed my arms over my chest and tried to keep the quiver from my voice. "I'm dead."

"We can't have that now, can we little lady?"

The Texan charm disarmed me.

He stood close. I had to look up and up to stare into his dark eyes. The man must be 6 and a half feet tall at least. Was he making fun of me? My brows furrowed. His words were calm and soothing, but something was off; like it was all an act. He held an edge behind the gentle attitude like he was moments away from exploding. I wondered if his friends realized. I had a radar for repressed rage. It was a hard-earned skill developed from working with Luís.

I shivered. The events of the day were finally catching up to me. Or maybe there was a draft from the now open bay doors. Taz took off his jacket and bundled me up with care. I'm sure I looked ridiculous. I wasn't used to people being nice. It confused me.

"Let's get you out of the way." He said and started leading me to a set of cars and SUVs. My legs gave out, and I stumbled. Before I even knew what was happening, he swept me up into his arms like I weighed nothing.

I yipped. "Put me down. I can walk." I didn't appreciate being manhandled, even if it was by the sexiest man I had ever laid eyes on.

Then he whispered something to me in Spanish. I always had some witty comeback, but the comment left me tongue-tied.

"You're mine to protect."

It was possessive and filled with heat. His eyes glittered with some emotion that I didn't understand. I didn't believe it was love. We had only just met. But it wasn't lust either. I was too tired to figure it out. After almost dying, I needed something to cling to; something to hope for. I held on tighter, enjoying the warmth and safety this man offered. Cuddling into his chest I smelled his earthy scent, a mixture of sweat and cologne. I allowed my body to go limp, relaxing for this moment in time. I knew it wouldn't last; nothing ever did.

Chapter 1

Six months later

Taz

I approached the safe house checking out the surroundings, following standard operating procedures. A deputy was on duty watching the witness. We had several witnesses for a high-profile case against Luís Lorenzo, aka El Lobo Rojo. But this one was critical. She was family. That meant she had the potential to do the most damage. The trouble was she was a pain. For multiple reasons. I didn't like how she made me feel. I had always been protective especially where women were concerned, but my feelings for her went beyond job responsibilities. It didn't make sense. While it was my job to protect the bastards that came through WITSEC, I didn't always like it. At least this one was easy on the eyes. She was also a pretty tough cookie. Rosa played the part well, but I could see a vulnerability that she didn't reveal to others. I noticed how her behavior changed when she was with me.

I hated the Lorenzos and had good reasons for that. That family took away someone I loved. I would never forget or forgive.

Deputy Williams buzzed me in after I knocked and then texted the correct code. The door opened and the deputy shook his head.

"She's in a mood today. I think she's gone stir-crazy."

A pot was launched across the living room.

"I said spices, pendejo. This isn't what I need."

She hurled a spice bottle at his head."

"I couldn't find what you asked for." The deputy complained.

"What kind of backward-ass place have you brought me to?"

A plastic stir stick sailed through the air. I stepped in the path, and I caught it.

"Now Ma'am, we talked about this."

The deputy took the opportunity, to scurry out of the apartment while he had the chance. I locked up behind him before making my way into the kitchen.

"What's with all the fuss?" I asked.

Her nose tilted up, and Rosa crossed her arms over her chest. Her V-neck T-shirt showed an obscene amount of cleavage. How could she make a simple T-shirt look so darn erotic?

"I need things." She blinked deep chocolate brown eyes at me.

Her slow perusal of my body felt tactile. Rosa's lashes were thick and dark. From her lust-filled gaze, they matched her thoughts. She had shared some of her fantasies with me. I'm sure it was to get a rise out of me. It had succeeded. In fact, I needed to adjust myself right now.

"You showing up like that, looking the way you do doesn't help matters."

She approached me slowly. Rosa didn't walk, she strolled, with seductive swishes of her hips.

"What does that mean?"

She slid fingertips over my pecs and down my abdomen. I caught her wrist before she went too far. The woman loved to play games.

"All sexy and macho, when I have no chance at you know."

"Know what?"

"Getting a release." She sighed dramatically.

ALBUQUERQUE ALIBI

I released her wrist.

Rosa stood back and gestured to my body. "It's not fair."

I grinned. She was always saying outrageous things to rile me up.

"Well ma'am, you can always take matters into your own hands."

"You think I don't?" She wiggled her eyebrows.

I had been teasing, but she sounded serious. The image of her had me swallowing hard. To know that she was doing something like that in the bedroom when I was in the living room guarding her, my neck suddenly got hotter than Hades. I went over to the thermostat and turned down the AC.

I cleared my throat.

"What is it you were looking for specifically, ma'am?"

"Stop calling me ma'am. It makes me feel old."

Rosa told me that repeatedly over the last six months. I had ignored her request to keep things professional.

"I need a treadmill." She said with hands on her hips.

"I thought you needed spices."

"Yes. I need those too. Cooking relaxes me." Rosa walked over to the cutting board filled with fresh vegetables. She slid a chef's knife from the block and chopped peppers and green onion.

"When I get irritated, I want to stab things." She pointed the knife in my direction and grinned. Her eyes sparkled with mischief.

My eyebrows rose. I walked to the other side of the island and relieved her of the knife.

"Not much of an incentive to let you play with knives."

"Oh please. If I wanted to stab you, I could have done so dozens of times."

I tilted my head.

She huffed. "Ok. Maybe once. You're fairly alert. The others not so much."

"That would violate your agreement.

She rolled her eyes and walked to the icebox pulling out a few chicken breasts that had been marinating.

I finished cutting up the vegetables she had laid out, wondering briefly if I needed to warn the other deputies. Rosa liked to make threats, but I knew they were empty. She had a flair for the dramatic.

"Why do you need a treadmill, Rosa?" I asked.

It felt personal using her name, but I rather liked it.

She froze staring at me with raised eyebrows.

"This body was not honed into shape without working out regularly. I've gained twenty pounds since I've been stuck here. You and your gang keep bringing me fast food."

"We can change up the menu if you like. But I thought you enjoyed the selection."

"I do. Obviously. St. Louis food is fattening as hell. Delicious, but fattening. I need to start cooking my meals. Less fat. More flavor."

I glanced at her body. I didn't mind the extra weight. I thought she looked better than before. When I had initially gotten her into the program, I thought she was too skinny. Working as a cocktail waitress, I knew she had to watch her figure, especially considering the amount of skin she had to show in her club outfit. At first, I thought she might have taken drugs to stay thin. I had worried we might need to send her to detox before putting her in the program, but her blood work came back clean. Even though she had been selling drugs out of Club Cuervo, she hadn't been taking them herself.

I blinked. "That's a mighty big item."

"This is a mighty big ass." She grabbed her behind. "And I need to get rid of it."

I tilted my head for a better view and grinned. I thought her ass looked fine. More than fine. I imagined taking her over my knee on more than one occasion when she'd get all uppity.

She huffed at me. "Then get me a gym membership."

"Now Rosa, you know that will never happen."

ALBUQUERQUE ALIBI

She shrugged. "Then you will just have to deal with my outbursts. I can't help myself."

I knew what we both needed. The sexual tension between the two of us had been building to a point where I could barely stand it. Not that I could do a darn thing about it. I needed this trial over, so I could relocate her and move on. I didn't have the luxury to get attached. There was something about Rosa that got under my skin. I was equal parts attracted and irritated.

My phone rang, and I looked at the number. It was the district office. They usually just texted, so it had to be important.

"Is your witness secure?"

It was Sandi Summers. She was an administrative support assistant.

"Affirmative," I said, glancing around the apartment. I still started re-checking windows, doors, closets, and under the bed. I shoved a complaining Rosa into the bathroom, shut the door, and locked it from the outside. It was something I had implemented because of her outbursts. She banged on it and swore at me in Spanish. Rosa had quite the vocabulary.

"What happened?" I asked, sitting on the edge of the bed.

"A witness was killed. One of Luís' men."

"Which one?"

"José."

Another essential witness for the prosecution. Although I had serious doubts he would make it to trial. Not that I thought he'd end up dead. I believed he would back out of testifying at some point. He was one of Luís' sicarios. José knew where the bodies were buried because he helped bury them.

"How?" I asked.

"The man snuck out of his room. We assume it was to buy cigarettes. He had been complaining earlier that his handler had gotten the wrong brand." Sandi blew out a breath. "He climbed out the bathroom window and down the fire escape."

"Didn't the deputy follow security protocols?" I asked. We had a series of checks. All entry and exit points were wired to set off an alarm if they were opened.

"The wire was tampered with. He figured José circumvented security."

"Where was he killed?"

"At the convenience store around the corner from the safe house. The local PD think it was a robbery gone wrong. There was a hold-up. The gunman escaped. We are waiting for security footage now."

"Does the SI believe it was just an accident?" I asked.

"No. The senior inspector thinks it was a targeted hit. The PD found a phone and cash on the body," she said.

These things didn't happen randomly. They were orchestrated. I had been doing this long enough to know. The deputy should have been better at his job. But this incident also identified a risk to other witnesses in the case. Whoever had targeted José had gotten the address to one of our safe houses.

"Do we have the phone?"

"Not yet. They are still processing it, but it looks like a burner."

"We need the last number called."

"Already on it. The Inspector is at the scene."

Not that I figured it would yield much. It was probably from another burner. But we could get lucky. Oftentimes criminals weren't overly bright.

"And the deputy?"

"Being questioned now."

"Has the accountant looked over his records? Does he think he might have been paid off?"

I didn't want to think along those lines, but it was necessary. If the deputy was compromised, then we needed to change passwords, locations; everything he might be aware of.

ALBUQUERQUE ALIBI

We had safe houses all over the city. If he was a threat, this could jeopardize more than just one witness. It could potentially risk our entire operation.

"He hasn't found anything unusual in his bank accounts." She sighed heavily.

I knew what was coming, but I asked anyway.

"Is there anything else?"

"Why do you have to be the one to guard her?"

It was my turn to sigh, "Ms. Summers, you know good and well that I don't need to justify my actions."

I had recently been appointed US Marshal for the Eastern District of Missouri. Before that, I had been Chief Deputy. Over the past decade, I worked in various positions within the USMS. I was currently one of the youngest US Marshals. The last thing I needed was staff questioning my command.

"It's just that you have so many deputies that could handle that sort of thing. It's beneath you."

I knew what the real problem was. The witness was attractive and just my type, ballsy and beautiful. Sandi knew this. We had gone on a few dates early in my career when I was young and dumb. It had been a mistake. Office romances didn't work, especially in my line of work. But she still occasionally pushed for more.

"Call me when you know more," I said.

She hung up. Sandi was moody, just like another woman in my life.

I sighed, staring at the bathroom door. As soon as I unlocked it Rosa would raise hell. She had every reason to. If I were in her shoes, I would too. I couldn't stand feeling cooped up and out of control. I scrolled through a list of treadmills. It was an excessive expense, and I didn't want the finance guy raising his eyebrows. I might just pay for it myself, just to get Rosa to calm down. I unlocked the door and she was ready for it. She launched herself at me and tackled me to the bed. I wrestled her easily, pinning her body.

"Enough of this. I know you are unhappy. But this is the way it has to be. You agreed to the terms."

She squirmed beneath me, but her smoky kohled eyes had dilated. Rosa was turned on. She rattled off a mixture of curses and compliments in Spanish. I grinned. I couldn't help myself.

Her chest pushed against mine. I held her wrists together above her head with one hand and balanced my body with my other arm. I didn't want to crush her with my weight, but I was still unwilling to move, afraid she might attack again. I wasn't worried that Rosa would hurt me, but she could injure herself, and that I wouldn't allow. Feeling her soft body beneath, I tried to focus on something, anything other than her pouty lips, and silky hair. Those dark eyes. The same ones I dreamed of when I slept. She rolled her hips and my jaw ticked.

"Don't do that," I whispered.

"Or what pendejo?" She pursed her lips. "Will you tie me up? Or will that just turn you on more?"

I was hard. She could feel it. There was no concealing my erection.

She rolled her hips again, and I thrust. It was automatic. We were aligned perfectly and it made her gasp. Rosa's eyes rolled back in her head.

"Again. Por favor."

It brought me to my senses. Still, I hesitated. I didn't want to move. I wanted to give her what she needed, what we both needed. I climbed off, eyeing her with caution. She reacted more like a wild animal most days. She did nothing for a moment and then curled into a ball.

"I hate you," she said. "Get out of here." She threw a pillow at my head.

I caught it and tossed it back on the bed. I turned and closed the door. My breath hissed out. I had almost done something unforgivable. She was temptation personified. As it

ALBUQUERQUE ALIBI

was, I had stepped over the line. That wasn't like me, but there was something about her. She pushed all my buttons. I should be focused on her safety, not worried about how she felt beneath me, warm and willing. Was Luís Lorenzo somehow orchestrating something from prison to get rid of witnesses? Or was his family? I needed a risk assessment on the deputy guarding José. Was he somehow involved? There were too many questions. I glanced back at the bedroom door and came to a decision. I wouldn't allow her to be next. Those bastards would have to go through me to get to her. From here on out I wasn't letting her out of my sight..

Appreciation

Thank you to everyone in my life who has contributed in one way or another to the writing of this book. My insanity or lack thereof is entirely your fault. Just kidding. I appreciate your acceptance of me just as I am, and allowing me to bury myself in my office/cave and not come out for days on end. To my parents, kids, and friends for your support, and endless supply of laughter that keeps me going. To my fellow author friends who understand that writing is our therapy and for being my sounding board whenever I need it. I'm amazed and humbled by your creativity and so grateful for your friendship. And lastly, for those within my inner circle that join me on the journey into the depths of the villain psyche. You always have a rope ready to pull me out if I ever go too far. I owe you more than you can ever imagine.

About the Author

Zizi Hart likes to sprinkle sizzle on her sass. Her muse takes her down shadowed, twisted paths, into her imagination and if you are brave enough to join her on the journey, you won't be disappointed. She writes a mix of fantasy, romance, science fiction, suspense, and adventure, wherever her muse takes her. But no matter what, you will always get a touch of humor and a feel-good story with a lot of heart. In her off-time, she travels the world connecting with nature and animals, getting distracted by decadent chocolates and is forever in search of the perfect brownie sundae.

www.ZiziHart.com

Thanks for reading!
Please add a short review on Amazon.
I'd love to hear your thoughts!